The Shame of John Slade

Phillip Drown

First published in 2024 by PipJay

The right of Phillip Drown to be identified as the author of this work,
in accordance with the Copyright, Designs and Patents act 1988, has
been asserted

*This is entirely a work of fiction. All of the characters and events depicted in
this novel are products of the author's imagination, or are fictitiously
portrayed*

A CIP record for this book is available from the British Library

ISBN: 978–1–7384816–0–6

www.phillipdrown.com

For daughters

one

Life changed after I was caught with the lollipop lady. However scandalous it was at the time, the very public shaming that followed turned out to be little more than a passing storm. For in a town like Tenderbridge, episodes of disgrace are as common as seeing dog poo on the pavement.

Take my ex-wife's best friend. Rather than splashing paint about in the art class she signed up for, Bea had instead been plunging around in the local swimming baths with the pool attendant, caught without bathing suits by a gaggle of old duffers who turned up early to their Aquafit class. And how I laughed when I found out. Because it was Bea who told Kirsty about me and Sadie, the lollipop lady.

Since the days of staring at Debbie Harry on the cover of record sleeves, I have always had a weakness for girls who wear too much makeup. Sadie had mounds of it. Combined with the sculpted body peeking out from beneath her hi-vis jacket, Sadie was incredibly sexy. Just like the song.

She clearly couldn't stand kids. It was the fathers that Sadie batted her fake lashes at each day, standing on the crossing with one hand on her hip, as if she was trying to sell her lollipop on some late-night shopping channel.

As any good lollipop lady would, Sadie moonlighted as a barmaid in one of the local pubs. Back then, I was a popular (local) musician in my thirties, so naturally I did what any singer in a popular (local) band would. It took only a lingering blink of her lashes to suggest that Sadie and I should go outside for a cigarette. We did end up having a cigarette, but only after Bea came stumbling outside to find me and Sadie going for it up against one of the picnic benches, vaguely hidden by an overgrown laurel.

There she was, trotting towards us, wobbling all over the patio in her stilettos, flirting dangerously with the shrubs. Attempting to point at us, she was performing some kind of strange street dance.

'You're for it now, you bastard,' Bea cawed from within a cloud of passion fruit-scented vape.

'We . . . were only . . . chatting,' I replied breathlessly.

The truth was, at the very moment Bea busted us, Sadie had been spilling filthy lines into the blue air while I yanked on her ponytail. Even as I was puffing out my lame defence, Sadie still had her palms spread out on the table in front of her. And I still had her ponytail in my grip.

'Oh, you and the lollipop lady,' Bea said, staggering towards us. 'That's poetry, that is.'

'It's not what it looks like,' I protested, zipping myself up.

'I can see her pulling up her knickers, mate,' Bea retorted, pointing in her disco dance fashion.

I looked, and Sadie was. Just simple white cotton briefs. That surprised me, given the low cut of her dress.

Staring triumphantly at me and the lollipop lady, Bea took another drag on her vape. A moment later her cheeks bulged. As I watched her vomiting into the laurel, I hoped that Bea would be too drunk to remember the episode in The Humphrey Bean beer garden. When Kirsty got home from work the next day, one look at her face told me differently.

Even though I found it hard to like a single thing about Bea, I could see why Kirsty would be friends with a woman like her. Kirsty is the sort of person who would be the first to throw a stone, and then frown upon someone who accidentally kicks a pebble.

When I first met her, she was my northern rose: fiery and confident, dressed up in an edgy, riot grrrl glamour. I would smile every time she opened her bud lips and coarse brogue slipped out, a contrast so endearing to me at the time. Yet as the petals began to fall, her prickles grew, until the flower that I had adored finally no longer bloomed. The faded bud of her lips only ever opened to reveal withering disdain. The decay of our romance. Not that there is really any excuse that can be made for a married man banging the lollipop lady from his daughter's infant school in a public place.

Excluding the occasional snog, and some light-hearted, mutual fondling with a few girls, Sadie was my first and only infidelity. Caught first time, pretty much.

3

But despite my protestations, I was defenceless: before spewing in drunken delight, it transpired that Bea had taken a shaky picture of Sadie and me.

Even though my love for Kirsty had long since evaporated, when she returned home that day, found me dozing in the backyard, and started spitting spiky shards of northern glass, I begged for the ground to swallow me; for the sun lounger to fold in half and file itself into the earth, with me plugged in its cushiony middle. Beneath being busted was the absurdity of hearing the words *"shagging the lollipop lady"* screamed over the rooftops, and the humiliation that people streets away would have heard it. But on top of it all, above it all, encompassing everything, standing shoeless in her favourite dress, hugging her doll so tightly, Ella had been watching.

It is not cheating on Kirsty that still wakes me in the night – to stay with her would have been to commit to a life of misery – but each morning, afternoon, every evening, night, wherever I may be, I miss my daughter.

It would be fair to say that I am a tormented man. But it's fine. I have ways of dealing with the torment.

two

Before Kirsty yelled at me in front of Ella and I was booted onto the streets, the three of us had lived together on the south side of town, close to the train station. If trains once rattled and chugged along railway lines, in modern Tenderbridge packed carriages shriek into the station with a tormenting regularity, deep into the small hours. Basslines beat through tight-knit terraced houses. Domestic arguments rain all day over the tiny backyards. Raised voices of drunk men and women fill the fuggy air. Kids on mopeds tear around the streets, all through the night. Others congregate in car parks, revving the engines of their thirty-year-old Vauxhall Novas and Ford Escorts. Along those streets, litter from the numerous fast-food outlets decays in the kerbsides. Cats and mangy foxes forage, fight and fornicate.

While the south side of Tenderbridge howls, the neighbourhoods in the north end of the town are greeted by morning birdcall. Those houses have gardens for the children to run around in; to kick a ball, bounce on trampolines, splash in pools and frolic in hot tubs. Kids on the north side don't have to play hide and seek in confined spaces, where the only place to hide is a grubby dustbin, later emerging from it smeared in bacterial sludge.

They lounge on their lawns, drink tea at a table and scoff scones in their summer houses. Electric cars are lined upon driveways, lawnmowers stowed in sheds, recycling bins parked in purpose-made stores, and all dwellers are rewarded for their Tory votes.

Within a year of Bea sending Kirsty the picture of me catching a piggyback ride on the lollipop lady, my soon-to-be-ex-wife and daughter moved in with Dan – a wealthy bachelor with a BMW and a four-bedroom house. Dan's house is in north Tenderbridge. And Dan only wears blue ties.

The divide of the town, from middle class to working class, is historic. In the nineteenth century, an outbreak of cholera plagued those living in the south side, possibly from playing hide and seek inside toxic bins. Guards stood sentry on the Great Bridge, separating the classes, protecting those that were more well-to-do from those who were literally dying in their own shit. The sentries are there no longer, yet the divide remains. In modern Tenderbridge everyone knows their place.

Having walked past the fried chicken shop, various vape stores, the kebab, the Poundland and the charity shops, I pass over the Great Bridge now. My tired, dirty town surroundings are replaced by the manicured river-banks, the cycle paths, the picturesque motte and bailey castle, and the world-renowned public school.

On this hot, sunny day, it is my walk of shame.

That I have to ask permission to see Ella – calling from my pay-as-you-go mobile phone, only to have Dan answer and tell me that my own daughter is at this club, or at that class, or at the house of some friend I have never even heard of – should leave me feeling approximately two feet small. And yet the greatest indignity is knowing that she is living a far better life than I could have ever afforded her.

The new gate, installed after some little oiks from the south side tried to thieve Dan's Beemer, has a security buzzer. Standing on the street, feeling like a chicken on a peacock farm, I am finally granted entry onto the pebbled driveway. It was these same pebbles that apparently betrayed the little oiks after I told them of a sparkling new BMW they could nick.

Kirsty opens the front door before I get there. I shamble towards her, hands in the pockets of my scruffy jeans, wearing my same old worn-out leather jacket, and with who knows how many days of beard growth. Once upon a time, when I found her voice endearing, Kirsty had liked my ruggedness. And yet now we must go through this routine, Kirsty looking me up and down disapprovingly enough times to ensure that her scorn registers. Yes, we are all disappointed and disgusted by John Slade. And probably I am the only one of us who doesn't give a shit about it.

'Couldn't you have washed?' Kirsty asks, her fake tan sparkling in the sunlight. I am getting a healthy dose of vitamin D off her radiance.

'Where's my girl?' I ask, as affably as possible.

'Come in,' Kirsty says with a weary lip-sneer. 'Shoes off,' she adds before my tattered boots have passed the threshold, let alone touched upon the palace pile. 'Ella!' she screeches, 'John's here.'

Sparing a bitter glance over her shoulder, Kirsty disappears into the kitchen.

Waiting at the foot of the staircase, I don't rise to the *John*. I refuse to show Kirsty that her snipes affect me in any way. And honestly, they don't. The mirrors in this house are huge.

I can't hear any movement upstairs. Although I guess you wouldn't hear the lightest shuffling about, unlike in our old two-up two-down terrace.

'Ella?' I call up the stairs, to no response. 'It's dad.'

And still, silence.

I amble through to the kitchen – big enough to fit the entire downstairs of our old house – and look at the digital clock on the cooker. 14:01. Bang on time, for once.

'Where is she?'

'Don't touch the surfaces,' Kirsty replies, pouring herself a glass of Chardonnay. 'The cleaner's been.'

The glass has cool, sweaty beads curving over its side. Catching my hankering, Kirsty takes great and deliberate delight in slowly taking a swig. And there it is, the tight-lipped smile, the one that comes with a slight tilt of her head. I know what's coming next.

'Perhaps Ella doesn't want to see you.'

Kirsty knows that comment does bite, deeply. After they moved in with wonderful, rich Dan, Ella's attitude towards me soon changed. No longer were there the carefree smiles, a bundle of joy who bounded my way as soon as I arrived. The child who spent her first years curled up on my chest. The little girl who would say *I love you* and gaze up at me with wonderment.

Who knows what is said behind the gates after they close at the end of my visits. I can only imagine the bitter poison that Kirsty is capable of drip-feeding to build up Ella's immunity to me. Or maybe Ella has forgotten being curled up on my chest, and only sees me as a scruffy bloke who turns up now and again, mostly hungover, if I turn up at all.

Through the open bi-fold doors, I see Ella skulking around in the garden. Her pet mutt, which has better grooming than I've ever had, is following her. I wave. Even across the broad expanse of immaculate lawn, I see Ella's eyes roll. Reluctantly, she begins to head my way. The dog, some little designer breed, traces her scent over the grass.

I catch the wisp of a sigh from between Kirsty's wine-moistened lips. Do I witness signs of distress?

'It's hard to get her to do anything at the moment,' Kirsty says, surprising me like never before by admitting it, betraying the image of the perfect life she lucked herself and my daughter into. Hidden within her expression is the reluctance to confess it, of course, but also a kind of pleading. It's a look I remember well, from the rare occasions when Kirsty was prepared to admit that she was in the wrong. I haven't seen it for a long time.

'It's as if when she hit thirteen a switch just went off in her,' Kirsty continues. 'I don't think I've seen her smile in a month. Maybe more.'

'Thirteen, is she?' I ask, still eyeing the wine glass.

Kirsty leans on the polished granite island, bigger than our old bathroom. 'Your daughter swore at me today,'

'Right, I see.' I slap my palms down on the island,

damn the cleaner. 'I can't see Ella without pretty much having to apply for a court order, but when she swears she's all mine?'

'Well, she didn't bloody well get it from me.'

'I didn't swear,' Ella says, stomping into the kitchen, wearing an expression so fierce that it makes her look oh-so-much like Kirsty. 'I called you a stupid cow.'

Ella sees me grinning, scratching behind my ear.

'And you, dickhead, you're just an embarrassment. Not only to me, but to *everyone*. Look at the state of you.'

That wipes the smile from my face. It is clearly something that she's heard her mother say, and we all know it. Even the dog is glaring at me, posh little twat.

'Dan's the only one who behaves like an *actual* adult around here,' Ella continues, glaring at us each in turn. 'He might be a prick, but at least he's got a job.'

I raise my hand to protest, to proclaim that I have got a job, *actually*. A proper job. Not just playing half-arsed cover songs to pissed people in local pubs. But Ella's not done yet.

'Dan's taking me and Keira to the Amex this weekend.'

'What's the Amex?' I ask. 'Other than a card in Dan's wallet.'

Ella looks my way, chooses to ignore me, and then redirects her invective back to Kirsty.

'When do you take me anywhere other than to your friends' houses so that you can gossip and drink gin?' she says, hands on her hips. 'Well?'

Wait a minute, since when did my little girl have hips?

The dog yaps at me.

I mouth *Fuck off* to it.

'I took you to the cinema to see Dumbo,' Kirsty says, uncharacteristically softly. She really is struggling.

'No, *mother*, you dumped me at the cinema so that you could get your nails done and go shopping. You didn't even pick me up! I had to come and meet you in the wine bar.'

Kirsty's mouth opens, but it seems that she sure isn't about to argue. I lean against the island, quite enjoying watching my tiny progeny popping off. What's not to like? While I'm *dickhead* – a standard acknowledgement in most places I go – behind my back Kirsty has become *mother*, and *you stupid cow*. God, I love this little brat. But what the hell is the Amex? When Ella stops for air, I intend to ask her. Again.

'And you,' she says, turning her untamed bollocking my way. 'What have you *ever* done but take me to the park? And always with a bag full of beers.'

'Come on, Ella, I took you to London that time.'

'Yes, you did.' Ella's voice is getting a bit screechy now. The mutt is sneering at me again, too. This is why we are a family better suited to the south side. 'Our one and only family day out so that you can go and see some band you like.'

'R.E.M.' I say.

'What?'

'We went to see R.E.M.' I repeat. 'In London.'

Somehow, I've dragged a fallen branch in front of the runaway caboose.

R.E.M. are my favourite band. They were Kirsty's favourite band, too, before the lollipop thing. They were our band. R.E.M. broke up a few years before we did, but

11

the difference is that they had thirty years of hard work behind them.

Do I see an expression close to hungering in Kirsty's eyes? Possibly it is just continued shock at the abuse piping out of this little daughter of ours.

'Dad, that was, like, eight years ago. I was five years old! And. It. Was. Shit.'

'Now, hang on,' I say, raising my voice, thumping my palm down on the granite countertop. At least she called me dad. I plan to turn that round on her in a minute.

'I hate both of you,' Ella shouts before storming out of the room, denying me the opportunity.

It turns out that you can hear people moving around upstairs in a house like this, if they are stomping hard enough.

'I can't believe she said that,' I say, shaking my head, resettling myself against the island. 'Yes, I get that they're not to everyone's taste, especially some of the early noughties stuff, but she can't say that about R.E.M.'

Kirsty bites her bottom lip. Her eyes move while she stares into the depths of the granite, as if watching a shoal of fish swimming beneath its surface.

'Kirst?'

She glances towards the ceiling, and then levels her worn expression upon me. 'Ella always behaves like this when she's got PMS.'

I think I sort of wince. It felt like I winced. And then I make three different tones of huffing noises.

'But she's . . . too young for that, isn't she?'

'Ella got her period over a year ago, John. While you have been off . . . doing whatever, doing nothing, our daughter has been growing up, you know. How can you not have noticed? In fact, don't answer that.'

'But she's so . . . *small*.'

Kirsty again examines the countertop. Even after a relationship that was strained to the very extremities, six years of living apart, a mutual dislike and distrust burgeoning in the years since, I can still read Kirsty. One thing is obvious: Ella is getting the better of her, and on a regular basis.

The thought of it almost makes me laugh out loud.

Kirsty looks at the dog. With the stubby tail drooping between the permed fur of its thighs, it leaves the room.

'We're moving to Canada,' Kirsty says.

Her words take a moment to filter through the air to me. Once they reach, those words swirl around my head, hypnotising me to dizziness. I try to understand what they mean.

'What?'

'Dan's company are transferring him,' Kirsty says. 'All of us. We're all moving to Canada.'

'*I'm* moving to Canada?'

'What? No, all of *us*, you stupid prat,' she replies, brushing me and my confusion aside with a wave of her fake nails. 'Me, Dan and Ella.'

'But . . .' Can someone do that, just take your only child and move to a whole new country without first checking if it's alright? 'Why *Canada*? It's so far away. Why not, fucking . . . Margate?'

'I don't think that Margate is a business hub for shipping companies, John.'

'It's by the sea.'

'Oh, I'll be sure to check with Dan, then. See if they'll

transfer him to Margate rather than Canada. Because it's *by the sea.'*

Again, Kirsty looks up at the ceiling, her eyes glittering with the reflection of the integrated lighting.

'Ella's been,' she waves her nails in the general direction of upstairs, 'like *that* ever since we told her. But it's decided, John. *We've* decided, between us, Dan and me. We leave in a month.'

three

When I have finished saying what I have to say, Darren seems baffled. The thing about Darren is that he looks baffled when he's reading the menu screen in McDonald's, so it's hard to gauge his reaction.

'Canadia's quite nice, isn't it?' he finally says.

'Yes?' I reply. 'No? I don't know. I've never been.'

'Hmm.' Playing with his beard, Darren frowns, as he always does when he's trying to grasp a thought.

Darren is the lead guitarist in our band. He has had long hair – like, ZZ Top length hair – and a scraggly beard ever since he could grow one. The long hair came before the beard. Playing guitar and taking part in epic games of Warhammer – a grown man moving miniature figures around for hour after hour – is all that Darren has ever been interested in. A great guitarist he may be, but Darren has never been the sharpest axe in the armoury.

'So . . . do they not want to go to Canadia?'

'Darren, that's not the point. My daughter is moving to Canada. *Ca-na-da*. As in, thousands of miles away.'

'We were going to go to Canadia on our world tour, remember? Follow the same route that Motörhead did in eighty-one.'

It's true. Years ago, after playing a passably good gig in the pub, we did talk about going on a world tour. We talked about lots of things. The reality is that we very rarely travel any further than the county borders. I don't know of many generic cover bands who get booked to tour the world, no matter how good they might be.

'You're still missing my point,' I say, looking into his wide, green eyes, brimful with the two-dimensional innocence of a cartoon character. 'I don't want Ella to move to Canada. I'll miss her. And there is no way that I could ever afford to go and visit.'

'It would be good, though. Like, if you could,' Darren adds, helpful as ever.

After leaving Dan's palace and sweating the entire length of Tenderbridge on my way to The Tap, I puzzled over what I could possibly do to stop Ella from leaving.

I could try and break up Dan and Kirsty's marriage.

That would only happen if he woke up skint one day in the next month.

Surely they can't go if he loses his job.

So, what, get one of the girls from the pub to phone the police and say that Dan had done horrific things to them? As if the police wouldn't side with the rich man.

It seems that the only possible way I can stop them moving to Canada is to kill Dan.

But what if Ella doesn't come and visit me in prison? I only see her once a week now, if I remember to make an appointment to go and get my weekly abuse from her and her mother.

'She called me a dickhead,' I say, taking a sip of my pint, smirking in spite of myself; still unable to decide whether to be proud of Ella's brazen effrontery, or if I should be offended.

'A dickhead?' Darren says. 'That's harsh, mate. You're not even the worst one in here.'

We look around The Tap. Old boys are cupping their beers or shorts and staring into space. Lads in polo shirts are perched on stools at the bar. Colourless morons and dole monkeys are sitting round the tall tables, drinking their hard-earned benefits away. A couple of younger fellas are playing pool, one of whom I recognise from the chicken shop.

I picture Dan leaning back in his tall leather chair, tapping a Montblanc against his walnut desk. His suit that I couldn't afford if I played thirty gigs a week. His watch that I couldn't afford if I played fifty gigs a week.

'Do you know what the Amex is?' I ask Darren.

'A bank, isn't it?'

'No, not that. And it's not a bank, exactly, it's a . . .'

Staring at me, possibly through me, Darren's mouth is open, his tongue resting on his bottom lip.

'Never mind,' I say, a pair of words that I often use when talking with Darren. 'I think that the Amex is a place. A place that someone can take you.'

'Hmmm.' Again stroking his beard, Darren surveys the cocktail menu painted on a supporting beam above the bar. 'Is it . . . a cinema?'

'That's the Imax. And I don't know what the Amex is. I was just wondering if you do. Whatever it is, Dan is taking Ella there this weekend. If he's doing that, then I should probably take her somewhere too, I suppose.'

'Brigh'on.'

I swivel to face an old boy sitting behind us. He has a proper outlaw's handlebar moustache, bristly whiskers and a flat cap. The weight of an invisible pipe turns down one side of his mouth. A crossword is open on the table in front of him. I am pretty certain that he's the source of at least one of the nasty smells.

'Brigh'on,' he repeats.

'Brian?' I say. 'Which Brian?'

'No, Brigh'on. S'where they play their 'ome games.'

'Games?' I ask. 'What sort of games?'

'S'eir footba' team,' he says in his old-fashioned Kentish drawl, a curious blend of cockney London and rural west country. 'Brigh'on n'Ove Alb-yon.'

'Ah. Cheers, mate.'

The man nods, and then returns to staring at his newspaper. His saggy-faced mate sitting next to him is just staring at the wall.

'Why is *Dan* taking my daughter to watch *football*?'

'Hmm.' Chewing on the inside of his cheek, Darren's narrowed eyes again stare away at the cocktail menu. 'Does she like football?' he eventually asks.

'I don't know. That's it, I don't know anything about her anymore. I didn't even know that she's started . . .'

Darren gazes at me with his usual absent expression, possibly wondering what colours he'd paint me to look like one of the elves in his fantasy craft game.

'Started what?' he asks.

'Never mind,' I say, tucking the PMS conversation away. 'She slagged off R.E.M. today, too.'

'Woah, mate. No one disses The Rem.'

'Yeah, I know.' Taking a mouthful of beer, I replay the scene in my mind. 'I didn't respond well.'

'What did you say?'

'Well, except for slapping my hand on the kitchen counter, I didn't get a chance. Ella just said that she hates us both and stormed out of the room. Our quality father-daughter time, as usual.'

'Said that she hates Kirst, too?'

I nod. No longer does it feel entirely amusing that Kirsty has lost control of our daughter; that her perfect world isn't quite as shiny as it seems. Although Ella did call Dan a prick. Sometimes I wonder if Kirsty only married Dan because he has some of my worst qualities – except for the one of never having any money in my pockets. Being a prick is the only thing that I can compete with when it comes to *Dan*.

The realisation that I will forever be losing the one thing I truly care about is settling in stages. The stage I am now in is making me fidgety. My skin feels cold; my stomach is spinning like an out-of-control tombola. I'm familiar with anxiety and despair, but never has it ever felt as crippling as this.

I down the rest of my beer and head straight to the bar. The standard solution.

'What else does she like?' Darren asks once I have sat back down, our fresh pints in front of us. 'Other than football.'

Now it's my turn to search the cocktail menu. There's one called a Rusty Duck. That must be a new drink that Kev, the landlord, has made up. His Frilly Dipper is legendary for inducing a painful amnesia. Thinking back over the years, trying to recall a single one of Ella's interests or hobbies, feels a bit like struggling through a Frilly Dipper hangover.

Surely I must have taken Ella to some things that she's enjoyed.

We went to the park so that I could drink.

We went to go and see R.E.M. because Kirsty and I liked them.

I used to take Ella to the soft play centre when she was tiny, but a menstruating teenager is probably past that stage.

When I was thirteen, me and my friends used to go to the local rec. While some of the lads were kicking a ball around, I would see how far the girls would go with me, offering them sips of my stolen booze.

The thought now terrifies me.

Suddenly I have a thirteen-year-old daughter.

Pushing aside that weighty reality, I pick through the things that the girls from the rec used to do to entertain themselves.

They definitely liked to go shopping.

I hardly ever have any cash. Who's the real hero if I take Ella on a day out to spend *Dan's* money?

Everyone likes the cinema.

But we'd have to get the bus there. What's more, on the way to the bus stop we'd have to walk past *Dan's* BMW. And then I'd probably only end up waiting for Ella in the pub, like Kirsty does.

Some of the girls used to go ice skating.

Most of the time I struggle to walk in a straight line with normal shoes on.

Bollocks to it, I'll just take her to the park. If any boys begin to circle us, I'm sure I'll be able to fend them off.

Darren sits suddenly upright, looking around like a meerkat that's just woken up. He prods a finger at me. 'You should take her away first.'

'It would be kind of illegal to move somewhere with my daughter just so that Kirsty can't, Darren. Even if Ella agreed to it, which she wouldn't. And if she doesn't agree to it, that makes it even more illegal.'

'No, I'm not talking about taking her away for good. Take her on a trip, something like that.'

Because I am so used to dismissing most of the things that come out of Darren's mouth, his suggestion almost escapes me. But as the idea of a trip settles in, the greater its significance expands.

'What sort of trip?' I ask.

'Dunno. Like . . . somewhere she's not been before. You just said you don't get any quality time together, so that's what you need. Just the two of you, where no one else can get in the way. Try and impress her. A camping trip, or something.'

Bloody hell, he's right. I know almost nothing about Ella anymore, and I need to learn while there is still a chance. I need to bond with my daughter. There is surely no better way than to remove Dan and Kirsty entirely – preferably without murdering either of them.

I'll show Ella exactly who her old man is.

I am Captain Reliable. I can do it.

I am not Captain Reliable, but I can do it.

Captain Football can piss off.

We have one month, that's plenty of time.

'That's it,' I say. 'It's a brilliant idea. I'm going to take her on a trip. Let's celebrate. Pint?'

Just as I'm saying it, Bea walks in with her pool attendant. While pool boy radiates youth, health and vitality, Bea looks as rough as mildew. She's sniping away; pool boy looks as though he's at the end of his rope. So I have a good chuckle, obviously.

Confused as ever, Darren is back to being baffled. Perhaps his one helpful thought has worn him out. Bea's presence turns me off the idea of having another pint here, so I suggest we go to The Humphrey Bean instead.

Rusty Ducks can wait for another time.

four

A hundred years from now, I wonder if people will look back at photos of Tenderbridge as it is today. I wonder if they will hang those pictures on the walls in pubs, the same way that we do with black and white photos of the Edwardian and Georgian eras: those olden days scenes depicting a classy motorcar easing along past the local grocer, the butcher and the tailor. Women carrying parasols, wearing bonnets and flowing dresses. Men in three-piece suits, sporting fine moustaches, holding the hand of a smart young lad, pointing at a floral display outside the town theatre.

If modern historical pictures were displayed in their place, they would instead show a single mother wearing a pair of leggings too small for her, bosoms busting out of a thin strappy top bought in a supermarket, barging the pushchair that she got out of a skip through throngs of unhappy, unhealthy people. Lads in football shirts revving mopeds past an obese bloke who is driving a mobilised scooter through a bus lane, simultaneously smoking a cheap fag and eating a burger that drips curry sauce onto his stained tracksuit. The faces of fury and the shops full of tat. And I'll be there, speeding past people, Darren lolloping along just behind me, the sole mission in life to drink my next beer as soon as possible.

Perhaps they will hang those pictures, but only as a reminder of what can happen if you simply stop caring.

The Humphrey Bean stands at the foot of the Great Bridge, the centre of the town divide; a last fuelling stop before reaching the more sober surroundings of the riverbanks and castle grounds that welcome the north side. Something in the window of the charity shop next door to the pub draws my attention. Darren continues for a few paces before he notices that I've stopped.

'Look at this.'

'You've already got a ukulele you never play.'

I glance at the little instrument with sagging strings and Union Jack laminate body.

'Not that. These.' I point at a pair of patterned urns with three different breeds of bird perched upon their curves. Painted green vines snake upwards from the bases, over the detailed ornamentation, creeping up over the lids. 'They're pretty, aren't they?'

'That yellow bird looks a bit deformed, if you ask me,' Darren says, smearing his finger over the glass. 'Its head is too big. And that one.' He continues tracing his finger up to make a smudged tick on the window. 'Half its wing is missing. Anyway, since when have you been into vases?'

'I'm not. And I don't think it is a vase. Vases don't have lids.'

'Neither do some toilets,' says Darren, 'but they're still toilets.'

I glance sideways at him. With his finger still pressed against the glass, his eyes browse over the objects in the window as if he is scanning a page trying to find Wally, when all he really needs to do is look at his reflection.

'I might get them for Ella,' I say. 'She loved birds when she was little.' Whenever we walked through the park, we always had to stop to look at all the birds. She could watch them all day, leaning over the side of her buggy. And I was never in a hurry to be anywhere.

'I'd save your money, if I was you. Usual?' Darren asks over his shoulder, walking the few remaining steps to The Humphrey.

'Huh? Yeah, mate. I'll be in in a minute.'

A few minutes later, I join Darren at a table towards the back of The Humphrey. A scattering of the regular faces are in the pub, as always. A nod here and a nod there. I see Jerry, another local musician. As ever, Jerry is wearing his favourite bowler hat. Since he read some book about a blues singer who wears one, I have never seen him without it.

We tried sharing a bill with his band Beat Les one time, but had a falling out when he insisted that they were headlining because they had an original song. There are few things as humiliating as being shoved down the order of a two-band line up in a crap local pub. Especially when most people consider the other band to be more shit than you are.

Unwrapping the tissue paper, I place the urn on the

table. It turns out that there are four birds. I point the extra bird out to Darren.

'That one's wing is chipped as well,' he says.

'It's a beautiful little thing.'

'Can't see what you see in it, mate.'

'As long as Ella likes it, I don't really care. I wanted to get her the other one, too, but they were asking thirty quid for the pair.'

'You spent . . . half of thirty quid on this?'

'Twenty,' I reply. 'It was thirty for both, but sold individually each one is twenty. If the other one's still there after I get paid, I'm definitely going back for it.'

'What's she going to do with it, then?' Darren asks, no longer interested in the arithmetic.

That's actually quite a good question. What would a thirteen-year-old girl keep in a decorative urn? I know what I would have stashed in it when I was her age.

'Hair clips?' I say. 'A bit of change? Doesn't matter. It's cute. She's going to love it.'

'I saw Sadie the other day,' Darren says, changing subject.

'Sexy Sadie the lollipop lady?'

I haven't seen Sadie around in a long while. We were never going to be exclusive, her and I, even if I wasn't married. Sadie was just my life-changing indiscretion that indirectly led to the heartbreak I've been going through ever since, that's all.

'Where did you see her?'

'At the Jungle Gym,' Darren replies.

'What the hell were *you* doing at the Jungle Gym, Darren? I'm surprised they'd let someone like you within a hundred yards of a children's play area.'

'Didn't I tell you?' Darren says. 'I'm working there now. Burning burgers and frizzling fries. Easiest money I've ever made. Full of yummy mummies, too.'

'In *Tenderbridge*? Are you sure?'

'Them from the posh houses, mate,' Darren replies. 'And the au pairs. They love it.'

'I bet they do, Darren.'

'Sadie's got another one on the way, by the looks of her.'

'I wonder which one of the lads it is this time,' I say, looking around the pub.

'Perhaps it's Toothy Charlie's,' says Darren.

We both look at him, leaning on the bar, laughing in the face of the bemused barman.

Toothy Charlie is pretty much the only one who laughs at his bad jokes. Any excuse to show off his massive dentures. He was originally called Toothy Charlie because of the grotesque condition of the few teeth he had. Like most of the blokes in the pub now, Toothy has the regular Peaky Blinders buzz cut around the back and sides and a nest of hair flopping about on top. He looks fifty, Toothy, but rumour has it that he's only in his early thirties.

Something that is definitely not a rumour, Toothy Charlie used to piss on his bar stool so that no one else could use it. Apparently he saw animals doing the same thing in a documentary – marking their territory with their urine – and had then gone around telling people, "I'm an alpha, mate." As grim as Toothy Charlie is, he's also a fucking idiot.

Perhaps sensing that we're looking in his direction,

Charlie sees us. As if it's an invitation, his beaming grin leads him to our table.

'Alright, Charlie?' Darren says, high-fiving Toothy.

'Dazzler.' Toothy Charlie nods to Darren. 'Roger,' he says to me. He's called me Roger since we first met, just because he thinks it's funny.

'Alright, Charlie,' I mumble.

'What's been happening, man?' Darren says.

'Oh boys, it's been terrible.' Toothy bites his bottom lip, making him look just like Conrad Veidt in *The Man Who Laughs*. He shakes his head, sighing noisily through the wet, spiky prongs sticking out of his nostrils. 'Terrible, I tell ya.'

'Why's that, Charlie?' says Darren, playing the game, as he always does.

'Well, first of all my wife got hit by a bus. That wasn't so bad in itself. I mean, she needed a bit of work done.' He waits a beat, all keen teeth and bright eyes. 'But the worst thing about it is, I lost my job as a bus driver!'

Toothy Charlie spits laughter, slapping his thighs, his side, the table – almost my shoulder, too, if I hadn't weaved out of the way.

As always, Darren laughs along at Toothy's joke.

Morons.

Now Toothy has his hands out, as if hushing a crowd before delivering an important edict. 'But listen, right. Listen, yeah. There are only two times that I haven't been able to understand my wife. Two times, yeah?'

'Yeah?' Darren says, smiling, gormless as a gargoyle.

'Yeah. I didn't understand her before I got married, and I don't understand her now!'

It's obvious that Darren doesn't really understand,

either, but it doesn't stop him laughing. I whisk Ella's urn off the table, safely away from Toothy's enthusiastic rapture, and carefully cradle it inside the tissue paper. Then I down the last of my pint.

'You off, Roger?'

'I am,' I reply, giving Toothy's merry dance a swerve.

'Thought you smelt bad,' Toothy says, wheezing.

'I thought I smelt bad, too,' says Darren.

'Oh, yeah, Dazzler?' Toothy says. 'Why's that?'

'I don't know.' Tears start spilling from the corners of Darren's eyes. 'I haven't been able to get an appointment with the doctor.'

Leaving them laughing at themselves, I amble out of The Humphrey into the muggy heat and the suffocating fumes that cloud the high street.

five

As a once-popular musician in a small town, people stare at me. When I enter pubs, or I am walking along the high street, or sitting on the swings in the park with a bottle in my hand, minding my own business, people know that they know me from somewhere. No one says hello. They just stare, like tribes peering at an explorer. Walking homewards with Ella's urn under my arm, those stares from strangers talk to me.

There's that quasi-talented bloke.

The one who is a bit of a waster.

Did you hear that his family left him after he was caught shagging the lollipop lady?

I don't need their judgement. I knew exactly what I wanted to do and who I wanted to be; the things I wanted to have. I used to fantasise about living in a house so big that I would have to kindly ask friends not to climb on the battlements when I was having a party. There are plentiful reasons to explain why it hasn't happened for me. There are many fruitless branches on my tree of excuses. These days I just ramble around, not really knowing what I am doing except for working on my beer belly – which barely grows anyway due to the meagre intake of food. All I know is how to keep my guitar in tune and that the sky is vast. I do still occasionally look in the windows of the estate agencies to see if there are any houses with battlements for sale, though.

Back in the dim light of my tiny flat above a takeaway, I sit Ella's urn on the coffee table. It doesn't look quite as alluring as it had in the window of the charity shop, when the beer had drawn me to it. One of the birds is staring at me, so I put the tissue paper over the top of the urn, quieting it, happier once it is hidden away. Why the hell did I waste twenty quid on that? Perhaps I won't go back and buy the other one, after all.

Sliding the phone out of my pocket, I make the call that I know will irritate me within seconds.

'What's wrong?' my mum asks, straight off the bat.

'Nothing's wrong.'

'What do you want, then?'

'I don't want anything, mum. I just thought I'd ring.'

'You never *just ring*. You aren't like Paul, phoning to see how I am. Or to ask if I would like to visit him. Or to say that he's bringing his family to—'

'Can you phone me back, mum? On the mobile,' I add, before hanging up.

Slumped diagonally across the sofa, eyes closed, I run my palm back and forth across my forehead, unable to decide if it is my head or hand that is sweaty. And then the crazy samba begins.

'Hi, how are you?' I ask, answering on the first ring. 'What have you been up to?'

'You're drunk.'

'I'm not *drunk*, mum. I've only had a couple of beers. I was in the pub with Darren, planning some gigs,' I lie. 'I saw Ella today.'

'Poor girl,' mum replies.

Always *poor girl*.

'She's started menstruating,' I hear myself saying, a tricky one to wrap my fat tongue around. I'm not sure why I said it, either. It seems like mum talk.

'I know she has, John,' mum replies. 'Ella's not a baby anymore. Just because you've not been there for half her life doesn't mean that she's the same little girl you left behind.'

'I didn't leave her behind, mum. You know it wasn't like that.'

'Poor Kirsty. She phones me more than you do.'

'Does she?'

Vindictive bitch. Maybe I'll phone her mum.

'Kirsty only does things like that to get back at me. Don't fall for it.'

'Oh, is that why she sends me flowers and a card on my birthday?' mum retorts. 'Just to get back at you?'

'Probably, yes.'

Shit. Does she? Grabbing an envelope, in a scribble that mimics my slur, I jot *buy kirsty's mum a*

What shall I buy her? I know.

kitten, I scrawl.

I toss the envelope back onto the coffee table. The updraft blows the tissue paper off Ella's urn. Perhaps I'll give that to Kirsty's mum. I doodle a poor impression of it on the unopened envelope, which reveals itself to be from the council. They are indefatigable.

'Mum, I'm not phoning to have an argument. Or to talk about *poor Kirsty* or *poor Ella*. I need help with something.'

'So, there is something you want.'

'I don't *want* anything, mum. I've decided to take Ella on a trip, that's all. Before she . . .' I stop breathing for a second. 'Did *you* know that they're moving to Canada?'

'They're what?'

'Dan and Kirsty are taking Ella to Canada. Moving there. For good.'

'That flash bastard,' my mother growls. 'What are they doing that for?'

I explain that the move is for Dan's job; that Ella has been playing up ever since Kirsty announced their news. For some reason I mention the PMS again, too. I can't help the grin that settles upon my face when I emphasise how much Kirsty has been struggling with Ella.

Poor her.

Mum starts slagging off Dan again. While she's blathering on, I put the phone down, grab a beer from the fridge and discreetly slurp away.

'So, I'm planning to take Ella on a trip before she leaves,' I say. *Interrupting*? I might have been. I wasn't really listening.

I realise that I'm staring at the urn again.

'To see me?' mum says.

'Um . . . yeah. At some point, mum,' I reply, hoping that Kirsty is already planning a farewell visit to see my mother in the house that I grew up in. 'But I also want to take her somewhere special. Maybe camping, something like that. Where was it that we used to go when we were kids?'

'We always went to that Butlins, if you remember. The one in Skegness. You boys loved it there.'

'I wasn't really thinking of a family resort, mum. They're more for families. It would cost too much, anyway.'

'Have you still not got a proper job?' she says, immediately jumping on my slip up.

Next, she'll mention—

'Paul's been made a partner in his firm. He's away with his lot on a boat, travelling between Italian islands, celebrating. Their Ben just got accepted into his first-choice university, too, wonderful boy.'

'That's fucking lovely,' I interject as soon as she takes a break from lavishing praise on my wonderful brother's family. Or my brother's wonderful family. A combination of the two. My wonderful brother's wonderful family. I slurp some beer down and cut her off again. 'Where was it you and dad took us that time? I think it was somewhere in Wales.'

'Oh yes, I remember. That was the Brecons.' I hear a sharp intake. 'It's *so* beautiful there. And if I remember rightly, you were about the same age as your little girl is now.'

'Was I?'

I begin to smile . . .

'Oh, no. You must have been younger than that.'

But I don't complete my smile.

I know what this momentary dead air means; the events by which mum has calculated the date. Neither of us says it out loud.

'You were a right handful back home,' she continues. 'But once we got there, you and Paulie ran about all over the hills, chasing sheep on your bikes like little herders. You canoed and climbed rocks. You had a lovely time. We all did. Even your bastard father.'

And there it is. Mum can never resist the moment where she gets to raise the dagger.

'Thanks, mum,' I quickly cut in. 'And, er—'

'No, it didn't cost very much, before you ask. Do you have any income at all, you lazy boy?'

'Actually, I do,' I reply. 'I'm a postman now. Started about six weeks ago.'

She doesn't need to know that I am already on my third warning. The first warning was for being continually late. The second for immediately being late again and turning up still drunk from the night before. The third was for always being late and crashing the postal van – messing around, even though I've had my licence taken away – and also still being drunk from the night before again. It is only because Brian, the drummer in our band, is my manager that I was allowed to have a second third warning. Brian's incompetence – although I think it is probably disillusionment, having spent his entire adult life working for Royal Mail – is a large part of why I wanted to work there in the first place.

Darren used to be a postman, too, but Brian did fire him after three warnings. It might have only been two, I'm not sure. Darren didn't care. As a session guitarist, he's making more money than any of us. That's why his job burning fast food at the Jungle Gym came as such a surprise.

Mick, the other member of our band, the bassist, owns a little village fishmonger's. He certainly knows his fish, Mick. Loves them more than he loves his bass.

It's only really me and Darren who consider ourselves to be proper musicians.

'It's great being a postman,' I say. 'The early starts mean that I have the rest of the day to work on music.' *Sit in the pub and talk about music.* 'I'm working hard right now. The band is going pretty well, too.' *Which isn't that bad a lie if "pretty well" can loosely mean "the band are barely rehearsing and haven't had a gig in months."*

'Just be sure you make the most of your time with Ella, alright? That bastard man, taking her to a foreign country, just to suit himself. Still, none of this would be happening if it wasn't for you and that lollipop lady.'

'Why do you have to mention the lollipop lady *every time* I phone? You don't know what it was like, living with Kirsty.'

'Don't know what it was like?' mum replies, snapping like a whip. 'Don't know what it was like? You're just like your father, you are.'

'Like my father?' I snap right back, squishing the beer can. 'Like my father? Mum, I made one mistake. Dad walked out on us.'

six

In the days following the lollipop incident, Kirsty hadn't allowed me to see Ella for more than a fortnight. I tried turning up at the door first thing in the morning, or after the pub last thing at night. I waited outside the house when Ella was due to arrive home from school. I even went to the school, but learned not to do that when Ella's teacher, Miss Eggleton, threatened to phone the police. And then Miss Eggleton did phone the police. And then I was escorted away by the police. It wasn't even my fault. Darren was the one who had been kicking off.

Because it was his idea to go to Ella's school, Darren insisted on coming with me. We left the pub, four or five pints in – I forget, maybe it was more – and the rest is sorry history. Kirsty and I were arguing all the time back then, so Ella already knew most of the words that Darren screamed at Miss Eggleton, but some of the other kids clearly didn't.

The situation with my mum and dad was entirely different. The initial separation was much more civil.

After lunch one Sunday, Paul and I were told to go and wait in our den – the garden shed – while mum and dad finished talking in the kitchen . . .

'What do you think they're talking about?' I ask.

'Dunno,' Paul says. 'Maybe dad's won The Pools.'

Paul likes to talk about The Pools, because it sounds like his name and it involves lots of money.

I have my stack of *Mexico '86* Panini swapsies in my hand. I can't believe my luck: I've got two spare Bryan Robsons. So far, though, England have lost one and drawn one of their two games, and Captain Marvel's just got himself injured.

Alongside Robson, we have posters of some of our other favourite footballers pinned to the walls in the den. Although Paul ripped down my Tony Woodcock picture. He said that he's gay because he has "cock" in his name. Recently, Paul has also started pinning up posters of bands and musicians that he likes.

The only other things in the den are our bikes, a flat football, Paul's skateboard and my new Aerobie, which I was given for my birthday. We're not allowed to play with it in the garden anymore, because the neighbours got sick and tired of us jumping over their fence to fetch it back. In the corner, opposite the sofa we are sitting on, is my tiny plastic chair, just like the ones we have at school. And just like at school, it hurts my arse if I sit on it too long.

'I can get a fiver for one of those Robsons,' Paul says, reaching over and snatching one of them from my pile. 'McGuilly needs one.'

'Cool!' I say. Because *everything* is cool when you've just turned ten.

'When McGuilly pays up, you get two quid and I'll keep three quid,' Paul says. 'A sixty-forty split.'

'No!' I try to grab the sticker back off him. 'That's not fair.'

'It's barter, you prick. That's how trade works.'

'No. Give it back to me, Paul.'

Paul keeps the sticker out of my reach, the same way that Captain Marvel shields the ball from the opposition. We start wrestling on the sofa. He has his hand on my forehead, pushing me away. I can feel my eyelids peeling back. A burning sensation prickles in my hairline.

'Don't call John a prick, thank you, Paul,' dad says, entering the den.

We stop wrestling and look up at him.

'I need to talk to you, boys,' he says. 'Sit in your chair, John. Shove up, Paul.'

Even though I know that the chair will hurt my arse, I do it anyway. Hopefully this won't take too long. Paul shuffles along the sofa, kicking my shins accidentally-on-purpose.

Dad sits down next to Paul, but he's looking at me, so I smile at him. I have only just had my birthday, but already I'm thinking about more presents. This is going to be so cool.

Stroking the new moustache that he's taken to growing, Dad stares at Paul's Pet Shop Boys poster. 'I'm not going to be living here with you boys anymore,' he says, popping the bubble that only a moment before had been holding so many amazing things. 'You're just going to be living with mum from now on.'

The smile that was stuck to my face is replaced by my open mouth. My stomach feels like it did when Paul kicked the ball at me the other day and it flew straight into my nuts. I make a sort of snot sound in the back of my throat, kind of like the noise we make when we're trying not to laugh in class after someone farts. Even if someone farted now, I wouldn't laugh. In fact, I'm closer to crying. The last time I cried, holding my nuts after the football smashed into them, Paul called me a pussy, so I try to hold it in.

'You have to live here,' I say, my voice a bit blubbery. 'Who's going to take us to football practice if you're not here?'

'Mum will have to take you,' dad replies.

Again, he attempts to smile, but I can see that he's sad. If it was a proper smile his new moustache would be a straight line, and not kind of turned down at the ends, like it is now. He squeezes Paul's leg. It makes Paul twitch.

Paul's eyes are narrowed, almost to slits, like he is thinking of saying something but can't quite think of the words. It's the same look he sometimes gives me at the dinner table, silently telling me that he's going to pay a visit to my room later for some beats.

'I know that it might be a bit of a shock,' dad continues. 'But the truth is I've been thinking about this for a while. See . . .' Now it is dad's turn to take a moment to think about what words to say. 'I've met someone else,' he finally says.

Paul turns his narrowed eyes towards dad. 'What?'

'It's true, Paul, I'm afraid. I've met someone else and I'm going to be living with him.'

Paul's eyes are properly open now. He's got that furious kind of look you get when you smell something bad. '*What* did you say?'

'From now on,' dad says, 'I'm going to be living with my friend Julian.'

Paul leans towards dad. He sometimes does the same thing just before headbutting me. 'Your friend . . . *Julian*?'

'Yes. Julian. The man I know from the squash club. And, well . . . We . . .' Dad looks at me. And then he looks back at Paul. 'We're in love with each other,' he finishes quickly, lifting his chin.

'You . . . *love* each other?' Paul says, now as if the smell has got much worse, like he has caught the first whiff of one of dad's Christmas farts. Realising that dad's hand is still on his thigh, Paul jerks back. 'Get off me, you gaylord.'

Dad tries to reach out to Paul, and Paul swipes his hand away.

'Seriously, don't ever touch me again,' he shouts, right in dad's face. 'Get out my way.'

Paul screws up my Robson sticker, throws it on the floor, accidentally-on-purpose stomps on both of dad's feet, and then storms out of the shed, slamming the door behind him. It bounces back off the frame and swings open into the day. Before disappearing inside the house, I see Paul kick the washing line. And then he is gone.

Now it's just us two.

I try to look at dad. It takes a few attempts to meet his eyes. He looks different to me now, and not just because of the weird moustache. For the first time, I notice that he looks a bit younger. His hair is longer than before, too.

These days he looks like one of the keyboard players on Top of the Pops.

He is smiling at me, but it still doesn't look like he means it. I've never seen dad look this sad. Actually, it's not really a *sad* look. I can't quite explain it. The closest thing I can think of is when I've been playing up and I'm not allowed to go and see my friends. The face looking back at me in the mirror after the anger has gone. Kind of hopeless.

'What does that mean, dad?' I ask. 'Are you joking? Because . . . you *can't* love other men.'

'You certainly can, John,' dad replies, smiling that sort-of-sad, floppy-moustache smile.

Leaning forward, it looks as if he is about to move towards me. I lift my knees. It makes the chair scrape on the floor. I hadn't noticed until now how tightly I had been gripping the plastic edges. Once dad has retreated and is sitting back down properly, I slowly lower my feet.

I watch as he looks around the den. His eyes settle upon something, then his gaze continues to wander, until we are silently looking at each other, once more.

'So . . . you really *are* a gaylord?' I ask after a bit more sad staring between us.

'That's not a word that I would like to use, John,' he says, using a tone that's a bit more like normal dad. 'And I don't think it's appropriate for you to use. But, yes,' he says. 'I would say that . . . I am now . . . a gay man.'

Later, I learned that dad's affair started in the showers of the squash club. Because I sit around and think about things, a lonely impression of a man who has too much time to himself, I wondered how common that must be.

It starts after a game, two men lathering themselves while praising each other's performance. They might mention their friend's physique. Perhaps that is then followed by a polite offer to soap their friend's back. If that's not too weird, you offer to soap them a bit more. Before you know it, the soap is forgotten on the floor and you're beneath the stream of hot water, pressed up against the slippery tiles.

I'm not quite sure how our friends got wind of it as quickly as they did, but there was no question that dad couldn't come and collect us from school anymore. Life became tricky for a while, and it stayed that way until we'd all matured a bit. Okay, until we'd matured quite a lot. It was much worse for Paul, though. He was already at secondary school.

In the years that followed, Paul became tough, hard-nosed, and determined to succeed. Since the day dad left to go and shack up with Julian, Paul has barely spoken to him. When they have spoken, it has never been friendly; quite the opposite. Whether it would have been the same if dad had left for a more vanilla affair, I am not sure.

At first, I had a similar reaction to the news, mostly bred by Paul's continued attitude and my own confusion. But as I grew through the years, finished school and gained independence, I was surprised to find that dad's love affair bothered me less and less, to the point that it developed into fondness.

Dad has always been a kind and gentle man – except

for when he was rowing with my mum. Initially, I wasn't overly keen on his new dress sense, all cravats and silk shirts, as if he'd accessorised from a pantomime dressing up box. But the most important thing, I've realised, is that dad seems to be happier now than he has ever been.

Just weeks after he moved in with Julian, dad quit his job as the marketing manager of the local council. And what a life he has had ever since.

To see them together, they're a right pair, swanning about living the high life. A visit to art museums in Vienna on Monday. Tea at Claridge's on Tuesday. Lunch and an overnight stay at *Le Manoir* on Wednesday. All followed by an extended weekend on a yacht moored off Antibes. Who wouldn't take a friendly bit of buggery for all that?

It is not only Julian's fashion sense that has been a great influence over dad. He never previously cared for the kinds of things that now make up their lives. The house they share in Henley is full of fancy ornaments and books on art. To walk through the garden is to experience a glimpse of one of the royal flower shows. Each blade of grass is perfect, as if measured by a ruler and cut by hairdressing scissors. Statues peek from within the canopies of ornamental trees.

When he was living at home, dad wouldn't have been able to distinguish a dandelion from a daffodil.

I recently learned that they do voluntary work, too, helping local charities, growing vegetables in community gardens. Next, they'll take up a placement in a National Trust property, learning all they can about the history of the place before guiding groups through galleries, rooms and gardens, pointing out the species and the genus of plants, trees and shrubs.

I like Julian a lot. He's funny, flamboyant and smart. In the seventies, he made a fortune selling patterned silk scarves, and the cravats that dad's taken to wearing. All he does these days is knock out a few new designs every now and then and wait for the money to roll in. If you see a celebrity, or a sultan, or anyone with a bit of cash wearing a silk scarf, Julian would have designed it.

On occasion, they come down and take me out to lunch, both finding it amusing as I get steadily pissed. Encouraging it, even, by plastering the bill with bottles of expensive wine and the very best cognac that the restaurant has. I didn't even know what a *digestif* was before Julian took me out for dinner.

Although I have never properly spoken with him about it, I have wondered if Paul's lingering resentment might have been caused, in part, by jealousy of dad's new lifestyle. Working hard, sometimes seven days a week, I think that Paul flirts with the status of millionaire. All that Julian has to do is doodle a few pretty patterns and send it off to Taiwan, or wherever, and then the rest – from manufacture to market – is done for him.

Having survived a marriage of my own, I can understand why dad would bond with someone who sees the light in each day. He met someone, told my mum, and he left. So it's unfair for her to compare it with what I did.

I was much more cowardly.

Either way, whatever the reason for the riot, there is always damage left behind.

seven

Ella's phone is ringing, as it usually does when I call her, although sometimes she cuts it off mid-ring. For anyone trying to get through to me, the probability will be that my mobile will have run out of juice, or I will have left it somewhere. An arsonist keeps hold of a box of matches longer than a mobile phone in my possession stays in one piece.

The latest phone that I am using is one of Ella's old mobiles. After nearly six months it is still in working condition, which is close to a record. After she gave it to me, I discovered some old pictures of her and her mates stored on it. When I can't sleep, or if I'm alone in the pub, I flick through them.

Grateful as I am for the photos, the battery on it is absolutely useless.

Ella picks up. At least I think she has.

'Ella?' A look at the scratched screen tells me that we are definitely in call. I check the volume. 'Els, are you there?'

I hear a full-on sigh, confirming that she is.

'What's up?'

Yet more silence greets me.

'Els? Are you alright?'

'Yeah, I'm okay,' she eventually replies. 'It's just—'

'I'm nearly out of credit,' I say. 'Can you call me back? On the mobile?'

As if I have a landline.

Another long sigh, and then I hear the sound of the connection clicking off.

This part never feels good. Reaching early-middle-age to find myself in a position where I have to ask my teenage daughter to call me back on her old phone is probably quite uncommon. It's worse if Ella doesn't answer; then I have to ring the house phone. Asking the wealthy stepfather if my daughter can please ring me on the mobile that he bought and has been handed down to me can be pretty humiliating. Or it should feel that way, but it is clearly not beneath me.

I grab a cushion, lie down on the floor and stare at a peeling patch of paper on the ceiling. I can see a galaxy within it. The mottled damp and mouldy patches as stars and planets around the spiders' web of an exploding black hole. A universe inside organic rot.

After a few minutes, Ella still hasn't called back. I look at the time. It's only just after ten in the morning. Other than speaking with Ella, I've nothing else planned today. It's wet outside for the first time in weeks, so I'll probably end up whiling the day away in the pub.

Now that I've started thinking about it, I find myself on the way to the fridge. Before I reach the kitchen, the funky samba ringtone chimes through from the other room, so I turn on my heel.

'Hey, Els. I thought for a minute that you weren't going to call back!'

Another long silence answers me. This is not unusual behaviour for Ella. These days she often sounds glum. Perhaps she always has, I can't really remember. It might be another PMS thing.

'I didn't want to talk in the house,' she replies, 'so I came out to the garden.'

Ah yes, the treehouse, complete with a four-foot wide staircase and glazing. Dan commissioned its construction when Kirsty and Ella first moved in. It has a bunkbed, a sofa and a telly for when Ella has friends to stay. If it had a fridge, I'd happily live in it. In the background I can hear the light thrum of rain upon its pitched roof.

'What have you been up to?' I ask.

'It was only, like, *yesterday* that I saw you.'

Ah, there's my girl and her usual disdain.

'So, you didn't watch any football on telly?'

Perhaps there is a satellite delay between north and south Tenderbridge. Or maybe the takeaway's massive extractor fan, rattling away beneath my window twenty hours a day, is interfering with the signal. I can feel its vibrations through the floor.

'Why would I watch football?' she asks.

'I just thought you're into that sort of thing these days,' I reply, quite casually.

'*No*,' Ella huffs.

'Oh right. I only ask because—'

'Yeah, Dan offered to take me and Keira,' she fires back. 'I probably won't *go*. Football's stupid.'

'Yeah, football is stupid. I agree.'

'I only said that I'd *go* because I'm so *bored*.'

'How can you be bored? Summer holidays are better than school, aren't they?'

The pitter-patter of rain coming through the phone and the drone of the extractor fan harmonise through the silence of her response.

To the fore, I can hear her breathing.

From years long passed, returning home late after the pub, I would crawl up the stairs and lean over Ella's bed to listen to her soft, sleeping breaths. The next morning, Kirsty would often find me asleep on the floor in Ella's room. Even though most of my memories have been blasted into oblivion, I will never forget those times. I think of them always.

'Don't you go to the park with your friends?' I ask once it's clear that she can't be arsed to answer my question. 'You know . . . in big groups, and stuff?'

'What are you *actually* asking me, dad?' Ella replies. 'You're being weird, *as usual*.'

'I'm just interested in what you're up to. I always am.' I shift the cushion behind my head and stretch my legs and chest. It feels like a hug. 'I think about you all the time, Els. I miss you.'

'And *again*, you saw me yesterday.'

'You know that's not what I mean. Even when I do see you, I know it's not going to be for long. It never is. And yesterday you stomped off, remember?'

I look around the room. Did I get myself a beer? I can't see it anywhere. I was certain that I went to the fridge.

'Are you *drunk*?'

'Ella, come on. It's not even eleven o'clock in the morning.'

'Doesn't usually stop you.'

'That's not fair.' I think about it for a second. I was literally just looking for my beer. 'Alright, that probably is fair. But no, I'm not drunk. Last night I couldn't sleep, that's all. I was thinking about . . . something.'

'Mum told you about moving to Canada,' Ella says. 'I can't believe they've just decided we're going, without asking me first. They think it's alright to take me away even if I don't want to. Pair of twats.'

'Ella! I know you're angry, but I don't want to hear my little girl talking that way. Like, I don't know . . . Like a merry-go-round mechanic.'

The biggest sigh yet, accompanied by a sound like something being dropped on the floor.

'I wouldn't have minded as much if we were moving to America. But Canada? What even is there in Canada?'

'Neil Young is from Canada,' I say. 'And Leonard Cohen.'

'Is that supposed to impress me?' she retorts. 'I don't even know who they are. And I don't give a shit about them. I am from England. My friends are from England. And I want to stay in England. I mean, I don't want to live with you, or anything – that's a fucking horrible idea – but I'm not going, even if I have to join a convent.'

I lean up slightly. '*Well*—'

'Dad, I'm not actually going to join a convent.'

'You could, though.'

'Why are you being a prick now, too?'

'Okay, Ella. Just stop, alright?' She does. She has. And again I can hear her breaths. 'Are you crying?'

'Piss off,' she says, the tears audible. 'I'm going.'

'No, wait!'

The battery might only just be clinging to life, but the screen is still alive. By the slightly choked air and slithery sound of thickened saliva in the earpiece, it seems that Ella has waited. The curiously massaging *brrrrr* of the fan hums on through the floor.

'I want to do something with you before you leave,' I say. 'I'd like to take you on a trip. Not to the football, a proper trip.' Now that I know Ella doesn't like watching a bunch of wallies fannying about like children, I simply can't resist. I presume her silence is an invitation for me to continue. 'We can go away somewhere. I was thinking camping, maybe?'

'Camping?' she repeats. I can't tell if her tone was littered with antipathy or propped up with interest.

'Yeah,' I say, as tenderly as I can.

'What . . . with you?'

'Yes, Ella. A trip for just you and me.'

'Are you planning on being pissed all the time?'

'*Ella.*' Examining the galactic patch of ceiling and my aroused taste buds, I scratch my neck. 'No, I'm not planning on being *pissed all the time*. We need to spend some proper time together, you and I. You know, before you leave.'

'Can you stop saying that? *Please.*'

'What do you think, Els? Just dad and daughter. It'll be fun!'

It sounds as though the rain on the treehouse has eased, maybe ceased. Through my mouldy old curtains, which are barely hanging onto the rail, I can't tell from my position on the floor.

'You promise not to get drunk all the time?' Ella asks with only moderate contempt.

'Yeah. I promise. Just fresh air and fun. We can go hunting for animals! Hunting, as in, looking for them,' I quickly add. 'Not, like, shooting them.'

'Will we have to stay in the same tent?'

'Erm . . . no?' I hadn't thought about that. I can't remember if I've ever seen a tent for sale in my shit local minimarket. 'You'll have your own space, Els. Promise. I was thinking we could go to Wales. I went there when I was a kid.'

'Dan took us to Sardinia.'

She is becoming so fucking much like Kirsty.

I grab the cushion and press it hard into my face. Once I am satisfied that it's out of my system, I return the phone to my ear.

'That sounds fun. But this will be *awesome* fun.'

'*Awesome fun.*' I hear her laugh. She's actually laughing. 'You're such an old loser.'

'Actually, people in town think I'm pretty cool, you know. Umm . . . some of them.'

'Only because they're all pissed, too. Or because they carry big lollipops around to make a living.'

Lollipops. I laugh with her, and it feels good. Leaning up on my elbow, I plump the cushion and then lay back down.

'Ella, what you said earlier. About staying here, in England. What if I could find a way to make it happen?'

'What?'

'What if there is a way that you could stay here and live with me? Maybe you could spend the summers in Canada and the rest of the time here with your friends. I could get a new place. If we lived together, I could teach you to play guitar. Do you remember you wanted to learn when you were little?'

A chemical pulse of happiness electrifies my blood. I've never considered the possibility of Ella and I living together again. I mean, I would have to change quite a lot of my natural habits, but this would be the best solution for everyone, surely.

'We could do anything you like, Els, all the time . . . Ella?'

This goddamn phone. It must have finally given up just when I was getting going, the cruel bastard.

'Els?'

I look at the screen. The picture of Ella aged eight? nine? thereabouts, is smiling back at me, her arm around some little blonde girl with a puffy face. Even though the last slither of battery life is flashing red, the screen is still glowing, defiantly so.

Ella must have hung up.

eight

Band practice is every Tuesday fortnight. Or that's when it's supposed to be. Often, we just go to the pub instead, where the conversation usually descends into an earnest debate about Warhammer. That's when I will leave the table to try and find someone to chat up. Normally I'll be about as successful as our band has been.

This is one of the rare rehearsals when everyone has turned up. Even Mick, who usually can't be arsed. But Mick is here, and, as always, Mick stinks of fish. Brian suggested that he should try washing with lemon juice, which apparently neutralises the pong. Mick countered that he has an intolerance of citrus. I think that he simply likes the stench.

We have just banged through a cover of *What's the Frequency, Kenneth?* – always a great loosener to warm us up. Seeing as we haven't practised together in well over a month it sounded pretty good, relative to our usual output.

Playing covers really is the easiest option for any

band. I'm the only one of us who has ever bothered to try writing original songs. It used to irritate me, arriving with a new tune, a recording of it sent out to the others days before, only to find that none of them had added a solo or embellishment on their respective instruments.

"It's just too dirgy to play in the pub," Darren said one time. I don't know from where Darren picked up the word *dirgy*. I suppose it is a very *musiciany* word.

"That's because it's recorded on a shit phone," I argued.

"I wouldn't be able to fit drums around that, John," Brian chimed in.

"You can! Think about what Hendrix did to *Watchtower*. Come on, let's jam it," I said, strumming the chords on my acoustic, nodding where the accents are. "See? Put a fill in there, Brian. And Darren, you could—"

"Shall we do *Big Mouth Strikes Again*?" Darren interrupted, already playing the opening chords. Right on cue, Brian started banging out Mike Joyce's simple drumbeat.

(Mick wasn't there that time. He was fishing. He didn't even make up some excuse, just **IM FISHING 2NITE** by text, half an hour after we'd all arrived.)

That was the last time I brought anything more than a new cover song to rehearsals. It's been a long while since I even attempted to write something original. Disinterest is as contagious as laziness – which actually sounds quite like a Morrissey lyric. Not that my bandmates would be willing to work around it.

'Have you seen the new Chaos Lord figure?' Darren asks Mick this Tuesday night, the last hammered-on D chord of *Kenneth* still ringing out.

'Yeah,' Mick replies from his usual position, sitting on the bass amp. When we could no longer tolerate the smell of fish, we had to insist that he stays away from us, near an open window.

'It's fierce,' Darren continues. 'Got one on pre-order. When The Lord is on the fortress alongside Mallex, you won't have a chance, mate.'

'I've ordered the Master of Executions,' Mick says, slowly looking up to reveal a secretive smile.

In the days when we used to be vaguely cool, Mick had an early-Dylan curly mop. Whenever he bobbed about with the bass, this amazing mass of hair would bounce around in a spongy mess of movement. These days Mick keeps his hair short. When he leans forward over his bass it reveals his growing bald patch.

Since those early years of girls and enthusiasm, we have all changed. I used to shove a pair of socks down the front of my pants, even when we were rehearsing, because I'd heard a rumour that Robert Plant did the same thing. Now I just wear a pair of cheap Y-fronts.

Darren looks as excited as a child with a frog in his bucket. 'When they arrive, we are going to have the war to end all wars. I promise you, mate, you are doomed.'

He thrashes out a power riff and begins whipping his hair around like James Hetfield. Mick starts jamming with it. *Jamming*. Brian joins in, busting out an amazing offbeat. Then seamlessly they segue into Tool's *Stinkfist*.

It's not even a song from our fucking repertoire.

But, I reluctantly admit, it does sound awesome.

I grab my jacket and pull out my phone, intending to search for the lyrics. The phone is out of juice – of course it bloody is. A buzz of irritation starts boiling behind my eyeballs.

Bollocks to this.

Leaving the three of them having the time of their lives, I pluck a can from the beer fridge and head outside for a cigarette. It's only because of these pricks and the general state of my life that I smoke at all.

Rehearsals are held at Brian's house in a village to the east of Tenderbridge, where the countryside is only a short fall over the garden borders. Out here, the fast-food outlets, and the scumbags who hang around outside them, are few. Following the fourth complaint from his new neighbours – and a friendly-ish visit from the bobbies – Brian kitted out his garage with soundproofing. Following another appearance by the police, we learned that the maximum volume Darren could turn his guitar up to was four. All of us have varying severities of tinnitus. And, what's more, the smell is worse because the window Mick sits beneath now has to stay closed.

After cracking the beer open, I remove my earplugs – oh, the things we learn with age, long after the grinning horse of knowledge has bolted. Leaning on the garage, exhaling smoke, I gaze at Brian's house on the other side of the paved driveway. Wisteria grows neatly up the walls and over the porticoed doorway, aesthetically hugging the latticed windows. Even though most of the lilac flowers have fallen, it feels eras away from my flat. A light is shining out of the kitchen, and also from one of the upstairs rooms, stealing into the deepening evening dark.

Brian has a lovely wife, two smart sons, a healthy dog and his job in management. Whenever I am standing out here, looking at his house, pissed off at the others, I think about that. Mick only comes to rehearsals when he can be bothered, a distraction from spending time with his fish. For Darren it's all a bit of fun, a playful diversion from earning proper money as a session musician – and, apparently, frizzling food at the Jungle Gym. And for Brian it's a chance to have the boys round, amusing himself with his hobby. None of them need to play gigs. Since the age of thirty, no longer have any of them dreamed about making it. Whatever the fuck that means.

The side door of the garage opens, releasing a gasp of the rocking thunder that my bandmates are making. Tucking his hair behind his tiny ears, Darren leans on the garage next to me and sparks up. Like a ping pong ball, he bounces to a rest.

'I thought that I'd find you out here,' he yells. Darren might be insanely talented, but he really is bewilderingly stupid. 'That was banging.'

'It sounded good,' I say perfunctorily.

'What?' he shouts.

I mime taking something out of my ears. Monkey see, monkey do, Darren discovers his earplugs and removes them.

'You want some?' he shouts more mildly, offering me a spliff.

I assumed Darren had lit a cigarette. I wonder how long it will take Mick to sniff out the skunk. The other two don't really smoke anymore, being family men, but Mick will sometimes join us if there is a reefer going around. We all know why those fishermen really love to sit out all day and night on the riverbank, just staring at the water.

The spliff tastes good, but I'll regret it tomorrow. I always do. What feels like a *jus* to complement the meat of my creativity after a few beers always turns into a blitz of paranoia and inactivity the next day. When temptation is presented to me, though, I am never thinking about the next day. I take a sip from my can and tug on the spliff.

'How's the Canadia thing going?' Darren asks.

'*Canada*,' I say, exhaling, tired of hearing the word Canadia only a little bit less than I am heart-strung by the news about Canada. Normally I let his gormlessness go, but my angst is running high, and the powerful skunk hasn't kicked in yet. 'It's pronounced *Canada*. *Canadians* live in *Canada*.'

On the occasions that I don't let it go, I always feel bad afterwards.

'Sorry,' I say.

'What for?' he says.

'Nothing, Darren.'

The light in the upstairs window goes out, drawing his attention.

Spiriting through tall shrubs, the orange glow of the streetlamp catches the blue smoke in devilish oriental patterns. Looking up further into the night, I can see the stars. I can't remember when I last saw them so clearly. I tap the ash off the end of the reefer and hand it back to Darren.

'There's not a lot to say about Canada,' I say, already feeling a little more pacified. 'But I did ask Ella if she'd like to go on a trip with me.'

'What, like, to the park, or whatever you said?'

'No, mate. A camping trip. Like you suggested.'

'Oh, mega. Yeah, I know.'

'I asked if she wanted to live with me, too.'

Darren turns his wide eyes my way. Within the misty cloud of smoke, the mask of his face is aghast. 'You did *what*? You asked her to *live* with you? Oh, mate.'

'What?' I say. 'What's wrong with that?'

'Well, it's a bit weird, isn't it? A forty-two-year-old man and a young girl living together.'

'Darren, she's my daughter.'

'Oh, yeah. Fair, mate, fair.'

I think Darren picked up that everything is *fair* from Jet Damage, his guitar sparring partner. Jet Damage (real name: Lee Potter) knows his way around a guitar like a blind man knows the smell of stinging nettles. But, like Darren, he has never been bothered to learn much else.

'It was a bit impulsive on my part, I suppose. I just kind of blurted it out, but have been thinking about it ever since. It's the only thing I can think of that might stop her moving away. But what if we fall out and it ends up like the situation with Kirsty? I don't know. I don't know what to do about any of it.'

I half-turn towards Darren. He's looking at the sky, his eyes moving from star to star.

'Did you see that shooting star?' he says.

'No, mate. I wasn't looking.'

'It might not have been a shooting star, actually. Just looked like one.'

He hands me the spliff. I take a drag, and then a sip of beer. And then again repeat the process in reverse. I hold in the smoke, and then breathe out until my lungs are completely empty.

'Maybe Ella and me living together is a bit weird,' I concede.

I continue to tell Darren about the call of this morning. Ella cried and I felt so hopeless, this little girl of mine being torn from her home, her friends. From me. But she had, perhaps thankfully, cut off the call when I mentioned living together.

After speaking with her, at first I had felt happy. But ever since I have been thinking about nothing else other than what my life without Ella will be. I open up. I tell him all of it. Except for the part that I have been trying to work my head around. The one that wonders why I have never tried to reach out to Ella in this way before.

And, God, I am starting to feel stoned.

'Tough, mate,' Darren says, having taken a while to process my tale. I wasn't certain he had been listening. 'Good that she doesn't like football, though.'

'I suppose, yeah. That is something.'

I rub my thumb across the top of my finger. It feels wet. In the orange light, I can see that it is bleeding from where I've been chewing on it so much today.

Because of the ten o'clock curfew imposed by the police, at quarter past ten we stop playing. Instead of messing around on acoustic guitars after practice, like we used to, our new tradition is to sit and drink a few beers.

These are not really band practices anymore, because there is nothing that we are practicing for. It's not like we've been booked to play any pubs, weddings or children's birthday parties – as we once did, disastrously. If there is anything worse than a drunk clown, it's a drunk band. After that particular show, Brian had quit for a few months. After all, it was his kid's party.

The garage has been transformed into a man cave that boy's dreams are made of. Hanging on the walls are framed portraits of The Velvet Underground and Nico, Debbie Harry (wearing only thick mascara and a t-shirt), R.E.M., 10,000 Maniacs, The Undertones, The Specials. Among them is a print of an original Leonard Cohen poem, and one of Lennon's sketches. Because it is Brian's garage, so it's Brian's rules, the biggest picture of all is of Madonna. Just off to one side, almost forgotten, is the framed poster of our one career highlight.

Growing up, quite a few bands we were into used to play The Angel Centre in Tenderbridge. Being a mouthy little chancer, somehow I managed to get us our first proper gig there, supporting Carter the Unstoppable Sex Machine. Finally, we were up on the stage ourselves, playing to our friends in the audience, sharing the bill with an actual, proper band. This was it. We had made it. We had youth, Mick had hair and we played only original songs – they weren't great, but we had at least been trying.

After the gig, Jim Bob from Carter told me that he quite liked *Strain Me* – my two minute punky love song, and a complete Johnny Cash rip off. Although, later that night, Jim Bob did also tell me to fuck off after I drank too much White Lightning and started flicking his floppy fringe.

Our feet were pressed firmly down on the bottom rungs of the ladder that climbs to stardom. And then Kirsty, babies and lollipop ladies entered my world.

These days The Angel is a fitness centre, which also

houses the soft play Jungle Gym where Darren works. When you're young, no one ever tells you that dreams are only things that end up being concreted over. I try so hard not to look at that poster.

As well as the beer fridge and soundproofing, Brian also installed a sound desk next to the drum booth so we could record our practices. If we have used it a dozen times I would be surprised. I look at it now, covered by a dustsheet. Some boxes have been put on top of it. Just like the pool table and dusty darts board we never use.

Sitting on leather sofas, we are facing each other over the Abbey Road crossing rug. Joni is chirruping away through the PA she's rigged up to. The chat is mostly between Darren and Brian. Totally monged, I just watch.

'I wonder how many burgers I've ever eaten,' Darren says. 'It must be thousands.'

'I reckon I've seen you eat more than a hundred,' Brian replies, scratching his short back and sides.

It's the only hairstyle I've ever known Brian to have, trimmed every fortnight in the same barbershop he went to for his very first haircut. Brian's old man used to be a copper, which is the main reason why their visits to his garage were always so cordial. As if inherited, Brian's hair is standard issue rozzer: the close buzzcut and the unfortunate widow's peak. Whenever he is pondering something, Brian can't help but fiddle with the fuzzy tuft of the peak, like he's doing now.

'What if you threw up the burger afterwards?' he asks Darren. 'I've must have seen you do that at least twenty times.'

'Fair, mate,' Darren says. 'Hadn't thought about that.'

'What about bags of crisps?' Brian says. 'How many

bags of crisps would we have eaten between us? What do you think, boys?'

'Well, I must have had at least one bag a day for the last twenty or thirty years, so . . .' Darren looks up at a collage of postcards that Brian bought from Covent Garden market in the nineties, the very same ones that used to be Blu Tacked to his bedroom wall. 'Lots,' he says after about thirty seconds, as if he'd been trying to work it out.

I find myself smiling. If I was only drunk I might join in, but I'm way too stoned to bother. I haven't even got the energy to move away from Mick's pong.

My mashed-up thoughts begin to wander. Skunk-numbed, my eyes drift to the Carter gig poster. So, this is the state that Spanky Macaca is in these days. From supporting one of our favourite bands in our late teens, to sitting in our early forties and talking about the food we've thrown up.

'I'm leaving the band,' Mick says.

I turn my moronic, stoned face his way. I am aware that my mouth is open, even if my eyes are barely.

'I can't keep doing this anymore.' Biting his bottom lip, Mick looks at each of us in turn. He stops when he gets to me and gives me a puzzled frown.

'You hardly ever turn up anyway,' Brian says.

Agreeing, I nod. The flopping head of a dashboard dog.

'Exactly. It's just not fun anymore. It's not fun for me, anyway. Not in the same way it was. So . . . I'm leaving.'

And with that, Spanky Macaca isn't even in a state.

For what will probably be the last time, Mick later drops me back on Tenderbridge high street. I drivel something about wishing him well with his fish, and then giggle.

'It will work out alright with Ella,' he says. 'In the end, these things do.'

Clinging onto the seatbelt, half-in half-out of the car, I harrumph and continue sliding onto the pavement. After a second attempt, the passenger door will still not close, bouncing back with each slam I give it. Leaning over from the driver's side with a bit of a glare, Mick drags the seatbelt inside the car and closes the door himself.

'Your car stinks of fish,' I yell as he drives off.

On the deserted high street, I stand alone. When we were young, there would still be small crowds of people making their way through the town after midnight, long after the pubs closed. Our streets of trouble and romance.

I gaze upwards. The wooly wash of orange streetlight obscures the stars and the cold night sky. The universe orbiting above me is a dirty mess. The pavement beneath me is acned with chewing gum and fag ends.

'This is my town,' I mutter, staggering forwards.

Walking lopsidedly, I hear footsteps following me.

I stop. They stop at the same time.

When I continue, they start again.

Trying to trick them, pausing mid-step, once more their echo falls dead.

Increasing my pace, I am close to freaking out when the pattering feet continue in time to mine.

Watching in a window opposite, I try to see the reflection of whoever is following me. Seeing no one, instead I peer over my shoulder. Already unbalanced, the toe of my boot clips an uneven flagstone and I sprawl onto the floor, landing on my shoulder.

Once I cease rolling around on the dirty ground, it is then that I realise the footsteps following me were the echo of my own.

'My fucking town,' I say, the Mayor of Tenderbridge, laid out on the filthy pavement.

Finally succeeding to let myself into the flat, I struggle with the battle between the prongs of the charger and the wavering socket. Once I have triumphed over that minor task, I stumble through to the kitchen, grab a beer and lean against the fridge. Just as I crack open the can, the lights go out and the buzz of the fridge disappears.

'Wankers.'

Fumbling my way to the cupboard, I insert the plastic key into the electric meter. Five pounds of emergency credit shows on the screen. The lights flicker on. The fridge buzzes back to life. From the other room, I hear the *ping* of an incoming text message.

In a pay-as-you-go life conservation is key, so I leave the sitting room lights off. In the darkness, I pull myself over the floor, a drunken commando crawl, spilling beer as I go. On my way I knock the coffee table. Something on top of it rattles, but I can't work out the silhouette that is standing there. It didn't fall off, so whatever it is survives my drunkenness, for now.

Reaching my phone, still splayed on my front, I see a text from Ella.

the trip sounds good :)

Staring slack-jawed at the screen, the only light in the darkness, a smile tries to rise on my weary face. My stoned, squinty eyes blink every few moments, and the text is still there. Ella has written this. My little girl. She even put a smiley face.

And then I notice what time she messaged me.

00:54.

Why the hell is my little girl on her phone in the middle of the night?

nine

At first, I think the flat is on fire. Then I realise that the shrill noise piercing my tinnitus is the alarm screeching out of my phone.

My eyes are crusty, stuck together with sleep grit. A squidgy pulse labours through my head. There is an uncomfortable sensation all over, as if my aching body is somehow laying cockeyed on top of me. I feel horrible. But I'm awake.

Hating the very thought of moving, I know I must get up. Today is a workday. That second third warning Brian gave me has really added extra clangour to my alarm. Nevertheless, easing my face from a drooled wet patch, I press snooze. Just in case.

The first light of day is reaching around the blackout blind. With the phone in my hand, I roll over onto my front. Ella's message is still there on the screen, which means that I didn't text her back. In the state I was in last night, that is very good news.

A sleepy smile leads my feet to the floor. And then a

spiteful headrush ripples throughout my soggy brain. Taking careful steps into the corridor that services all four doors of the flat, I see that I left the kitchen light on. Plodding through, it turns out that I also left the fridge door open. I quickly check the meter. Somehow, in the last five hours, just under, while I was passed out, I have used one pound and twenty-three pence of emergency credit.

'Bastards.'

And why does my shoulder hurt so much?

I arrive at work only twelve minutes late, which isn't really late at all. Ploughing a wavy line directly through the sorting room, I find Brian in his office. I thought that the mirror told me *I* looked bad this morning. Brian is clearly as seasick as I felt when my phone first started yelling at me. His eyes are puffy and his face looks less full of colour than usual, both glum and pained. These days, the elasticity of the skin takes a real beating after a night of drinking.

As per the ritual, he glances at the cheap clock with loose, bouncy red hands hanging askew on the wall.

'That was good last night,' I say.

And then I remember Mick left the band. Alongside how brain-dead I feel, I doubt that Brian would appreciate chatting it through right now. Perhaps if we don't mention it then it never really happened.

Tugging on the tuft of hair in his widow's peak, I see a faint shiver pass through Brian. He picks up a slightly squashed water bottle from his desk, his hand shaking as he lifts it to his mouth. A loose drop dribbles from his chin, onto his crooked tie. I can't remember whose idea it was to open the bottle of Jack. Probably mine. Well, if you will leave a bag of grain in the chicken run . . .

'How are you today?' he asks, a tricky smile breaking the gutter-lines at the sides of his mouth.

'Not too shabby,' I reply.

This morning I was grateful to find the beer that I opened when I got home last night was on its side in a flowerpot, watering a dead plant. The burnt leftover pizza for breakfast was a treat to discover, too.

'I've definitely been worse. How about you?'

'It's going to be a long day,' Brian replies, nodding slowly, then thinking better of nodding. 'I need hot food as soon as possible.'

Brian's phone starts ringing. Without even thinking, he presses a button, silencing it.

I could be a manager.

I pull out a chair on my side of the desk. Sitting down feels good.

Brian looks at the clock again.

'You've got to be out on your route within the hour, John,' he says, being Manager Brian. 'Mrs Acles phoned to let us know that a catalogue she was waiting for was put through the wrong door.'

'Did she? She must be ordering more kinky toys for Ken.'

After a brief and frail laugh at my joke – Joyce and Ken Acles are both fast approaching ninety – Brian says, 'Please don't give her a reason to call today, John. I'm not sure I could handle it. The catalogue was left at number nineteen, so remember to double-check, okay?'

'I'll knock on the door,' I reply.

And I will. When she answers, I'll repeat my kinky toys joke. She loves it, Joyce. Leaning back in the spongy chair, I stretch out my legs and link my hands behind my head, mindful of my sore shoulder. On mornings after our rehearsals, Brian doesn't know how lucky he is to have an office job, rather than walking the beat.

Flitting between the water bottle and a paper coffee cup, this time Brian decides on coffee. After drinking a mouthful, the coffee doesn't look as if it was entirely well received.

'Come on, John,' he says, still wincing. 'I don't want the post going out late again today, mate.'

'Actually, Bri, I have something I need to ask you.' I had meant to speak privately with him last night, before Darren revealed the doobie and my brain turned to absolute porridge.

'You're not going to quit, are you?' Brian asks, now looking really agonised.

'No,' I say, with a chuckle. 'I can't stomach the smell of fish. Can I have your coffee, if you don't want it?'

'No.' Brian drinks from the cup in defiance of my envy and his distaste. 'You can't. Now get to work,' he says with a bitter smile, which quickly turns to pain.

'That isn't what I wanted to ask you.'

I cross my legs. The movement unsettles my stomach. Another vertiginous wave of light-headedness rocks the chair. I've yet to carry kilos of post nearly four miles this morning. My diagnosis of *not too shabby* might have been a little premature. Clearly my hangover hasn't yet begun. I am probably still pissed – it's happened plenty of times before, like when I took the van for a joyride in the car park and crashed it. I make a mental note to pick up a can of G & T from the corner shop.

'I need some time off,' I say, avoiding eye-contact with Brian, looking instead at the framed poster on the wall.

DON'T MESS WITH POSTMEN
WE KNOW WHERE YOU LIVE!

Some of the lads will pay back awkward customers with late-night parcels through their doors. If not bodily, usually pornographic. Always absolute filth.

'I'm taking Ella on a trip,' I continue. 'Before she moves away.'

Fiddling with the tuft, simultaneously scratching the back of his head, Brian begins chewing the inside of his mouth, making little smacking sounds. My mind starts to drift, wondering whether coppers ever go to work with hangovers. I decide they must do.

'When?' he finally answers.

'End of next week?'

Brian takes a deep breath. Even sitting six feet away, I can smell the nasty coffee and rotting guts carried within the exhalation. I blow my own horrible breath into the fetid cloud, trying to defeat Brian's stinky expiration like one of Darren's model armies.

'You know you're supposed to give a month's notice, John.'

'But I know that it's flexible, too.'

'It's flexible when we have cover. Kerry's on maternity leave, two others already have holiday booked in, and Jason is still off sick.'

He is more than off sick. After finding out that Jason was going at it with one of the wives on his route, the aggrieved husband had been waiting for him with a log. Jason was lucky to survive the beating that the husband gave him. The attack hospitalised him for nine days, with three broken ribs, a fractured skull, and heavy bruising over more than half of his body. There was a rumour that his testicles had been close to rupturing, not that they could tell until after the swelling had gone down. Word has it that Jason told his girlfriend he was hit by a van. The silly sod. He decided against pressing charges. We've filled up his locker with knickers for when he's back at work.

'I'm not sure how I can make it work, John. You know we're already short-handed.'

'I need this trip, Bri. In a month Ella will be gone. I won't get another chance. I might never see her again, I don't know. It's just . . . *hopeless*. The whole thing. I don't know what to do.' My voice is cracking, close to tears – mostly because of how weak in the head I am today after smoking Darren's powerful Super Skunk. 'I will quit, if I have to,' I add. And I meant it. I think. I haven't really thought that far ahead. As much as I am indifferent towards this job, or any proper work, I kind of need even a little bit of income, I suppose.

Can I quit and then reapply after I get back from our trip? Brian would know, but it doesn't feel appropriate to ask him right now.

'For fuck's sake, John.'

Brian heavily exhales. My hand is already up by my nose, building a protective bridge over it. As soon as I remove my hand, there he is, breathing at me again. If this continues, I might have to be signed off sick with Jason anyway.

'The end of next week?' he asks.

'Yeah. Well, next weekend. I'll need the Monday, too. And the Friday. But I'll bring you back a sheep.'

By the look on his face, Brian might have just smelt his own breath. 'A *sheep*?'

'Yeah. We're going to Wales.'

'John.' Brian leans forward, his elbows on the desk. I roll my chair backwards a bit. 'Have you already booked it, before checking with me?'

That is a very good point. I must look where there is to stay. If I was going by myself, I would be perfectly content to just rock up and find the closest field to sleep in. I've done it before, when I have been in no fit state to walk home. This trip has to be a bit more special than that, I suppose.

'You know that I wouldn't do that, Bri. But I will do anything I can to spend time with Ella before she leaves. I only found out that they're moving a couple of days ago. I had no idea how upset Ella is by the whole thing. Kirsty's not getting on with her, either. And what's more, *Dan* offered to take her to the Amex. The football Amex.'

'Right,' Brian says, a bit perplexed. I can see why he would be, I'm talking absolute shite. 'Look, John, I'll see what I can do. I'll ask Dan if he can fill in on your route—' a different Dan; not a Dan who is in any way the cause of my current distress '—but no promises, okay?' he says, seeing the smile about my face.

'Cheers, Bri. You're a legend, mate. I really appreciate it.'

'Now you *have* to get to work,' he says. Another check of the clock and a DT-like shiver.

'Yes, boss.' I stand up and salute. For a moment, I think about going around the desk and giving him a kiss, but then I think about how much he stinks today so decide against it.

Walking towards the door, something else I meant to ask Brian last night pops into my head. 'Oh, *Brian* . . .'

The phone begins to ring. Brian stares at it. Once more thinking better than actually answering the call, he again silences the phone and sips from the bottle of water. It looks as if even that is causing him distress. He raises his eyebrows, and then winks. I think that the wink was a throb of discomfort, rather than him being playful.

'One more thing, mate. Have you got a tent I can borrow?' I say. 'Preferably two tents?'

ten

It is another blisteringly hot day, which made this morning's route even more hellish than usual. I don't often stop so many times, sitting down to carefully sip my G & T. My shoulder doesn't hurt quite as much as it did, but I had to use my other one to lug the post around town, so now that is feeling a bit tender. It's funny, walking twenty miles and more each week, everyone tells me how healthy I must be becoming. If I have to do it much longer, I swear that this job will kill me.

Following the hungover trudge with my mailbags, all of the post delivered late, I chatted with Dan – good Dan from work – and he said that he would be happy to cover my shifts. Top man, Dan from work. Loves a beer, loves a laugh and a joke, loves the cookies and sweets his customers give him. While we were chatting, Dan from work told me that he once booked a weekend in Wales for him and his girlfriend. It cost over a hundred quid, *each*. And that was only for the travel fares. Maybe I should just take Ella to the park. Why did I have to be so stupid and mention a proper trip before I found out how much it would cost?

Back at the flat, I go straight through to the sitting room, open the cupboard doors, sit down on the stained carpet, and start pulling my records, CDs and tapes out of the cupboard.

Over the years I've got rid of most things I own, sold for pennies to the thrift shop that used to be in town, or trying to barter it for junk in charity shops. Most of my other possessions have either been given away, lost, stolen or trashed. The only things I've managed to hold on to in any quantity are the most cherished bits of my music collection. There is not much left to talk of – certainly compared with someone like Brian, who has always been careful with his possessions, like the post-cards on the wall of his garage – but these treasured pieces, the albums that hold the greatest memories, time capsules of my life, are all I have left.

I don't know how long I have been sitting here, just looking at them, thumbing through them, trying to select the ones I can live without. Here's my *Automatic for the People* record, signed by Michael Stipe.

It's wasn't actually Michael Stipe who signed it. I did. To try and impress a girlfriend. Her favourite band was Take That, so it meant precisely nothing to her.

'Can I do this?' I ask the collection, my life's diary of girlfriends, passions and inspirations.

I feel like Noah trying to decide who gets to go on his boat.

'I can't do this.'

Heading to the fridge to grab a beer, I see the urn sitting on the coffee table. Today I like the silly little pot a bit more again. But then, before my next blink, I begin to wonder if charity shops have a returns policy. Another twenty quid towards the trip would be very welcome.

After getting the beer, I sit back down and recommence putting my life's collection into piles of ones that I have decided to sell.

How can the door of the new record shop be closed on a day as hot as this? The faded record sleeves dangling inside the window are folding in on themselves. Beneath the sleeves, alongside a sign that says **WE BUY AND SELL RECORDS!!!**, is a poster advertising the upcoming anniversary reissue of *Monster*, possibly my favourite R.E.M. album. Boot me when I'm down, why don't you.

I feel sick – not just for the weight of the two knackered bags for life that I've carried here, and not entirely because of my hangover, which has definitely settled in now. I roll my shoulder around in the socket, finish my beer, drop the can on the pavement and open the door.

The question of why the door was closed is answered as soon as I walk into Sound All Round. A jet of cold air and lounge music, both fit for the atrium of a midmarket chain hotel, blasts me. I wasn't entirely sure that I liked the name, but I definitely don't like what the new owner has done to the place. The walls have been painted in soft lilac tones. There are two small bistro tables, covered by blue and white gingham tablecloths. The many lights hanging from the ceiling have ugly, care home-cream lampshades. My dislike is already well-founded before I notice the display of teapots lined upon tiered shelves, splendid in assorted colours, presumably for sale. With only a few boxes half-full of records and CDs shoved against the walls, the music most definitely seems to be secondary.

The coolest thing about this place is the picture of a painfully miserable Robert Smith hanging on the wall, looking like he's had to go to work the morning after one of our rehearsals. Next to Robert Smith is a framed poster of the Sound All Round logo. A stick boy and stick girl are standing on a record deck, holding hands, while LPs, CDs and cassettes pour from the sky all around them. Apparently it can be mine for **ONLY £20!!!** (*Or framed for £45!!!*) the small print beneath tells me. The new owners certainly haven't held back on originality and exclamation marks.

Leaving the powerful air conditioning unit behind me, I skirt around a bloke skimming through a box of seven-inch singles. As I brush past his padded bomber jacket – arctic attire that all customers should be issued with as soon as they walk in here – he whirls around. I should have known it was Simon, an obsessive music and memorabilia collector that I know from the pub. He wears that jacket everywhere he goes, even on days as hot as this one. Simon glares with leonine defensiveness, shielding the seven-inches from me. Satisfied I'm not after his quarry, he continues scurrying like a weasel through the records.

The only other person in the shop – or tearoom, or whatever it's trying to be – is a man sitting on a stool, carefully cleaning a record behind a counter made from an antique sideboard. I lean the bags against the counter and clear my throat. The man half-glances up, glares at me, says nothing, and then continues to scrub away. I wonder how he would have responded if Brian had come in here and breathed on him.

I watch as he carefully slides the record back into the sleeve. It's an Everything but the Girl album I've never owned. I find myself about to ask him how much it is, but the phantom weight of the bags reminds me why I am here.

With a sigh, he finally looks up, cocking his head to one side.

I note that he's not wearing a band t-shirt.

'Yes?' he replies by way of greeting, finally making eye contact.

'Are you the owner?' I ask, friendly as can be.

'Yes,' he replies in a breathy voice.

Presumably this is the man of the triple exclamation mark. I can't help but wonder to where that enthusiastic magnification has now disappeared. This is nothing like the banter you get from a half-pissed postman on your doorstep first thing in the morning.

He places both of his hands on the counter with a soft thud. I notice the slightly longer thumb nail on his right hand.

'Are you a guitarist?' I ask.

'What can I help you with?' he replies.

'My name's John.' I smile the broadest smile that a sweaty, hungover man can. 'I'm a guitarist, too. In a local band. Spanky Macaca? You might have heard of us.'

'I haven't,' the man replies. But I think that I notice something like recognition glinting in his eyes. Or maybe he's already heard that Spanky Macaca all-but-broke up last night.

'What's your name?' I ask.

'Russell,' he says after a delay of huffs and puffs and sideways glances. 'Look, I'm terribly busy.'

'Yeah. I can imagine,' I say, smelling the bluster of a thriving shop in the freezing air. 'I've got some bits and pieces that I'd like to sell, Russell.'

Heaving the bags onto the counter, I start removing the records. Russell takes over from me, as if his technique of taking records out of a bag is better than mine. To be fair to him, it probably is. He is definitely handling them with more care than I usually do. I need not turn around to know that Simon's attention has pricked up.

Even though I left a few records at home, my heart lurches to see them all laid out on the counter, with some moody prick ferreting through them, and a weaselly prat behind me sniffing out a bargain.

'This is *your* collection?' Russell asks in different tone, a friendlier fashion.

'Yeah. Except the Simply Red ones. They're my ex-wife's,' I say, suppressing a snigger.

'And you're . . . a *musician*, right?' Russell says. Then he smiles. Hovering over the collection of my lifetime, moody man actually *smiles*. At first, I return that smile. But then I realise that Russell is being condescending, or facetious. Possibly both.

'Look. If you knew what this means to me, Russell, selling off almost my entire music collection . . .'

I pause, thinking carefully about what I want to say. While I do, I glance again at the bric-a-brac adorning the walls. The teapots and the local parish cake sale tablecloths. The patisserie display case, and the muffins and pastries lined up inside it.

'Here's the thing,' I say. 'I'm taking my daughter away on a trip. Just a little break, but I could really use some extra cash. Don't get me wrong, I don't *want* to sell these. But I would really appreciate it if you would consider buying them from me.'

Russell sucks his teeth. 'We just don't need any more stock.'

I take a quick scan of the half-empty boxes. Perhaps if I was trying to sell him teapots, or some other chintz. Maybe I should have brought the urn with me.

'Let me have another look,' he says.

Russell slides the pile of records to one side. Next, he brushes the cassettes towards me.

'Only selling new ones,' he murmurs.

When I first walked in, I noticed the rack of tapes on the wall. Surely there really would be more chance of selling a teapot. Even a chocolate one.

Goosebumps start to appear on my arms. The process as Russell carefully examines every CD and record, and then checks them again, is painfully slow. The chillout music makes the whole process seem longer, hypnotising me, brainwashing me, until finally . . .

'Okay!!!' There they are, back again, the trio of exclamation marks. 'These I can't use, I'm afraid,' he says, sliding the second tallest pile, that of CD singles, towards me. 'I can give you ten for the CDs, five for the seven-inch singles, and . . .'

Leafing through the records for a third time, Russell begins to hum a little tune. It's as irritating as his oddly handsome face. Then it turns into, 'Bob, bob, bob.'

So far, we're up to only fifteen quid.

I look up at Robert Smith. I know how you feel, Bob. Bob, bob, bob.

'And thirty for the records,' Russell finally proclaims.

'Thirty? For . . .' I count through the sleeves that Russell has propped up on one side, against an acrylic cabinet displaying vegan snacks. 'Only thirty quid for fifty-three albums?'

'Like I say, we just don't really need any extra stock. We're full to the rafters. So that's what they're worth to me.'

'They're worth much more than thirty quid, mate. I mean, this one . . .' I find the copy of *Automatic*. 'Look. It's signed! By Stipe!!!'

'Let me see that.'

My count of goosebumps increase. Even though my hungover stomach is blobbing about, and my toes are twitching with mixed impatience and gut irritation, I can't help myself but smile as I watch Russell keenly checking out my handiwork, running a finger over the inky swirl I made on the cover.

I survey the row of coffees and fruity green teas on a shelf in the corner.

'Do you sell beer?' I ask.

'No,' Russell replies.

Finished with *Automatic*, Russell starts looking back through the rest of the records. He takes them out of the sleeves, checks each matrix code and every minute mark. He gently brushes a thumb, barely touching the surface, over the Portuguese reissue of *Green*. It's a rubbish pressing, the record itself as floppy as a flexi disc. I only bought it because it seemed exotic at the time, having a backup copy that had been printed in a foreign country.

I notice that his eyes keep being drawn back to *Automatic . . .*

Five minutes later I am carrying my bags, still heavily weighted, towards the door. I hold it open for a pair of young mothers and their pushchairs, shiver beneath the air conditioning unit, and then head back out into the day.

'Ladies!!!' I hear Russell effusing as I close the door behind me. 'A cup of the usual?'

Having wasted nearly half an hour of my day in the weird little record-tea-ice chamber fusion shop, I forgot how warm it is outside. The goosebumps retreat and my pores open.

When I was stuffing my music collection into the bags earlier, I had been thinking that I would be walking out of Sound All Round with a couple of hundred quid, minimum. But in the interminable wait for Russell to shatter my illusions, I have at least thought up a different plan to fund my trip.

I really should have thought of it sooner.

eleven

Wandering back down the stinky high street with my bulging bags, I receive a text from Darren. He is off work sick, apparently, so has gone to The Humphrey for a pint. I message back, telling him that I am only a few minutes away. First, I dip into the newsagent's to buy a scratchcard.

I find Darren at the back of the pub, staring at a triangular prism-shaped menu advertising meals that would make most tramps think twice. Even when he notices me, something between the connection of his eyes receiving the image and his brain telling his head to follow is clearly wired incorrectly today. With sore eyes, and his open mouth visible as a droopy hole in his scraggy beard, he looks even more desperately gormless than usual.

'You alright, Darren?'

'Uh? Yeah, mate,' he replies. 'No.'

On the table in front of him is a cup of tea and a beer.

After a late, boozy night, he sometimes does this: tea for the caffeine kick and beer as a sugary softener.

'I thought you were sick,' I say. 'Pulling a hangover sicky?'

'Huh? Erm, no,' he replies. 'I did go to work but had to leave early. I've, eh, broken my finger.'

Darren lifts his left hand. Strapped to his index finger is a splint that looks like a futuristic wireless computer mouse. For a guitarist a broken finger is a snapped ankle to a long-distance runner, so his expression of a stoned puppy with a hurt paw is understandable.

'Shit, mate. How did you do that?'

'Eating crisps,' he replies miserably.

'How can you break your finger eating crisps?'

'Well, there was this tin of corn oil on the floor, yeah? I accidentally kicked the tin over and hadn't picked it up yet.'

'Why not?'

'Because I was eating crisps.'

'Okay.'

'So, there's this tin of corn oil on the floor, right? And I didn't know the lid wasn't on.'

'Was it you who left the lid off?'

'Huh? Yeah, it was, yeah. But I didn't know it wasn't on. So I wanted to finish my crisps before I, sort of, like, picked the tin up?'

'And by now there's corn oil on the floor?'

'I, er . . . yeah. There was, like, a sort of little puddle? But I didn't know that the oil was still glugging out all over the place.'

'Right,' I say, trying to keep up.

'Then Debbie from tickets calls me over. She wanted to show me a video of her dressed as an astanaut—'

'Astronaut.'

'That's right, yeah — roller-skating over a bridge on a crazy golf course. So, I was going over to see the video, still eating my crisps, and that's when I slipped on the oil. Went straight over and landed on my finger. Didn't even know it was broken until I took my hand out the packet.'

Even though Darren looks as miserable as Robert Smith, I can't help but chuckle. 'No one else I've ever met could injure themselves eating crisps, Daz. Unlucky, mate. How long will it take to mend?'

'Well, I sprained my wrist, too, didn't I, so can't play for about six weeks? I'm supposed to be playing with Bruno Mars at the O2 next month. Obviously can't do that, now.'

Darren often drops things like this into conversation. A text saying:

turn on the tely im on jules

And there he'll be, dancing around in the background of Jools Holland's studio, playing guitar for some boyband or other.

When Clapton put on his *A Night of Guitars* concert at the Royal Albert Hall, Darren was invited to play. For the show's encore, all the guitarists came out to perform a version of *I've Got a Rock 'n' Roll Heart*. From the third-row seat he got for me, I watched Darren jigging along between Gilmour and Knopfler. At one point, he got so carried away that he ripped into an amazing spontaneous solo. Jimmy Page turns to him, laughing his head off. And then they're trading licks. *Jimmy fucking Page*, standing there, bouncing his knees up and down like some grandad who has won the bingo, loving it. Then Brian May ruffled the back of Darren's hair, and Darren just shook him off. BB King didn't like it much, though, sitting at the front in his wheelchair, looking along the line at this crazy hippy.

That occasion meant precisely nothing to Darren. He's invited to those kinds of things all the time. Except for the Carter support slot at The Angel Centre, my biggest claim to fame is when I snogged the neighbour of the cousin of one of the girls who was in B*Witched, just before they made it big for two minutes.

'Why are you smiling?' Darren asks.

'Just thinking about Jimmy Page.'

'Oh, right.' He nods unhappily. 'Yeah, I do that.'

'I'm going to get a drink. Want one?'

'Nah,' he replies, looking at the beer and his cup of tea. He does look proper sorry for himself.

When I am halfway to the bar, Darren calls across the pub that he does want a beer, actually. And a packet of cheese and onion crisps.

It is only when I am sitting back down that I notice he's wearing a Manson t-shirt. Not Marilyn Manson, but Charlie. On top of Charlie's head is Christ's crown of thorns, snaking threads of blood slithering down his forehead.

'Did you wear that to the Jungle Gym?'

'What, this?' Darren points at Manson, right in the eye. 'Yeah, mate.'

His attempts at opening the crisp packet are intriguing. After a few efforts, I reach over and open them for him. Even then, he tries using his splinted finger to pluck the crisps out of the bag. Finally thinking better of it, instead he uses the damaged hand to hold the bag. Brave soldier, sitting there stuffing his face, straight back on the horse.

'Are you sure you're okay with that? You haven't got crispophobia, or anything?'

'Potnonomicaphobia,' he says.

'What did you just say?' I ask, gobsmacked by all the syllables that came out of Darren.

'Potnonomicaphobia,' he repeats. 'It's the word for a fear of potatoes.'

'How the hell do you know that?'

'My sister had it when we were young. She got better, though. What's in them?' he asks, pointing at the bags.

'Almost my entire music collection,' I say, my sullen expression mirroring his. 'I was going to sell it.'

'Sell it? Why would you sell it?'

'Cash. For the trip.'

'But you can't.'

'Yeah, I just found that out. You know the new record shop?'

'Russell's shop? Course I do,' Darren says. 'I asked him for a job.'

'What did he say?'

'Told me they're over-staffed at the moment,' Darren replies, spraying crisps over his drinks and into his beard. 'Good bloke, though. And I love what he's done with the place. So rad.'

'It is rad.' I stand my bags up better against the table, a bit slouched as they were. I wonder what is the average life expectancy of a person who invests in a bag for life. 'He was only going to give me forty-five pounds for this lot.'

'Seems fair,' Darren says with shrug.

'Forty-five pounds for a collection that I have spent my entire life acquiring *seems fair*?'

'Yeah,' Darren says. 'Your music taste is bunt.'

If I can't stand a lot of the words Darren uses, bunt is the worst. I think it must be another one that he picked up from Jet Damage (Lee Potter).

'You can get rid of *Fables of Construction*, though,' he says. 'That's a shit album.'

'It's not shit, Darren,' I say, unable to stop myself from raising my voice. 'And it's *Reconstruction*. *Fables of Reconstruction*.'

'*Automatic* is their best album.'

I'm tempted to tell Darren that, other than a fiver for the Simply Reds, *Automatic for the People* is the only record that I did leave behind in Sound All Round, after settling on twenty pounds. It was signed by me and still had the original *Our Price* £5.49 sticker stuck to the front. I saw that as a good profit – a portion of which has already been invested in beer and crisps. I might sign all of my records.

'I'll give you thirty pound for the lot,' Darren says. 'Right here, right now.' He's getting his wallet out – being mindful of his poorly finger.

'But thirty *pound* is less than Russell offered me, though, Darren. And you think my music taste is *bunt*, remember?'

'Oh,' he says, fingering the wallet with his bionic

finger. 'I've only got ten.' He's looking at me expectantly, like we might have a deal.

'I've decided that I'm not selling them,' I tell him, reaching into my pocket. 'Hence the fact that I didn't sell them. Anyway, I've got to go. There's something I need to do. After I've done this.'

Darren watches closely as I scrape the foil from the scratchcard, absorbed in the process. When I'm mug enough to buy one of these addictive little horrors, I always get a flutter, telling me that this is the one. I scratch them so carefully, the teasing anticipation of each reveal, hoping that the next number will be the one to match, or the next fruit, or whatever.

As with every time, no win.

'You can have that,' I say, sliding the scratchcard over the table, getting my bags together.

'Cheers, mate!'

This must be a record for the amount of weight one man has carried around Tenderbridge in a day, while hungover. As I am leaving the pub, wondering if you get paid for a winning entry into *Guinness World Records*, a look over my shoulder tells me that Darren is yet to work out that the scratchcard I gave him is worth less than the card it is printed on. I would love to be there when he attempts to cash it in.

twelve

On my way back to the flat, I stop to buy a pack of ice creams. While I am at it, I pick up some antacids, a ten pound top-up for my mobile, and one of those air freshener things with the thin bamboo sticks. The ice creams are for the sugar, the pills for my bubbling belly, and the air freshener is a complete whim. Hopefully it will help to mask the grim damp smell that skulks throughout the flat. I should really buy one for each room, just in case I get lucky.

The moment that I walk through the front door, I crack open an ice cream. A hail of mottled chocolate falls, leaving little droppings all over the place. Beneath the chocolate, the ice cream itself is covered with spiky, crystallised icicles. Not only does the cheap imitation taste bad and hurt to eat, it smells a bit funky too, so I throw it, uneaten, into the sink. I should have chosen lollies. The irony makes me snort.

Deciding instead to medicate with beer, I put the antacids in the cupboard. The air freshener I leave on the side, stuck to a sticky spill. I should probably focus on cleaning the place before splashing out on unneeded luxuries and dreaming about bringing a girl back here.

Turning out my pockets on to the coffee table, I find that I have only one pound and eighty-five pence left from my trade with the record shop. *Automatic for the People* was with me for over twenty years; the cash didn't even singe my pocket. Of all the purchases, the only thing I really needed was the top-up.

Among the change and pocket-fluff I spy the electric key, which I had also meant to buy credit for. Sprinting to the cupboard, the meter tells me that only two pounds and seventy-nine pence of emergency credit is left. How can ninety-five pence of electricity have drained in such a short time when there's not even been anyone here? Maybe the blokes from the takeaway downstairs have wired their extractor fan to my meter, blatting away outside my window, as it does for all waking hours, as well as a great deal of those when I'm trying to sleep. The only solution is to turn off the lights and sit in the semi-dark. Even that will probably cost me twenty pence an hour.

Reaching out to a silhouette upon the coffee table, thinking it's my beer, I am surprised to find a weighty object in my hand. The bloody urn. That's twenty quid of electricity just sitting there, doing nothing, looking pointless. In the blueish glow of the mobile phone screen, I find my beer next to me on the floor. At least beer never lets me down.

I reluctantly plug my phone into the wall and watch the pennies slipping past my eyes.

All day I have been thinking about Ella's message, and why she sent it so late last night.

And then I remember about the band.

And then, after pressing the call button, I wonder whether I really can live without *Automatic* . . .

'My darling boy, how are you?' dad lavishes down the phone, giving colour to the darkness.

'Can you call me back, dad?'

'Of course I will, my dear boy. Of cou—'

I slump back against the electric two-bar fire, screwed to the wall in front of what was probably quite a nice surround until some unscrupulous landlord bricked it up. When it costs twenty pence an hour to sit in a room with the lights turned off, there's no way that I ever use the fire. It's uncomfortable, it digs into my back, so I lay down on the floor instead. The industrial rumble of the extractor fan massages its noisy, oily hands beneath me. My stomach grumbles. The cheesy taste of the ice cream is still in my mouth, so I slurp down the remainder of my beer. And then the funky samba rings out into the dark, smelly room.

'How are you, Johnny? It's so good to hear your voice,' dad says.

I can just picture him there in his garden, wearing a summery shirt, perhaps complemented by one of Julian's cravats. I hear a thousand different breeds of bird singing and chattering away in the background. I close my eyes. I can smell vanilla. The river breeze blows back my hair, allowing warm sunlight to add colour to my forehead – easy to imagine because of how hot it is in the summer living above a takeaway.

'Johnny?'

'Yeah, sorry. I'm alright.'

'Alright? Al-*right*? My boy cannot be just alright. You're a poet aren't you, of sorts? Give me better than *alright*.'

'I am wonderful, father,' I reply, monotone. 'My soul does twinkle with joyous effervescence.'

'That's more *like* it,' he says.

In the darkness, I smile. Every time I talk with dad, no matter my mood, I smile. Since he and Julian joined the Henley am-dram society, neither of them can settle upon a single timbre for longer than a syllable.

'*No, it's Johnny,*' dad calls out, away from the mouth-piece, a sprinkling of actorly affectation making it sound like he is saying *John-eh*. '*My darling progeny.*'

'*Send my love,*' I hear Julian tweet in the background, which dad then relays to me.

'And mine to him,' I reply, 'the old fruit.'

'*He sends all of his back to you, sweets,*' I hear dad call out. And then down the phone to me, 'You cheeky boy.'

I really am there now. Dad shaded by a straw fedora, drinking peach schnapps on a swinging love seat, while Julian deadheads the petunias for the second time today. Not a single mechanical sound allowed to disrupt the peace.

The strange father, son and father's boyfriend raillery continues for a while longer. Julian will occasionally join the conversation from a distance, with interjections such as '*Tell him about the do at Hidcote, and our chinwag with Monty Don about paradise gardens.*' And '*Tell Johnny what happened that time I babysat for Tony Blair.*' Apparently, Julian had wanted to read infant Tony an Oscar Wilde book for his bedtime story, but infant Tony threw a wobbler and insisted that Julian read from the memoirs of Sir Anthony Eden. A passage about the Suez Crisis made little Tony emit a sleepy chuckle, so Julian says.

'Tell Johnny I always said that he was a little tinker, that Tony.'

'That's probably among the nicest things Blair has ever been called,' I say, which is then relayed to Julian, making him guffaw. 'Er, dad, while we're on the phone, I was just wondering—'

'How much do you need, sweet boy?' he says. 'You know that you only have to ask. When people recognise your genius, you'll get all your rewards at once.'

I refrain from telling dad that being able to sing a bit like Bryan Ferry, and filling notebooks with half-finished songs about how sad I am for myself is not really a constituent of genius.

'Then you can pay back the hundreds of thousands of pounds you've had from me over the years . . .'

'Dad—'

'I just told John that he's got to pay me back the hundreds of thousands that he owes me,' dad calls out to Julian.

'The sprinkles that go on the top of iced cakes?' Julian retorts. *'I told you not to lend him any more of those.'*

God, I yearn to be there with them. That is what my one wish in the world would be right now. Perhaps they could adopt me, if it is possible for your own father and his boyfriend to adopt a forty-two-year-old man. Maybe I could live with them, move in their circles, possibly even get a sugar-daddy of my own.

In fact, none of those things would really be my one wish.

'Ella's going to Canada, dad.'

'Oh, Canada is lovely,' dad replies. 'What a lucky girl. We went on a cruise through the Northwest Passage a few years ago. It was so pretty. Oh, and I'll tell you who was there, we had that Jane McDonald as the evening entertainment. She was ever so good. I've never seen anyone knock back as many Pornstar Martinis as she did. She's a *riot*. Swears like a northern hod carrier. It was so much better than when we had that *Boyle* woman, when we were in the Canaries. After a few pints of bitter that Boyle *sings* like a hod carrier, I tell you now.'

'But Ella's moving to Canada, dad,' I say when he's finished. 'Not just going on a cruise.'

'Good for her,' he replies. 'A few weeks is never enough anywhere you are in the world. Except for maybe East Anglia. *Do you remember our trip to East Anglia that time, darling?*'

It sounds as though Julian has moved a little further away from the phone. From what I can catch, it seems that the Norfolk locals didn't take too kindly to a pair of old benders swanning about, dressed up like dandy dumplings.

'Dad, trips are great. Holidays too. But you are missing my point. Ella is moving away from me. To live. Forever. Against my will.'

There is a silence. I don't need to check my phone to know that dad is still there: I can hear the birdsong. After a moment I hear him smack his lips.

'Sorry, this is a fine day for schnapps,' he says. It seems that this day is fine enough for a second sip of schnapps. 'I remember very well being away from my children, when you were little. It was heart-wrenching. Just horrible.'

'Dad, you were in the next county. Your boyfriend drove down in his Rolls Royce whenever you wanted to see us. Ella is moving *thousands* of miles away. And I'll never be able to afford to go and see her.'

'Do you need money to move there?' he asks, now sounding a bit panicked. 'Do you?'

'No, dad. I did think I was moving there at first, but it was just a misunderstanding. All I want is to take Ella on a trip before she leaves. Maybe later I might think about moving there, but right now I just want to spend some quality time with my daughter.'

I briefly explain about the work relocation, and that Dan – wealthy prick Dan – and Kirsty have agreed to commit to a new life far away and let's none of us give a single fuck about what the lonely, erstwhile father thinks. How many times must I repeat the same lines to various different people?

'So, I just need a few hundred pounds to get things going. I'm not paid for another few weeks, and I have come to the conclusion that the bank is never going to let me have another credit card, ever again in my life.'

'You don't need to pay me back, Johnny. Think of it as making up for the birthdays and Christmases I missed,' he says quietly, I suppose so that Julian doesn't hear. Not that dad ever once forgot to send presents to me and Paul, if he hadn't managed to visit us in person. I wish that I could afford to just throw money at my various different problems. 'Let's call it five hundred, shall we?'

'I definitely do want to pay it back, dad. I can't just accept handouts whenever I want them. I'm in my forties now.' *I should be hanging out on yachts with celebrities, catered for by famous chefs, like you and Julian do*, I feel like adding. 'But if you insist, then alright, I'll take it.'

'Well, we were going to have a trip down to see you soon,' he says, schnapps-tongued. 'Maybe you can take us out for a lovely lunch somewhere instead of paying us back.'

'There's a lovely takeaway downstairs,' I reply. 'I'll take you there.'

It can sometimes be a good thing, that takeaway. When I slide steaming across their window on my way back from the pub, they occasionally give me free chips. If I am too hungover to move, or too broke to buy food, the smell alone can be quite filling.

'You are such a funny, sweet boy,' dad says. 'I really don't know why Kirsty couldn't make it work with you.'

'Because I was caught boinking the lollipop lady,' I reply. 'Remember?'

'Oh yes, of course. *Boinking the lollipop lady*.' He titters at that. It even makes me snigger.

Julian must be back with him again – I heard the clinking of glasses. And then we end our call and I open my eyes to land back in my dark, sweaty, smelly world.

thirteen

When I woke up this morning for the second time – the
first awakening being at three-something, shivering on
the cold, silent sitting room floor – I went straight to the
meter cupboard to find that the emergency credit had
almost run out. By the time I returned from work with
the key, loaded with a fresh ten pounds, it had run out.
And then I found the disgusting ice creams on the side in
the kitchen, melted over the counter and dripping down
the cupboard doors. At least the beers in the fridge were
still cold.

Casually peering at the cast-off junk in the window of
the charity shop, I see that the other urn is no longer
there. Inside, the usual crowd are browsing through the
tat: the aged and the odorous. To my surprise, I also see a
fairly well-to-do lady in there with them, holding up a
fake fur coat.

I wipe my sweaty forehead and wander in.

Since the dawning of the internet era, charity shops
must have benefitted more than most. It used to be

possible to find armfuls of outrageously good deals and funky junk – funky not just for the originality, but also because of the smell – but bargains can be found no longer. These days, they're all bashing away on laptops to see what this shit sells for online. I don't even bother looking at the price of Bowie albums anymore.

The well-to-do lady is now trying on the faux fur, studying herself in a mirror, smelling the armpits. Even though she wrinkles her nose, she seems to like the fit. It's no surprise that this woman has trotted over the bridge to come charity shopping on the south side. By comparison to the unappealing alternatives, the best clothes in Tenderbridge are found in charity shops. I can just picture her wearing that coat to a parents' evening at the posh school.

Swinging my carrier bag, I swerve over to the glass counter and plonk the urn down. The lady behind the cash register is not as old as some that work in here, maybe about fifty. Her aquamarine eyeshadow and pink lipstick are so bright that I wonder if she might have accidentally used kid's face paints. It's a surprise she didn't sweep aside the faux fur for herself.

Her name badge tells me that she's called Bridget.

'What can you give me for this, Bridget?' I ask, partly unsheathing the carrier bag from the urn.

'What do you mean?'

'I bought it in here the other day,' I say, prodding sharp glances at the urn, encouraging Bridget to do the same, 'but it doesn't fit my collection. So I wondered if you have a returns policy?'

'What's that, lovely?'

'I want to return it, Bridget.'

With lots of crinkling-cheap-carrier bag fuss, Bridget lifts Ella's urn out of the bag and onto the counter. 'It's an urn, is it?' she says.

'That's what I've been calling it. My friend thought it's a vase. But it's got a lid. And he's a moron.'

'I think that an urn is a vase, lovely. It is nice, isn't it.'

'You can buy it off me for twenty quid, if you want.'

'Oh, you,' Bridget says, flapping a hand at me.

'No really, I mean it. I bought it from here, so, you know . . . I want to sell it back.'

'That's not how charity shops work, my lovely,' she replies, giving me a long, slow wink.

I think that Bridget here might be flirting with me. In my past, I've achieved quite a lot by flirting, even if my sights are not usually set upon women quite like Bridget.

'I like your dress,' I say, directing a nod at the shapeless, bright green monstrosity she's wearing.

I notice there are little fishes swimming between big blue leaves. Perhaps it is supposed to be a big, green pond. Whatever it is, it's absolutely fucking horrible. Not even my mum would wear it. Julian probably would.

'That looks like . . . *No*. Are you wearing Alexander McQueen?'

'This?' Bridget says, putting her hands on the top of her ample bosoms and giving a little twirl. 'No, lovely, I got this from the Sali Army sale at our church.'

'Oh, I see. It's *stunning*,' I add with a flourish that would make dad and Julian applaud.

'Thank you,' Bridget says.

I do wish she would stop wheeling about. Not that I can stop watching.

I scratch my chest. These are the same clothes I was

wearing yesterday – the usual pair of jeans and a faded-to-grey Guinness t-shirt that I got free from some pub when they were doing a Paddy's Day promotion. Like me, the clothes could do with a good wash.

'So. Bridget. I bought this urn from here, all in good faith. Vase? Whatever. And this pretty little bird here has got a chip in its wing. See? And this lovely fella' – I turn the urn, showing Bridget the bloke on the top with the tiniest mark in his feathers – 'he's got one, too.'

'Oh, yes, I see. It is pretty, though.'

'Are you *sure* that you don't want it for yourself?'

I lean my hip against the counter, pressing my advantage. Am I going to end up trying to shag Bridget just so that I can get some cash? I don't think I really want to, but I might be able to do it if I have to. It could end up being another one of those weird things to add to my memoir.

Someone behind me clears their throat. It's the lady with the faux fur, which is draped over her arm, now also holding a boxed set of wine glasses.

'Nice coat,' I tell her, before returning my attention to my vamp.

'I really don't need any more vases,' Bridget says.

'But do you have one as pretty as this, though?'

'I just don't know what I'd use it for.'

'What if the shop buys it back for fifteen? You could put it on sale again for twenty and then the shop would make an extra fiver! Can't say fairer than that.'

'I really can't do that, my lovely,' Bridget says, after a fleeting moment of thought. 'It's not the policy.'

The faux fur woman clears her throat again. 'May I

just buy these, please?' she says, in a class of voice not usually heard south of The Humphrey.

With the urn in my hands, I turn to face her. Greeting me is an expression that the Queen might have given if I had walked into the room at the precise moment she found out Windsor Castle had caught alight.

'Would you be interested in this?' I carousel Ella's urn around for her, displaying each of the four birds. 'Isn't it lovely? Bridget and I think so.'

'No, thank you,' she replies, punctuated by a tight-lipped grimace. *No*, thenk *you*.

'Suit yourself,' I say, turning my back on her. 'So, are you sure there's nothing we can do, Bridget?'

A bit pouty, she shakes her salt and caramel bob.

Lifting the urn above my head, I get the attention of the other browsers. 'Would anyone like to buy this lovely little urn?' I ask. 'Possibly a vase. Just one careful owner.'

The lid pops off and bounces from my head, onto my shoulder, and down onto a three-foot long orangutan teddy slumped against the counter, before finally dropping to the floor. By the time I have retrieved the lid and straightened up, everyone has gone back to examining the stained pots and musky clothes.

The faux posh lady's nose is pointing into the air, flared nostrils of distaste. She looked less repulsed when she was smelling the armpits of her new old coat. In fairness, I wouldn't have wanted to smell myself with my arms up after a hot morning walking my route, either.

Popping the top back on what is now indisputably my urn, I find myself thankful to see that no more bits of wing or bird seem to have broken off. Hmm, on second inspection maybe a tiny piece of wing.

fourteen

I cross the road with my urn and my carrier bag, open the door of the travel agency, and am greeted by the loveliest row of smiles I have seen since I was popular in this town. It takes me aback, a welcome as rare as this. Maybe they were expecting someone else.

'Ladies,' I say, raising my invisible hat. That's what I intended, at least. What I actually did was wave the carrier bag in front of my face and get a powerful whiff of my armpits. I head straight towards the prettiest girl and sit in the chair opposite her.

'Hello, sir,' she says in her perfect travel agent's voice, even if her accent is a long bridge from Mrs Faux Fur.

'Hi, Kelly.' I am loving all of the name badges today. Everyone should wear one.

'And how may I help you, sir?'

Sir again.

I am Sir.

'Sir?'

'Sorry. Erm, I need to book a holiday?'

'Wonderful, sir. You've come to the right place!' Kelly gives a proud shake of her boobs. I think she did. I might have imagined it.

The other girls are still watching, still smiling. Even the older one. Unlike most people, these girls don't look away when you stare at them. I love this place. I knew that one day I would find my harem. And here it is, right on my front door, hidden in plain sight on one of the grubbiest high streets in the south-east of England.

'So where would you like to go today, sir?'

'Wales,' I reply. The other girls get back to work. 'But not actually today.'

'That's lovely, sir,' Kelly says. 'I love Wales.'

'Me, too. I'm taking my . . .'

Kelly gives a keen nod. 'Sir? You were about to tell me who you're taking away.'

'Just . . . a friend,' I say. 'I'm taking my friend.'

'Very good,' Kelly replies. Using a mouse, she taps at something on her monitor. 'And where abouts in Wales, sir?'

'To the Brecon Beacons,' I reply. 'I went when I was a kid, so I wanted to take my . . . friend there. Because it was such . . . fun.'

'It sounds fun, sir.'

'You can call me Sir John. Sorry . . .' I scratch under my armpit. I really stink. 'I mean, you can call me John. You know, if you want.'

'Certainly, John.'

'Kelly's a nice name,' I say, but I don't mean it.

Kelly takes a break away from her screen to smile at me. A professional smile? It's hard to tell.

'And how were you planning to travel to the Brecon Beacons?'

'The cheapest way,' I reply. 'Because I, erm . . . my friend? They're on a bit of a budget.'

'I understand. It can't be very easy for your friend,' she says with solemnity.

Are you kidding? She lives in a big, posh house on the north side of town, has her phone bills paid for, and doesn't even get told off when she's acting like a little shit. But, well, she is menstruating now, so . . .

'It's not easy,' I reply. 'No.'

'Aw.' Kelly pauses and gives me possibly the most sympathetic look I have ever been witness to. It's quite unnerving. 'Do you know where in the Brecon Beacons you want to go, John? With your friend?'

'Er, how big is it?'

Kelly turns her monitor around to show me a map zoomed in on the south of Wales. Then she uses one of her mind-boggling nails to draw an outline around a big green bit. 'That's the Brecon Beacons,' she says. 'This area here.'

'Hmm. Yes. I see.' I stare at the big green patch, not really knowing what I'm looking at. Scratching away again, I can now properly smell myself. I lean my elbows in towards my belly, sitting here like a ventriloquist's dummy. And then I confidently decide: 'We'll go to the middle bit. As long as there's a pub nearby.'

'Oh, yes,' Kelly says. 'There has to be a pub nearby. You can't be without a pub.'

'I can't,' I say. And then smile as an afterthought.

After asking a few more questions about our wants and needs for the trip, Kelly finds a campsite in a place called Danwylliarwean. Having struggled to pronounce the name, Kelly girlishly jokes about the malapropism with her colleagues. While she does, I lean back in my chair – about to put my hands behind my head before the stench reminds me not to – and bathe in the delight of female laughter.

How can I have lived in this town for so many years and not know that this place existed? While I've been getting pissed just over the road, here these girls have been, every day, waiting for me to come in and book a coach and camping holiday.

'There'll be two changes in Cardiff, John, and then when you get to Brecon, local services will take you on to Dan—' *bloody Dan* '—wylli-ar-we-an. I don't think it's really pronounced like that. Do you, John?'

'I like the way you say it.'

'Oh, do stop,' she says, feigning a blush.

Would it really be that bad if I take Kelly to Wales instead of Ella? Ella and I could still have a trip to the local park. Or perhaps she would be happy enough with the urn.

'And that all comes to a total cost of . . . Just one moment, please . . . Thirty-seven pounds per person.'

'Thirty-seven pounds!' I cry, sitting forward.

'Oh, I'm sorry,' Kelly says. 'Is that too much?'

'No, that's *amazing*,' I say, already calculating how much of dad's cash I'll have left over for beer money. 'I thought it was going to be hundreds.'

'Oh!' Kelly says, clapping her hands. 'That's great!'

'It is great!' I say. 'You can come, if you want! I'll pay.'

'Lol. I don't think my boyfriend would be too happy about that,' Kelly says. And then she properly laughs.

With devilish mania forking out of her eyes, she shares her joke with the other girls, while I sit here and shrink, a pile of smelly washing.

Slumping in the chair, my foot nudges the carrier bag.

'Hang on,' I say, brightening again. 'Are child tickets cheaper?'

Kelly's hilarity drops like a broken Venetian blind.

This new expression is the one that girls in the pub usually give me when I slide along the bar towards them at the end of the night.

'Is your friend a child, John?' Kelly asks, stony-eyed.

'Well, um . . . She's—'

'Is your friend a female child, John?'

'No, it's . . . Well, it's . . . It's my daughter I'm taking away. It's just . . . I wanted it to be a surprise? I only told you I was going with a friend so it didn't . . . ruin the surprise. In case you . . . maybe . . . spoke to her.'

'I see. Well, if you just pay a small deposit today, I'll keep the details of the booking on the system here and you can pop back in and we'll get this all finalised. Or you can pay in full now, if you'd rather.'

While we settle up – even less than the original quote, with the concession for Ella – there seems to be a tiny hint of repulsion simmering within Kelly's tone. It's as if we have been through an entire relationship in about fifteen minutes.

'Before you go, John,' she says, surprising me by becoming the animated travel agency girl again. 'There's something I wanted to ask you.'

'Go on,' I say uncertainly.

'Did you play a show at my friend's birthday party?'

'*May*-be,' I carefully reply. 'I am in a band. Or . . . was. When was it?'

'Last year,' Kelly replies. 'It was for her twenty-first.'

So Kelly is only twenty-two. Frail is my perception.

'You were great!' Kelly continues, softly bouncing on her chair. 'Proper dad rock,' she adds, bursting my tiny bubble before it can grow.

In the involuntary response that humans simply can't help, when the door opens I turn my head. A roomful of bright and smiley smiles greets Bea and her beau. Bea is wearing leggings and a stretch top. Judging by the confidence on display, pool boy must have got her working out. By my estimates, it really hasn't started to show.

Seeing me sitting here, looking miserable, old and smelly, Bea reciprocates the glare I welcome her with.

'We want a holiday somewhere hot,' she announces before she's walked more than two steps into the travel agency. 'To celebrate our engagement.' And there she is, flashing the tacky diamond around the room. 'We were thinking Barbados,' she brays loud enough to ensure that everyone hears. 'Maybe St. Loocha.'

A fearsome grin of triumph whistles directly towards me. It hits, too, striking me right between my baggy eyes. I can't stay here a moment longer.

There can't be that many people who leave a travel agency feeling depressed after booking a trip for less than a hundred quid, but I do.

A few paces down the high street, I stop.

'Ah, *bollocks*,' I say, loud enough to startle strangers.

When she sees me walking back in, Kelly smiles.

They all smile – except for Bea and the beau.

'Hello, sir!' Kelly says.

'Hi, Kelly!' I lean on the chair I was sitting on and reach beneath it. 'Forgot this,' I say, shaking my carrier bag at her.

Holding the urn that I wish I had never seen, I storm back out of the travel agency through the trail of my own pong.

fifteen

Following the dispiriting victory of my visit to the travel agency, I take a walk beside the river, the stretch of water that scrambles past the castle embankments, beneath the historic Great Bridge, and onwards towards perfectly picturesque towns and villages.

The towpath that runs alongside the river isn't quite as scenic. Broken bottles and crushed beer cans pepper the route. Rubbish peeks through the flora. Every sign and bin is covered with offensive graffiti. The snakeskins of used condoms, dog-ends and discarded poo bags litter the pathway.

I come here because it leads out of town, where the traffic and the bustle of chavs can no longer be heard. Despite the litter, the air is clearer, with more to capture the senses. Back in moderately happier times, Kirsty and I always said we would move out to one of those pretty villages further downstream. Almost twenty years later, I don't even have a spare bedroom.

When I am suitably clear of the town, I sit down on

the riverbank, crack open a beer and take a good, healthy glug. After checking no one is around, I begin laughing manically. Out of breath, I stop, catch up with my lungs, and then laugh again, as loudly as I can.

From behind a tall shrub on the opposite bank, an elderly couple appear, both of them wearing expressions that anyone would upon discovering a madman – part panic, mostly for their own safety, I presume, as no river could stop a hysterical lunatic; part shock, because the laugh was so demented that it would make Joker look no more harmful than Ronald McDonald; and a third part of concern, because someone that sounds as mad as I do really should have a carer or registered nurse with them.

The phone is already in my hand, so I plug it against my ear and laugh in a more subdued manner. I wave at the elderly couple, point at my phone, roll my eyes and shrug.

A small dog comes into view, struggling along behind them. It only has three legs: one more than most people, but one less than most dogs. I wonder how that feels, in the grand scheme. I watch the three of them hobble on, until they are gone.

I often do this laughter routine before phoning Ella. But my forced hysterics were a fruitless waste of idiocy, though, because Ella doesn't pick up.

I call the house phone instead and Kirsty answers.

'Hi, Kirst. Call me back,' I say and hang up.

A duck waddles along the path behind me, looking a bit pissed off. I wonder if it has just been told that its family is migrating to Canada. I pour some beer on the path for it, but it only stops and glares at me. It must be really pissed off.

It's no surprise that Kirsty phones back straight away. She almost always does. I would probably phone back someone that I don't really like if I had nothing to do all day. It's become our routine.

'What do you want, John?'

'Is Ella there?'

'No. She's at summer camp.'

'What's she doing that for?' I ask.

'What do you mean, *what's she doing that for*?'

'Why is she camping? She didn't tell me that she was going camping.'

'A summer camp is not camping, John. It's a course at the public school. Ella's doing a computer tech management course, if you really want to know. Some of her friends are doing it, so Ella wanted to go. Dan's paying.'

'Of course he is.'

'What do you want with her?'

'Just to talk. Did Ella tell you about our trip?'

'Yes, she did. And actually . . .' Kirsty sighs like a donkey into the mouthpiece. 'Actually, I think it's quite a good idea.'

'So that you can get some peace and quiet for a few days?'

Kirsty hesitates. I feel the phone heating up against my ear. I hadn't *intended* it to be a dig, but she obviously wants to tell me off. I don't mind if she does. It really is the perfect afternoon for a beer and an argument.

'She's still being difficult,' Kirsty says, turning down a bicker. 'So yes, some peace and quiet would be quite nice.'

'I can't wait,' I say. 'I've already booked it.'

'You've *booked* it?' she says, sharpening up. 'When for?'

'Weekend after next.'

'The one after this one?'

'Yes, as in, there's this weekend *next* and then we're going away on the one *after*. The one after next.'

'I wish that you'd checked with me first, John. We're supposed to be going shopping that weekend.'

'Can't you go shopping when you get to Canada?' I reply. 'There must be shops in Toronto, and . . . some of the other places in Canada.'

'That's not the—'

'Nova Scotia,' I interrupt. I'd been wracking my brain for just one more place.

'What?' Kirsty does sound very weary.

'Nova Scotia is another place in Canada.'

'You do know that Nova Scotia is a province and not a place, don't you?'

'Well, it sounds as though Nova Scotia must have lots of shops, if it's a whole province.'

'You're being childish, John.'

'I am,' I cheerfully reply.

'Next weekend is very short notice.'

'The weekend after next. Anyway, I'd say telling me that my daughter is moving away forever in a month is quite short notice,' I retort, trying to remain cheerful. My idiot laughter tactic really does work. 'In fact, I'd say that is barely any notice at all. Especially for something so big, like moving to a whole other country.'

'Alright, John. That's fair. I understand why you'd think that.'

'It's good of you to understand, Kirst.'

'Please don't. Not today. It's not easy for me, either.'

Taking a swig of beer, I watch the skaters and flies buzzing about the reeds. It must be easy being one of those. Insects must have a pretty simple life. Just as I'm thinking it, a big fish jumps out of the water and eats the exact fly I was looking at. Maybe not that easy, then.

'Are you still there?' Kirsty asks.

An unexpected thought carries me back through the years. I'd be pushing the pushchair through the park, and Kirsty would phone me if she was having a bad day at work. Calling just to hear my voice; to reassure her that everything was alright. In those days I was making about four hundred pounds a week playing gigs. I felt like I had made it; I was getting paid and getting laid, and that was enough. Telling Kirsty that *everything is alright* was simple to say. It's at times like this, reminiscing on those days, the ones of romance and purpose and not a care in the world, that I realise just how badly I've screwed it all up.

There's no way that I would ever share any of those private thoughts with Kirsty, though. She'd only agree with me.

'John.'

'Yeah, I'm here.'

'Does Ella know she's going away next weekend?'

'Weekend *after* next. That's why I was calling. To tell her. Can you get her to call me back?'

'After summer camp she's got dance class. Then she's having a sleepover at Josephine's—' *Josephine. That's a new one. With a name like that, she must come from the north side* '—But it'll be fine. We can rearrange the shopping trip. Where is it you're taking her? Ella said something about *Wales*.'

'We're going to the Brecon Beacons!'

'Brecon Beacons? What are *you* going to do with a thirteen-year-old girl in the bloody *Brecon Beacons*?'

'Lots of things,' I reply. Even though I still don't have a clue what we'll do when we get there. The big green patch that Kelly circled her insane nail around was . . . well, *big*. There must be lots of things to do.

'Anyway,' I say, 'it's better than just taking Ella to the football.'

And then Kirsty surprises me by laughing. Properly laughing.

I'm still pretty good at this job, it seems. I wonder if we would have kept in touch if we didn't have a kid together. Just phone each other every now and then for a decent row. Kirsty could afford to pay me four hundred pounds of Dan's money each week, calling up for an argument any time she wanted. I wouldn't mind. I'd probably do it for half that.

'Did you know that Bea's engaged to pool boy?'

'Yes,' Kirsty says. I can *hear* her eyes rolling. 'She's over the moon about it. But I won't be holding out for a wedding invitation.'

'Oh? Have you fallen out?'

Like Bea's tits, those two fall out a lot.

'No, not at all. I just think that the chances of them staying together long enough to make it to the church in one piece are *pretty* slim. Rumour has it,' Kirsty part-whispers, 'that *pool boy* still has a habit of slipping into the girl's changing rooms, if you get my meaning.'

Ah. I hadn't expected this conversation to cheer me

117

up quite so much. Ruminating on that after we hang up, I open my second beer.

The duck has returned. It's in the river now, gliding back towards the town.

'Slim pickings out here, mate,' I call to it.

The duck doesn't bother responding, just paddles on.

I'm glad it seems a bit happier.

The same people that walked along this river path in former times, those of dainty parasols and tweed suits, I wonder if they were happy. They might have had the same problems back then – like disillusionment, existentialism, unhappy marriages – but the black and white photographs simply couldn't capture them.

A picture of a family strolling beside the river in the sunshine today would make a handsome image to hang on the wall of a pub in a hundred years. It wouldn't necessarily mean that, after the shutter has clicked, they didn't sometimes want to murder each other. Or maybe even have sex with someone who is employed by the local infant school. It's quite a reassuring thought.

My second beer is finished, so I throw the empty cans into the river, grab my urn and do like the duck.

sixteen

Nothing much outside the usual routine happens over the next week: I work not very hard, drink a fair bit, and wander about muttering to myself. With the day that we leave for our trip fast approaching, a sober sprinkling of anxiety has been dousing the drunk euphoria of my anticipation.

Except for by text, there hasn't been much contact with Ella, which also isn't unusual. The only change is that, lately, most of her messages have been coming through close to midnight. When I was her age, I was in bed by half-nine, reading music magazines until I fell asleep with the plugs for my Walkman still in my ears, probably only months away from discovering what else I could do when I was alone in my bedroom.

There has only been one telephone conversation with Ella, brief as it was. Monosyllabic and morose, she finally sparked to life when I asked for about the fifth time if she was looking forward to going away with me.

"Stop *saying* that," she moaned. "You've asked me,

like, *a thousand* times. I've already said I'm coming with you, haven't I? And I'd better have my own tent."

I didn't exactly lie when I told Ella that she does indeed have her own tent. Inside the huge, heavy red bag that Brian dropped into work the other day, the tent we're taking has a separate two-man compartment at each end. I would like to see *Dan* compete with *that*.

"It's going to be fun!" I told Ella.

"Stop saying that, too. You're such an idiot. And can you *stop* calling it a tour."

Over the duration of our call, I did say quite a few times about how fun our trip is going to be. And calling it a tour doesn't make it sound more exciting, apparently. That I'm an idiot is a given. The closer our trip comes, I've been wondering more and more who I am trying to convince about the fun.

Throughout these interim days, one of my idle maunders led me to The Tap – there's no way that I would go to The Humphrey by myself, just to have Toothy Charlie latch onto me, telling jokes that aren't even worthy of a Christmas Cracker bought from the mouldy ice cream shop. The new landlord, Kev, took over The Tap a few years ago. One of the first things he did was fill the jukebox with good rock music and a bit of ska. The baize of the pool table is no longer stained and torn. None of the chairs or stools wobble, where almost all of the old ones used to regularly tip pissed locals all over the sticky floor.

A new clientele has found its way onto the shiny, polished floorboards. Unlike The Humphrey – which remains a den of iniquity, where even someone as grim as Toothy Charlie can find a bird to nosh him off in the toilets – there is way less illicit behaviour in the beer garden than there used to be. Even so, last Christmas Day, when I had nowhere to go, one of the barmaids and I managed to knock one of Kev's hanging baskets off the wall. Being winter, the basket was only full of dead plants and dry compost, but in the New Year things were a bit frosty with Kev. I have never known if it was for the corruption of the barmaid or for the hanging basket.

The temporary cold shoulder might even have been for grabbing one of the guitars while the band were on a break and bashing out a very drunk and emotional cover version of R.E.M.'s *The One I Love*. The next morning, I found out that someone had filmed the entire episode and put it online. When I next met Darren, he showed it to me. There I was, all over the place, thrashing hell out of some poor dude's Fender. The cameraman joined me on the floor, capturing every moment as I slobbered into the microphone I'd knocked over. The video didn't end until Kev grabbed my foot and dragged me away.

It was Christmas, I was drunk, and my emotions got the better of me. Unlike the old days, I wasn't singing the song for Kirsty.

Before I invaded the stage, I had earlier lifted the Christmas tree out of its pot and waltzed it around the pub, so Kev's anger might have been because of that. Or possibly for my behaviour around the buffet. It could have been for many things. But I think that probably it was for the hanging basket.

Even though I've never joined in with a single piece of social media, and don't entirely understand what it is, that video isn't the only time that I've trended. Like the weather, the lingering disgrace of my humiliation always blows away after a few days.

Kev is already pouring me a pint, as they do when I walk into most of the pubs in Tenderbridge. With an assorted wardrobe of plaid shirts and different shades of regular fit Levi's, the only fancy or fandangle about Kev is his tall, textured quiff and his designer cropped beard, both trimmed twice a week.

''Ello, mate,' he says, his handshake crippling me.

'How's it going, Kev?' I reply, discreetly massaging my hand.

'Very happily. Had a splendid workout last night.'

Kev doesn't often have a steady girlfriend. With his natural charm and a bar full of booze, why would he? He is like the me that I want to be.

'How about you?' he asks. 'What's happening?'

'Not a lot,' I reply, checking again that my wallet is in my pocket. 'Just getting ready to take my daughter away on a trip.'

'Getting out of town, huh? Good for you, mate.'

In this town, I've gone from having a status similar to Kev's, to now being the bloke who never does anything or goes anywhere. No longer known as a musician, but as a postman.

And a layabout.

And because of the lollipop incident.

'Where are you taking her?'

I finish glugging a steady gulp of beer, and *yet again* recite the tale of Ella moving away. And then I slag off Dan and Kirsty for a while. Mostly Dan.

'Get this,' Kev says. 'I knew a bloke who split up with his girlfriend, and then seven years later finds out that he's got a six-year-old son he never knew about. How about that for a busted coil in the old machine?'

'What did he do, the bloke, when he found out?'

'He already knew the kid,' Kev says with a chuckle. 'Just didn't know it was his. It turns out that the object of his four-year-old daughter's infatuation, an older boy at school, was actually her half-brother.'

'Another tale of Tenderbridge,' I say.

'Sounds like it,' Kev replies, 'but this bloke was from Maidstone.'

'Ah.'

Somehow, I am already on my second pot. Kev never allows anyone to go empty.

'Did I tell you about the time I took Ella for her first haircut?'

'No.' Smiling, Kev leans forward, his elbows on the bar. 'Tell me.'

'Well . . . I'd been drinking.' I lift my beer and take a few hippo gulps to demonstrate my point. 'It was just me and Ella that day. We didn't have anything else to do, so I decided to take her to the barber. She was only, I dunno, two? three? when boys sound like girls and girls can look like boys. I don't remember why I asked them to give her a short back and sides, though. I guess I thought it would be funny. And it was funny. The thing is, it was Ella's nativity play a few days later. There's my little Mary, Mother of Jesus, looking like a gypsy boxer.'

A couple arrive at the bar as I am recounting my tale. Kev simultaneously serves them while listening to me prattling on. From the couple I receive a slightly sneering look. Perhaps I'm their postman.

The beer is perfectly cold and refreshing. Unlike the old landlord, Kev knows how to keep his lines clean. I watch him refilling my glass again. The lovely, frothy stuff can't pour quick enough to match my thirst today. My beer-loosened happy place.

'It's messed up, mate,' I blabber on. 'The whole thing. Bringing someone into the world, doing the business with someone you don't really like anymore, and then unconditionally falling in love with the little brat who doesn't really like you. It's a strange feeling.' My hands are all over the place, describing my babble with invisible shapes. 'There's suddenly this *thing* you're supposed to be responsible for, and . . . it's love, mate. True, unlimited love. Not only the love, but you share every moment of its pain. It's like having a second heart that moves and thinks in its own way. And then when that heart finally detaches, you still want the feel of it. The beat. This . . . *intense connection*. This *thing* you were never even sure you wanted, you suddenly find you can't live without it.'

Kev's eyebrow slopes up into his smooth, tanned forehead. How can anyone work in pubs for fifteen-odd years and still have skin as good as his? There is not even a single fleck of grey in his beard, the prick.

'Is this because of your girl moving away?' he asks. 'That this feeling is coming up stronger?'

'A man can't live without his heartbeat, my friend,' I say, draining my latest pint. 'No one can. But why would anyone deliberately put themselves through all that? If they knew all the other shit that was coming their way, would they still do it?'

Elbows on the bar, Kev leans towards me and looks me directly in the eye.

'Not everyone takes their daughter for a short back and sides, mate,' he says.

My God, he is good.

'Oi, *Kev*,' I'm saying later, now on my whatever-number beer, before the Six O'clock News has been broadcast.

Kev is busy with another punter, so he signals me to hush for a moment.

I've received all kinds of looks from people who have come up to the bar. I stare at them until they look away. If they're remotely pretty, I complement my stare with a soggy smile.

Kev closes the till and heads back over. 'What?'

'Kev. I used to be popular,' I slather. 'I was. The bloke who plays and sings in a band, that was *me*. I was a man with fans, like . . . *Elvis*. I made a sex tape once. Did I tell you?'

Smiling, Kev shakes his head, his eyes twinkling.

He loves my stories, Kev.

'I did, yeah. It's on the computer. *Elvis* never made a sex tape. He never got that far. But me, I did. And now I'm no-no-nobody. Even the most important person . . . I'm taking Ella on a trip!'

'I know, mate,' Kev says. 'You told me.'

'I am.'

He doesn't replenish my drink this time. Instead, he puts a glass of water on the bar in front of me. I glare at it. Spin the glass around. Push it away. And then I pick it up, down the water and sling the glass over the bar. Kev catches it at about knee height.

'I've still got it, *Kevin*. I still have *fans*. They stand in front of me and they say . . . John.'

I catch the attention of my reflection in the mirror behind the optics. A blurry zombie is staring back at me, blotchy-red and sallow-eyed. My usual alcoholic veneer.

'*Kev*,' I loudly whisper.

He nods.

I signal for him to come closer, but he doesn't.

'Kev . . . I don't even have a band anymore.'

'What? Have Spanky Monkey broken up?'

'It's Spanky *Macaca*. Like Monkey, but *Macaca*. Come on, Kevin, you should know that. *Ever'one* should.'

'And you've broken up?'

'*OhIdunno*. The others, they just want to play with themselves.'

While I am giggling, Kev puts another water in front of me, this time in a plastic cup. I burble into the cup and water spills down the front of my ancient Elastica t-shirt, making me laugh hysterically.

Kev is eyeing the mess I'm making. As long as it's water, he won't mind.

'Everything's breaking, Kev,' I say, staring into the cup that I am trying to crush, but can't crush. 'I just want to play some songs but nobody wants to hear me. Like the boy with the horn.'

'Why don't you do a solo show?' Kev says. 'In here.'

'Really? Can I play some of my own songs?' I ask, water soaking my front. 'To my fans.'

'Course you can, mate.'

126

'What . . . now?'

'No, not *now*, dickhead,' Kev says, plucking the cup from my hands. 'Tell you what, not an open mic night, you can do your own show. A solo night. What name will you go under?'

'My name? My *name*? My name is John. You know that, Kev, mate. You're a fan. Oi! Kelly saw me play. She said so. *Oh, she said so . . .*' I start singing.

And I'm still singing as I walk down the road, having been told by Kev to shut the fuck up and get out.

I received a text from Kev the next day to remind me about the solo show – and also to check that I made it back home to my stinking flat okay, which I must have. Because there were only a couple of days to prepare – and because I couldn't be bothered to practice – I didn't attempt to play any of my own songs in the end. But I was in a great mood. I didn't even cry, only choking once on *Sad Professor*.

A beer wasn't poured for me as soon as I walked into The Tap that night – I turned up nearly an hour late, and a bit tipsy, anyway, so it was fine. Nor was I paid, but that's alright, too. If I could have settled every back-dated bar bill by rattling off a few half-arsed songs, I'd be much better off than I am.

Kev seemed to act a bit funny towards me, though. I received a bit of the old slant-eye from the punters, too, even the ones that I don't really know. It was as if there was a big joke that everyone was in on except me.

It's Tenderbridge. I'm used to that in this town.

But the show has left me with a healthy buzz; a fuse to ignite my growing excitement for the trip. Now that it is only the day after next. As in, just over a day away.

seventeen

This morning I took Dan – not-a-dick Dan from work – a two pack of beer as a thank you for covering my shifts while I am away. It was originally a four pack, but ask a heron to guard your pond, and all that . . .

I finished work a bit early, so rather than spending the afternoon in the pub, and the disasters that would inevitably lead to, I decided to go shopping for bits and pieces for the trip. My first stop was going to be the beer shop, but I quickly thought better of it. Instead of puffing around town with them now, it makes much more sense to pick up the beers on the way home. And my supplies would only end up being decimated.

Just as I am heading into my usual local minimarket, I think about the mouldy ice creams. Arriving at a camp-site with out-of-date snacks and stomach cramps would be about as well received as Mick's fishy aroma. With dad's cash in my pocket, I instead wander further along the high street to one of the very slightly more upmarket places, where the lights and the fridges work properly.

'Sausage rolls and other precooked meat,' I sing under my breath, browsing the aisles – something that I tend to do when shopping, rather than waste time writing lists. Not only does it make shopping more bearable, but it also adds lucidity to my purchases. I'm basically the Dylan of shopping. *'And other shit a teenage girl likes to eat. Tampons, tampons, should I buy her tampons?'* I sing, staring at the alien boxes of girl-stuffs I've stumbled upon.

'Do you need any help, sir?'

A little woman wearing a lime green apron is looking up at me. Her wonky squint says that maybe she heard me singing about tampons. These sorts of things happen to me often enough to not make me blush, even if an early-middle-aged man singing about feminine care products while staring at them is a bit of an odd thing to do. Whatever. There is no way I am the only weirdo in Tenderbridge who walks around singing about tampons.

'Sir?'

'You can call me Sir John,' I say. And then I notice her name badge. 'If you will, Jill.'

'Right,' she replies, backing off. 'Just let me know if you do need any help.'

I refocus my attention on the products on the shelf in front of me. Some of the boxes are pretty and pink, while others are more intimating shades of regular pharmaceutical packaging. My little girl is now a part of this world. That thought sobers my fascination to quite an uncomfortable extent.

What else has she got to learn to live with?

I take in the bewildering volume of products. Cups and creams and cleaners, pads and powders and wipes. Look at this one: *Vagisil*. If there isn't a product on the market called *Cockisore*, I think to myself, wandering away from the aisle of intrigue and fascination, then I'm definitely taking it on *Dragon's Den*.

"*What does it do?*" one of the magnates will ask me, probably the bloke with no top lip.

"*Exactly what it says on the box, mate.*"

I am definitely going to be more empathetic towards women from now on.

Emerging from the shop with two bulging carrier bags, a querying goggle from the little woman, and no tampons, I automatically begin to walk towards the pub.

Shaking my head, I turn homeward.

And then my feet swivel in the direction of the pub.

And then they face homeward again.

To anyone watching from the opposite side of the street, I must look like a harrowed man, pacing back and forth – which is exactly who I am and what I am doing.

'I can have a beer,' I tell myself, muttering my way to the pub. 'Just one beer. No damage done.

'*There must be something else you have to do,*' I chatter, heading back home. '*You haven't packed a thing. And where is your rucksack?*

'Packing won't take more than a few minutes. And the rucksack will be where it is. I've only got three rooms to check. Just one beer. Come on, I went *shopping*.

'*Simple question: have you ever had just one beer?*

'There was that time when I was out with dad and Julian—

'*And what happened after that? They bought a bottle of Chivas Regal. A night that ended with the police shaking you awake on a swing in the park, still cradling the bottle.*

'But I'm not going to buy a bottle of Chivas Regal,' I

argue, shambling up the high street. 'Just a simple beer in a simple pub. I deserve a reward for going to a proper shop and not a shithole, don't I? It is dad's cash I'm spending, remember.'

Momentarily glancing up from my meanderings, I notice an older couple walking towards me. Oh Jesus, it's the same elderly pair who were strolling along on the other side of the river last week, freaking out after they saw me laughing my head off at nothing. I smile, nod to them, roll my eyes and shrug, just like last time. But unlike last time, I have two heavy carrier bags in my hands, so I can't get my phone out and pretend that I'm speaking to someone. They give me and my bags a very wide swerve.

'Look, I'll go to a pub I don't know,' I continue. 'One where I am not familiar with the locals. Just slip in, have a quiet beer in the corner. Sit there and think about the trip.'

Before the conversation with myself has ended, I am already opening the door of a pub that I never go to.

The clientele in here are not proper locals. There is not a single pair of leggings or football jersey to be seen. While I have forever been trapped by the lure of cheap booze and women who might give me a second glance, this must be what it is to drink on the north side of the town.

Located by the river, balconied double doors open above the lazy, low water. The reflected brightness of the summer sky floods over the ceiling. In the absence of the usual temptations, there is a different snare in which I soon find myself captured. The peace and quiet of the dozy river. The sound of voices speaking normally; no shouting, swearing, or soap opera drama. Sitting here in the relative silence, I'm *enjoying* myself.

Such is my enjoyment that I end up having six beers. I have also sneakily snacked on two sausage rolls, three Tunnock's tea cakes, and a couple of bags of crisps from my stash for Wales. So that's dinner sorted, too.

With the late summer sun yet to set, a flash of inspiration strikes. Finally heading homeward, I brag about it to my Good Angel. If I hadn't had those beers, there is no way that I would have thought of buying a torch.

I spend the next few steps attempting to justify going back to the pub, to see if it inspires any other purchases that we might need for the trip. But even my Bad Angel thinks that would be a liberty too far.

eighteen

There are four signs sticking out of the lamppost, gold text on a black background. I've been staring at them for a couple of minutes. Three signs point to north Tender-bridge, encouraging visitors towards the *Castle & Tourist Information*, the *Sportsground & Play Area*, and the *High Street & Swimming Pool*. A single, much thinner sign offers a choice of destination in the south side: *Local Shops*. Whoever chooses to follow that sign will quickly realise they've been mugged off. If not actually mugged.

Having picked up the torch on my way home from the pub last night, I had every good intention of famil-iarising myself with the tent's instructions. To get in the mood for the trip, instead I drank a few beers while watching *Countryfile*, followed by a few episodes of an Attenborough documentary.

My Good Angel has only just stopped giving me an earful for waking up hungover. For despite the drunken night's sleep, tossing and turning and getting up to go for a wee every other hour, I somehow managed to make it to the railway station on time. Early, even, which has allowed me the opportunity to amuse myself with the lamppost.

Dan's BMW pulls into the taxi rank in front of the station. Standing here with my carrier bags, rucksack, and the massively heavy tent bag, it feels like Dan is the dad dropping off one of my friends – albeit a friend who isn't really interested in me, which only increases my impression of feeling like the schoolboy I once was.

'Ready for our tour?' I ask Ella, the moment she gets out the car.

'Stop calling it a tour, John,' she says. 'I've already asked you not to.'

Sometimes I am dad, but I'm back to being John. Still, it's less offensive than some of the names she calls me.

With arrogance oozing through the tiny holes of his pale blue polo shirt, Dan emerges. I watch him strut the length of his car and take a pink wheelie bag and shiny new rucksack out of the boot.

'You're looking fit and healthy,' Kirsty says, startling me in more ways than one. I wonder if she noticed me glaring at her wealthy benefactor.

'Everyone looks fit and healthy by the end of the summer,' I reply. Kirsty, of course, has her orangey glow all year round, a few tones softer than Bea's smouldering twilight. 'But thanks,' I quickly add, because it is too early, too public, and I'm too tired. 'It's always good to be out in the fresh air. Which we're going to get plenty of, hey, Ella?'

She mumbles something that I can't hear. Her hair is a tangled, wavy mess covering half of her grumpy face. Even when she was a little kid this girl hated mornings.

135

She pulls up the hood of her yellow raincoat and hides within it.

'Alright, John?'

Over my daughter's shadow, Dan looks down his sharp, smooth nose at me. I reluctantly shake his manicured, city-boy-plump hand. It is as bronzed as his shiny face – unlike his other hand, which spends most of the summer tucked up inside a golf glove.

'Do I get a kiss goodbye?' he asks Ella.

'Piss off, Dan.'

Did she say Dan? Through the mess of her hair, she might have said dad. The more I think about it, the more it sounded like dad. Damn the sharp howl of tinnitus that tortures me every day, especially after a few beers the night before. So mostly every day.

'*Ella* . . .' Kirsty says, in a patient but warning tone.

Dan doesn't seem to mind. With Ella's bags dropped beside mine, he's laughing it off on his way back to the driver's side of his car. Would anyone notice if I charge at him and push him in the path of an oncoming bus?

'Yeah, you can piss off, mate,' he says to a cabbie, who is yelling something and waving a fist towards the no entry sign. 'I'm about to move it, you prick. What does it look like I'm doing? Go and be a cabbie back in your own country, if you don't like it.'

So, not only is Dan a wonderful role model for my little girl, but he is also a BNP sympathiser. It wouldn't surprise me if he is a proper fascist. Perhaps the blue tie he wears to work is just a cover up so that he can fit into the serene backdrop of the north side.

Back in the Beemer, he revs the engine, showing off

the immensity of how far he can push his foot down in an otherwise idle car.

'I get a kiss, my darling warling.' Kirsty grabs Ella to her cleavage and pecks her beak onto the hood of Ella's yellow coat, searching for a way into Ella's cheek. Ella's taking it. Or I assume she is. It's hard to tell beneath the huddle of Kirsty. 'My little scwunchie.'

That's a new one. And where has the once-adorable Northern accent disappeared to lately? It comes out on the phone to me, alright. If I moved to the north side, I wonder if I would start shaving more than once a fortnight, and wearing a clean pair of jeans more than once a season.

'You take care of yourself, okay?' Kirsty tells Ella. 'I've checked you've got everything you might need.'

Ah, girl talk. I smirk secretly. If only they knew of yesterday's adventure down the supermarket aisle.

'And you've got your money?'

Money? I wonder if Dan gave Ella more cash than my dad gave me.

'Your sleeping bag and pillow are packed into the rucksack,' Kirsty says. 'You've also got your special blanket in there, okay?'

Ella prods a scowl at me. I don't know if it cries, *Please rescue me!* Or even a chummy, *This is* so *embarrassing.* Or perhaps a confidential, *We both know I'm too old for a comfort blanket, but this woman just can't seem to accept it.*

Stupid, isn't she, I thought-talk back to Ella.

And then I interrupt myself: *Sleeping bag? Pillow? Blanket?* One of the three would be excellent. None of them is a most definite oversight.

Why didn't Brian check I had them? Wally.

'Dan's also put a camping roll in there, so you'll sleep like a little angel.'

While I'll be sleeping like a Hell's Angel.

'The train's due in ten minutes, Kirst,' I say. 'If we miss that, we'll miss all our connections.'

Kirsty gives me a look like I just casually mentioned the lollipop lady.

Sensing her moment, Ella twists from the raptor grip she is held in, squirming to free her shoulders, but Kirsty instantly regrips her talons.

'Make sure that you SMS me every evening as we agreed, okay?'

'Yes, mum.'

'Nine o'clock every night. No later. Just to let me know you're alright.'

'I *literally* just said I would.' With the final word, Ella rips herself free.

'Have you got the tickets?' Kirsty asks me.

What's this tone she's using, as if I'm a binman who needs reminding to collect the rubbish?

'Of course I do. But they're not tickets, they're printouts. Brian ran them off for me,' I say, a bit smugly.

Unlike the tent and my personal sleeping arrangements, those printouts I have checked obsessively. Even since arriving at the train station, four times I must have made sure that they are still in the pocket of my rucksack where I left them. I do sort of want to check again.

'Alright,' she says. 'Well, you make sure that you take care of my little girl.'

'I will definitely make sure that I take care of *our* little girl,' I reply.

Saying *our* makes me feel a bit dirty, somehow. Especially with Dan sitting only a few feet away.

He is ugly, actually. He might have a healthy fake tan, but he is definitely uglier than me. A bulldog whose face has been dipped in creosote.

Wait a minute, everyone keeps telling me that I have a healthy tan. I'm the only one who knows that I feel like shit all the time.

The taxi driver blocked in by Dan sounds his horn, so of course Dan replies with a much longer, more aggressive blast of his. He yells again at the taxi driver, as well as anyone else who looks his way. And then screams a swearier version of *Get a move on* to Kirsty.

The last pouty kisses are rained down upon Ella, followed by a quasi-tearful wave goodbye. As soon as Kirsty closes the car door, Dan screeches out of the taxi rank, a few feet ahead of a passing truck, sadly.

I grab my rucksack, scoop up the carriers, and lift the tent bag to knee-height. I am sure it's got heavier since I arrived at the station.

When I returned home last night, I did open the big red bag once. All in, I've got twenty-four beers stashed in various places: a few in my rucksack, some more in each of the carrier bags, but most of them packed in with the tent. I hope that Ella remembered to bring something to drink. I only had room for one bottle of water. I don't want to break my stupid back.

'Ready?' I ask. 'Come on. We've got to get the tickets.'

'You told mum you already have the tickets.'

'For the coach, yeah,' I say with a wink.

Ella looks at her bags and then at me, close to buckling beneath the weight of my load. With a sigh, she lifts her rucksack and primes the handle of the wheelie bag. And then we step into the station, just me and my girl, off on our trip.

Sweat breaks out all over me. Not more than a few pigeon steps into our journey and already I am puffing and panting and clammy and smelly.

'Ella,' I say. 'When did your mum start referring to text messages as SMSs?'

'I don't know,' Ella replies. 'I think she's got brain disease. If she's even got a brain.'

That's my girl.

This trip is going to be so great.

nineteen

I can't recall if I have ever been able to sleep in the same way that Ella does. On each leg of the journey – from Tenderbridge to London Victoria; by coach to Castle Street in Cardiff; a fifty-minute ride to a bus station across the city; and then a smaller bus onward to our final stop – as soon as Ella slumped down in every one of the seats, she was away with the fairies. I am pretty certain that she sleepwalked between the terminals in Cardiff.

I don't mind. I can't remember the last time that I spent this long alone with her, even if she has had her eyes closed for most of it. As the hours and scenery pass by, I've been happy to just watch her. Not even the kid on the other side of the gangway of the earlier coach journey, zapping something on his handheld gaming device, could distract me. Too captivated was I by this girl to care. Although I did throw half a cocktail sausage at him.

Ella's hair is not in its usual place, covering her face,

instead tucked behind her ear. It is almost inconceivable that this is the same person whose bed I used to sleep beside after I crawled home from the pub. I try to work out what I have been doing since the tiny thing I could hold in one hand became this teenager. That little girl with the cheeky grin, pigtails bobbing around her head, wearing a dress so tiny that it fit her teddy bears. I don't have a clue who she is.

Content with just turning up and being amused by her grumpiness, I don't remember ever stopping to consider that Ella has thoughts of her own, feels certain ways about things. She decides for herself when to add a smiley face when messaging me, and the other times when she feels compelled to tell me to fuck off.

I notice the soft, almost invisible cilia on her top lip. The freckles in the shape of wings scattered over her button nose. A tiny pimple hidden beneath her jaw, under the spongy curl of her cheek. The barely perceptible creases of smile-lines in her dimples. Here is the only real thing to show from my years of doing not a lot.

I look for clues that might reveal what Ella will become as a woman. High on her cheeks, her skin has a natural blush, a pink wash over her pale skin. Her eyebrows steeple over her sleeping eyelids, the shape of birds flying through the sky of a child's drawing. Her ears so small and unlobed, all Kirsty. Did I even know that she'd had them pierced? And the gentle whisper of sleeping breaths, so like all those years ago.

That detached heartbeat I told Kev about.

What a hopeless father I have been. Put both hands in the air if you agree . . .

Every person in Wembley Stadium lifts their arms.

Standing in the wings of the stage, a beautiful young woman waves both of her hands above her head. "But I love you anyway," she yells. "You old twat," I think she adds. Of course, I can't hear her because Wembley is going wild.

Dad and Julian are standing next to her. Beside them, Paul is grinning. He gives me a thumbs up and shares a joke with dad. On Paul's other side, mum is shaking her head at dad's dancing. But she's smiling.

I notice that mum is wearing one of the Sir John t-shirts that sells out every night at gigs. In fact, they all are. Even Julian, beneath his pastel-pink beret. In one hand, the beautiful young woman is also holding the charity shop urn.

"I'm going to play a cover song now."

The rest of the band leave the stage and I stand alone, just me and my guitar in the Wembley spotlight. Peering through the blinding whiteness, I see Kirsty and Dan sitting in the cheap seats. And . . . yes, Bea is sitting next to them. Can't see pool boy, though.

Kirsty has grey roots growing through a bad dye job, her skin blanched and lined. Dan is wearing one of my old jackets, and has a bandage around his head. Bea's bum has grown so big that she needs two seats, and even then each cheek is over-spilling them. All three of them are looking everywhere except for the stage.

"This song is dedicated to the most special person in my life," I tell the crowd, who have hushed to silence. "It's called The One I Love . . ."

Girls begin to weep. Mothers and daughters. Even some of the men, big burly men, in floods—

'John.'

'What? Who's that?'

'Dad!' Ella sticks a finger into the side of my face. 'Wake up. We're here.'

'Eh? What? Where? Wembley?'

'What? No. The bus driver just said this is our stop.'

'Merthyr Tydfil?' a voice from the front of the bus says.

Sunshine is pouring over my sweaty face. I rub a thumb around the inside of my eye. A beer can standing between my thighs drops to the floor, spilling bubbling amber fluid beneath the seats. Using the headrest in front of me, I pull myself upright.

The bus driver is leaning over his seat. With his dark hair and slightly dangerous-looking eyes, if Cary Grant had been a bus driver, he would have been this bloke.

'Merthyr Tydfil?' he says again.

'No, mate,' I say. 'Daniwylliwhatnot, that's our stop.'

'Danwylliarwean?' Cary Grant says.

'Yeah,' I agree. 'Something like that.'

'This is the stop for Danwylliarwean.'

Kicking the can away, I grab the carriers and rucksack from beneath my seat, and then I lift the massive, slightly soggy tent bag.

'Definitely the stop for the Danwilli place?' I ask, just to be sure before we disembark.

'That's right,' the bus driver says. 'It's only about fourteen miles from here.'

It's like I've woken up in a foreign country.

'That can't be right,' I say. 'Doesn't the bus go . . . directly there?'

'This is the closest stop,' he says. 'You can get a taxi from here to Danwylliarwean.'

'Taxi? Do bus tickets cover the fare?'

'Oh no,' Cary Grant says with a chuckle.

As if I had been joking.

This is bloody Kelly's fault, I think, lugging the bags off the bus. I hope that everyone in that travel agency is as useless as Kelly, and Bea ends up spending her engagement holiday cooped up in a chicken shack on the Isle of Man.

I had pictured bowling up at a holiday park with rolling hillsides and mountains in the background, like when I was a kid. With its yellowy-beige fascia and graffitied covered seating areas, Merthyr Tydfil bus station could've been lifted straight out of south Tenderbridge. Taking Ella to a car park in Tenderbridge wouldn't have cost me, or my dad, a penny.

Ella hugs the hoodie's baggy arms around her. Even though it must be mid-afternoon, it is definitely colder than it was in the open double doors of the pub by the river yesterday.

Staggering a bit, I pull my charity shop leather jacket out of one of the carrier bags. A fair few empties clatter onto the tarmac.

'Are you pissed?'

'Huh?' I grunt, struggling upright.

'You can't even get on a *bus* without ending up *pissed*?'

'Nuh. I'm not drunk, honey,' I announce in my slurry, slightly emotional-sounding voice. 'It probably seems that way because I've just woken up. I had a couple of drinks while you were asleep, that's all.'

After a few attempts, I finally manage to fit my arm into the correct sleeve of my jacket.

However I try to focus on my new surroundings, the glow of the Wembley spotlight confuses my eyes.

'What was it that bloke said?' I ask, with a shiver.

'What *bloke*?'

'The, erm . . . the bus one.'

'We have to get a taxi from here to Danwylliarwean,' Ella says, looking around the car park.

'Say that again. You sound just like the bus man.' I can picture my smile. I've seen it in the mirrors of innumerable pub toilets. The wet one that hangs off my face.

Without a further word, Ella walks off.

One of the reasons I so enjoyed watching her sleeping was so we didn't fall out straight away. It turns out that all it took was for us to both be awake at the same time.

'Hey!' I call after her. 'Els!'

'Follow me,' she says, without looking around.

'I'm just going to get rid of these, sweetheart.'

I count nine empty beer cans into the rubbish bin, then penguin-walk my bags over to the taxi that Ella is standing next to. In the driver's seat is one of those overgrown baby sorts. He must be about six foot four, but has the face of a toddler. If he's ever had to shave, then Kelly is a genius.

'He'll take us,' Ella says.

'How much, mate?' I ask, leaning in through the open window.

'To Danwylliarwean?' the cabbie says. ''Bout twenty quid, mate.'

'Twenty? Are you sure?'

It turns out that toddler-man is only approximately sure, so twenty-two pounds lighter later, we arrive at a set of low stone buildings hidden in the crook of a valley.

Sticks of pines, green and yellow and red, rise up the hillsides. Sheep trail over the waves of undulating fields like plump white ants. The sky, a shade similar to Kurt's sonic blue Jag-Stang, is dotted with liquid spillages of clouds, zooming overhead. A vaster landscape I struggle to recall. Quite simply, this forgotten place out in the middle of nowhere is stunning.

Breathing air fresher than I have ever imagined, I dare to check what Ella makes of it. She is spinning around, arms out to her sides, drilling upwards into the watery mass of sky, swimming in it, and smiling all the while. When she stops, she staggers to the side.

'What do you think?'

'I love it,' she replies. 'It's wild, but so beautiful. It's nothing like back home. Look at all the sheep!'

So, perhaps I could have just taken her to a zoo. But I don't think that I would have seen that smile at any zoo, the one of complete abandon. The same as the one from the side of the Wembley stage.

I couldn't really have imagined a better start to our trip if I had bothered to plan it.

twenty

A couple appear from a doorway on the side of the largest cottage. Hand in hand, they head towards me. I pick up the tent bag and waddle in their direction. Even though I'm not quite as wobbly as I was at the bus terminal, I can picture how shabby I must appear, emitting a moan or a grunt with each step. And with my handful of carrier bags.

'Hello, traveller,' the man calls before reaching me.

I suppose that I do look a bit like a traveller. Can't expect to be called Sir everywhere I go. I drop the tent, lean the bags against it and huff *Hi*.

'Welcome to The Cannock,' the lady says. 'My name is Nell. And this is Andrew, my husband.'

'I'm John.'

'Pleased to meet you, John,' says Andrew.

I love the Welsh accent. It's so friendly and welcoming. Such a far step from the gravelly smoker's rag back home.

Both of their grips, the toughened country hands, are stronger than mine. Even though Nell has dyed blonde, straggly shoulder-length hair and is wearing a zipped-up fleece, she strikes me as a woman who would travel from north Tenderbridge to do her shopping. And with Andrew's slightly-too-long salt and pepper locks bothering his mildly amused, heavily lidded eyes, he seems like the sort of bloke who would be a local representative for the Liberals. The V-neck sweater shawled over his shoulders only adds to the semblance. I would guess that they have fifteen years on me, but their faces are largely unlined. These days I look more like a dry riverbed with each passing season.

'Have you got an army coming to stay with you?' Nell asks, indicating the huge red bag.

'Just the two of us.' I gesture towards Ella, halfway up a field gate, bathing her face in the sunlight. The gate rattles and shakes beneath her while she tries to get the attention of a sheep. 'Els, come over here and say hi, sweetheart.'

With only the slightest measure of teenage stroppiness, Ella slowly acknowledges my request.

By the time I turn back round, Nell and Andrew's expressions are not quite so smiley anymore. Nell's lips are parted, as if she forgot what she was about to say. She sucks a great gulp of air, holds it in, looks around a bit, and then puffs it out. Andrew just looks like he wants to rough me up.

'Ella is my daughter,' I say, calculating the reason for their altered manners.

And their easy smiles reappear.

Nell claps her hands together. 'Of *course.*'

'Of course you are,' Andrew agrees. He puts his arm around Nell and gives her a loving squeeze, which she clearly does love. Isn't it all very lovely now they know I haven't stolen a random child away into their peaceful countryside.

I get that with my beer fatigue and twice-broken, lopsided nose – one drunken accident with a stiff door, and another a drunken accident with a guitar, and just generally walking into things, or falling off them – set against Ella's cute button nose, pretty smile and freckles, we might not exactly look like father and daughter. And that is before accounting for my scruffy appearance and general demeanour. But even so, to resolve that because of the polarity in our appearances I must have snatched a grumpy teenager away to a campsite in the middle of nowhere seems an odd presumption to make. Anyway, surely paedophiles are more likely to be caravaners than campers.

'What are you planning on doing while you're here, my lovely?' Nell asks, directed to Ella.

Ella looks to me for an answer.

Now they're all looking at me.

'Wander around a bit?' I say with a shrug. 'See some of the countryside?' I add because none of them seemed entirely satisfied with my first response.

'Well, if you need recommendations of places to visit, then don't hesitate to ask,' says Nell. 'We're over in the main cottage here, so just give us a knock.'

'Where *would* you recommend going, Nell?' I ask, seeing as she offered.

For the next few minutes, Nell and Andrew pass their

favourite local places of interest back and forth: abbeys, castles, and other heritage sites, such as the Roman city, the priory, and the stone circle. They tell us about the museums, towns, and the entertainment attractions. And they emphasise just how easily accessible these wonderful, amazing places are by car.

'And how accessible are they if you don't have a car?'

'Oh.' Andrew looks at Nell, who looks at him, both of them as perplexed as when they thought they had a predator and a runaway to stay. 'You've come all the way out here without a vehicle?'

'He had his licence taken away after he drove his car over a bowling lawn, when they were about to start a national tournament,' Ella, my lovable little assassin, says. She folds her arms, challenging me to disagree.

I chortle, roll my eyes, and shake my head. 'That isn't what happened.'

'What did happen?' Andrew asks, folding his arms, too. Maybe he was once a politician. Maybe he still is. Anyway, there is no way that, down the pub, one of his cronies hasn't recounted a tale of the time they drank a few too many sherbets and acted like a bit of a bell-end.

Bollocks to it. I'll just tell them the truth.

'Well . . . I *did* drive over a bowling lawn,' I carefully begin. 'But it wasn't my car; it belonged to a pal. And the bowling lawn was being used to host heats for a regional croquet tournament at the time, not a national lawn bowls tournament.'

Because I was driving off-road, not on a public highway, I contested that I should be let off. But the police disagreed, advising me to not continue challenging the charge for such a futile technicality, as I could consider myself lucky not to be going to prison. Because—

'He was drunk,' Ella says.

'Anyway,' I quickly interject.

I explain to Nell and Andrew about how we came here by bus; that my divvy travel agent neglected to mention that the bus wouldn't actually drop us at our intended destination but at the closest stop, just over fourteen miles away.

'You do really need a car to visit most of those places,' Andrew reminds us. 'But, well, you can see what surrounds us.' He gestures towards the fields and hill-sides. The peaks of the mountains on the far horizon. The sheep. 'If you came for the countryside, you've got it.'

'There's the reservoir behind us, just over these hills,' Nell says. 'Or from here you can walk to the fells easily enough. Everyone who visits heads out to see the water-falls at some point. You'll have plenty to do without a car.'

'Or if you did want to take a bus, it only takes forty minutes, or so, to walk to the nearest village,' Andrew tells us, picking up the baton. They'd make great travel agents, these two. Unlike my actual travel agent.

'How far away is the the local pub?' I ask as casually as I can, avoiding Ella's eye.

'That'll be in the village,' Andrew replies. 'So forty minutes, by foot. It's easy enough to navigate your way there on your map.'

Cars, buses, maps, sleeping bags. The things you need to know. I thought that I had been pretty clever when I bought the torch – if I even remembered to pack it. Perhaps

I have become so set into town life, where everything I want is readily available along one utterly disgusting street, that the world surrounding it has been reduced to nothing but an extension of that same ease of access. Never could I have imagined that the closest pub would ever be a forty-minute walk away, wherever I was. And who would guess that a map would be needed to find it?

It turns out that Nell and Andrew keep a supply of spare maps for visiting townies, so Andrew goes to grab one for us. His walk is immaculate, seeming to slide over the ground, rather than to be ruffled by having a gait. It's unfair to liken him to a politician. His easy manner is a bit more regional weatherman, content with his twenty-four grand a year and a single measure gin and tonic after work on a Friday.

While he is gone, Nell explains, mostly to Ella, a bit more about the facilities they have here. There are toilets and showers in the main buildings, recently renovated, where there is also a payphone, if we need it. They've just converted a store cupboard into a little library, too, so we're welcome to sit in the lounge and read any books we like throughout our stay.

'Or,' she says, now speaking mostly to me, 'there are some colouring in sheets, if you'd prefer.'

When Andrew returns, map in hand, Ella and I are pointed down a track that leads into a scrubby paddock, about the size of four lawn bowls pitches. I expected that the campsite would be bulging with tents, a Thursday morning before Glastonbury Festival, but we discover only two. The smaller tent is in the shape of a bright blue polytunnel, and the other one is covered by a thick, green canvas rainfly, the sort of tent that the army or boy scouts or pretentious twats use.

Both tents appear to be empty. No one is around. Maybe the other campers are in the small restaurant that Nell told us they open twice a day. And Andrew afterwards confirmed that, yes, they do sell booze.

I really do love this place. Especially now we don't have to panic about the pub.

twenty-one

My third attempt at constructing the tent ended with another messy confusion of pieces bundled in a heap. While I was waving poles about and treading mud all over the fabric, Ella had been studying the instructions, so we agreed that she should take over. I had to put my beer down to help whenever there were bits too tall for her to reach, but otherwise I was perfectly content to just watch her go. Working together, we had the massive tent up in no time at all.

If the blue tent looks like a tiny tunnel, and the green canvas tent resembles the one in which Captain Scott froze to death in Antarctica, then our tent is a massive slug. A massive slug with an entrance hall.

'Is this it?' Ella says, hands on her new hips.

Chomping on a sausage roll, which even my alcohol-wearied taste buds pick out to be quite repulsive, I shrug.

'You said you were going to bring two tents.'

'You haven't eaten all day, Els,' I say through my

mouthful. 'You must be famished. Would you like to go and get something in the restaurant?'

'I had a packet of crisps when you were snoring on the bus.'

'That was hours ago. I'm sure that Nell and Dan will fix something up for you.'

'It's Andrew,' Ella replies. 'Not Dan.'

'I said Andrew.'

'No, you didn't. And anyway . . .' She reaches into the tent bag and pulls out a bundle of string. 'We haven't attached these yet.'

'No one uses guy ropes, sweetheart.'

'People who don't want the flysheet to blow away in the middle of the night do,' she counters.

'How about we do that after getting you something to eat?'

'Don't worry, dad, you don't *actually* have to help. And you didn't *actually* tell me why you didn't bring two tents.'

'Brian lent us this out of the kindness of his boring heart, Ella,' I say, pointing my sausage roll at the slug. 'Each of us having our own compartment is the same as having two tents. In fact, it's better, because we have the middle bit to put our stuff.'

Ella puffs her cheeks, an earnest little hamster, and she again inspects the entrance.

'I'll still be able to hear you snore,' she says, standing in the hallway, looking out.

'Then I promise not to snore.'

'Dad, I only woke up on the bus was because you were snoring.'

'That's because I was sitting upright. I don't normally

snore. Not if I'm lying down.'

'You snore every single time you fall asleep,' she says. 'When you used to sleep next to my bed, you always snored.'

Now that Ella is speeding along the lane that heads to Grownupsville, I have never considered that she might remember those days, too. I feel my heart flutter. I almost choke on my mouthful of beer. 'You remember that?'

'Yes!' she replies. 'I *also* remember when you turned up at Dan's for my tenth birthday party and started snoring in the middle of the barbeque.'

'Ah, I was sitting upright,' I say, earning a reluctant smile.

The moment that Ella dips back inside, I throw the empty beer can at the foot of the tent and dip into my bag. When she steps outside a few blinks later, there's no way she could know it's not the same beer – although, because it's warm, froth is hissing out of the top, running down the can and over my fingers.

'Alright,' she says. 'Tell you what, if you don't snore I'll ask mum about not going to Canada. And then *maybe* we can find some way that I'll come and live with you.'

We shake on it. An absolute deal – probably because I'm on my third beer of the evening, and not considering the repercussions of living with a thirteen-year-old, right now. Especially when everyone already seems to think there is something a bit unsavoury about us spending time alone together.

Ella's latest promotion for the use of guy ropes is interrupted by a young couple walking past. They are wearing cagoules and hiking boots; the girl has a plastic-covered map hanging around her neck. Before heading towards the little tunnel tent, they give us a wave. In reply, I raise my beer can. They didn't seem to think there was anything odd about us.

We pitched our country pile as far away from the others as possible. Each of the three tents has claimed its own corner of the paddock, with the entrance track on the far side. I think of the rattling, buzzing extractor fan in the takeaway beneath my flat. That will be banging away right at this moment. Out here, all I can hear are the sheep and the choir of birds.

'Do you *ever* stop daydreaming?' Ella asks.

'Huh? No, I don't. What's up?'

'The guy ropes?'

'Just show me what to do, kiddo.'

It turns out that Ella is indeed best left to install them by herself. It looks great when it's finished, our massive slug, proudly dominating our corner of the field.

By the time Ella has finished her mac 'n' cheese, and I've washed my oggie and chips down with a couple of Andrew's strong Welsh beers, the sun has turned Kirsty-orange. The earthy, washed scent of moist field air breezes around us as we head back to our slug. A few golden leaves fall from the trees alongside the paddock, carried to the ground on the dying rays of the day.

The young couple are sitting on camping chairs outside the door of their measly little tunnel, leaning over a stove. Again, they give us a smiley wave. This time I just nod. We learned from Nell and Andrew that the group in the green scouts' tent are off on a cycling tour for a few days, using the campsite as a base. So tonight it's just us and the young couple.

Everyone seems happy enough to stay out of each other's way here, embracing the peace and quiet. When we get back to Tenderbridge, I am definitely going to look into whether living in a tent is allowed. If Brian needs his tent back for the odd weekend, I'll just ask if I can kip in his garage. I doubt that he would allow me to housesit. He's known me too long for that to happen.

'I'm going to go straight to bed,' Ella says.

'Okay, Els,' I reply, halfway into a carrier bag. 'Let me know if you need anything.'

Ella frowns. She kicks off her boots in the entrance hall and pauses for a moment. 'I'm glad I'm on this trip with you,' she says.

'It's our tour, baby,' I reply, the slurred words dropping out of my sloppy mouth.

'I asked you not to call it that, dad,' she says. 'Please.'

'Last time.' I give her a wink. 'Promise.'

'Okay.' Still, she stands there, giving me a blank look.

'What?' I ask.

'Nothing. Night.'

'Goodnight, Els.'

So as not to disturb the young couple – however tempted I am to go over and ask if they have a guitar that they want to pass around, or a doobie, or something – I retreat to the far side of the tent. The sun deepens and drops away beyond the mountains. Stars spin into the sky, even more abundant than they are above Brian's garage. The twinkling sheet of them is startling. The universe around them darkens as I gaze upwards.

These same stars have watched over every change of

my life; all of my dreams that evaporated towards them, buried by orange streetlights. And yet here they still are. I do desperately need to go for a whizz, but so transfixed am I that I leave it until my bladder hurts, and until my beer is finished.

Nobody bothers to use guy ropes for good reason: no one ever remembers to step over them. Even in a field with only a single tent in each corner, and space enough for a hundred more, one of the ropes hooks my foot and I fall face first into the tent. I hear poles snapping, pegs pulling up. Not sure which way up I am, I slip and roll over the top sheet, tangled and disoriented, every single movement making the struggle worse. I gather myself and try again, thrashing around in the cocoon of ropes and nylon. The fabric fights back, refusing to let me go. It is then that I feel the warm, strangely reassuring comfort of piss filling up my trousers from the inside.

When everything has settled and I cease writhing and weeing, something inside my jacket digs into my ribs. So I did remember to bring the torch.

Finally managing to untangle my limbs, I flash the crappy thing in the vague direction of the young couple, thankful to discover they have gone to bed. Guided by the wimpy light, I find my way inside the slug. The wavering glow highlights the extent of the damage. It couldn't look worse if the U.S. Air Force had given our lodgings a nice, friendly bombing.

Fortunately, Ella chose to sleep inside the wing that I didn't crush, and somehow my blundering doesn't seem to have to woken her. I'd be surprised if she's had her eyes open for five hours today.

I unzip her compartment. My nose presses into the

softer fabric of a fly screen. In the torchlight, through the mesh, she is facing away from me. I hear the soft purring sound of years gone by.

Shuffling backwards on my knees, I lay down in the hallway, struggle out of my soaked jeans and put my jacket over my legs. It's cold. It's uncomfortable. I smell of wee.

Not exactly how I imagined our first day ending.

A hand is on my shoulder, attempting to roll me from side to side.

I try to open my eyes.

It must be late. There is no clattering extractor fan. No orange glow peeps around the blackout blind. Just the smell of moist grass. And this excruciating white light shining directly into my face.

Something pokes me in the eye.

'Sorry,' Ella's voice says from somewhere above me, a haloed silhouette. 'You moved.'

A sucking, crinkling sound crackles from my cheek as the groundsheet peels away from my face. It is the only warm bit of my body. The worst sensation is the stinging coldness around my crotch. I attempt to sit up, only to discover that my entire right side has gone numb, so I flop back down.

'You alright?' I croak.

'*I* am, yeah,' Ella says. 'Why are you in the middle bit?'

A moment of heavy thinking, and then I remember how I came to be in the entrance hall, haven't got my trousers on, and it stings down there.

'Tell you in the morning.'

'Here.' Soft material pushes into my forehead. 'Take my blanket. You were shivering. Take it.'

'Thank you,' I say, taking the sweet-smelling sheet from her. "Thank you, Els.'

'I'm going back to bed. Please can you not open my compartment again?'

'Huh? Sure,' I say. 'Did I?'

A momentary pause, a jingling sound, the light of the torch on her phone dancing, and then the zipper begins to slide closed.

It stops somewhere above me.

'By the way, you were snoring.'

And then Ella zips the zip all the way.

While I arrange the blanket not-very-well over my lower half, it takes a moment to realise the significance of what she said. Having demolished half a tent, wetting myself, and then for my teenage daughter having to lend me some of her bedding so that I don't freeze to death, it is probably for the best that we don't live together.

Through the canvas of her compartment, I can see the gentle glow of her phone. And then I hear the whistling sound of a text message sending. In the middle of the night.

twenty-two

Ella woke up to find one end of our slug looking rather worse for wear. Before that, she had discovered me – who was definitely worse for wear – in the hallway in my pants, still snoring, half-covered by her blanket, and with my feet in the arms of my leather jacket. Having neglected to zip the front door closed behind me when I returned last night, my compromising position was laid out in full view to the glory of the new morning.

Over breakfast, with a quite thick head, I explained to Ella that I went out for a whizz in the night, tripped over a guy rope and landed on the tent, mangling one end of it, isn't daddy clumsy, ho-ho-ho. There is a rope burn on my leg to prove it, too. I didn't deem it necessary to tell her that I wet myself in all the excitement. And she didn't ask why my jeans were damp when I pulled them on for breakfast. I don't know if Ella noticed, but I could definitely smell a vague scent of piss.

'Have you got the map?' she asks when we're just about ready to leave.

'It was here somewhere.'

'Yes, I know it was here somewhere,' she says, a bit impatiently. 'But have you got it now?'

Eventually, we find the map tucked inside the pocket for the tent's instructions. When Ella admits that it was her who had put it there for safe keeping, she gives me the most adorably guilty smile. She doesn't even shrug off the hug that I feel overwhelmed to give her.

This morning she has been incredible: smiley, chatty, friendly, bossy. Back home, she sometimes won't give me more than a grunt, yet out here she lent me her comfort blanket. She simply laughed when I told her my slightly amended confession about the demolition job on the tent. And then she'd said, still in good humour, that no, there is absolutely no fucking way that I can share her compartment tonight. All after I had broken my snoring promise to a prodigious extent.

Although I chucked the empty beer cans into the woodland, hiding the evidence, Ella must have a suspicion that I drank quite a lot yesterday. As a thank you for this morning's easy demeanour, and also for last night's blanket, I stow only five beers into my tatty rucksack – alongside a jumper, my leather jacket, a bottle of water and snacks. I don't recall buying bananas, but apparently did.

At breakfast, Nell and Andrew asked what our plans are for the day. We told them that we are going to visit the fells, seeing as it is what most people do.

"And while we're at it," I added, "we're planning on hunting for animals, too." I then reassured them that I meant hunting as in, "Just out looking for wildlife; not hunting animals like fat Americans or royals."

It was then that, even though we had woken up to another fine Welsh morning, Nell had advised us to be prepared for all possible weathers.

"You'll probably be alright," she reassured in her lovely accent. "I've checked and there is only a thirteen percent chance of precipitation today. At worst, it might start picking. But it does look as though we'll be in for a wet and windy night."

With our simple plan to head for a stroll, check out the waterfalls, a bit of animal spotting thrown in, we'll be back long before any storm hits. Although, I advised Ella, it will probably be wiser for us to spend quite a lot of this evening in the bar area.

'Right.' I sling my packed and zipped rucksack over my shoulder. 'Got everything you need?'

'I think so,' Ella replies.

'Then let the tour commence.'

'How many times do I have to ask you not to *say* that? It's really irritating.'

'But tours are supposed to fun,' I continue as we set off through the gate behind the Cannock site, heading to the hills. 'Little Mix go on tours.'

'Firstly,' Ella says, stopping after only a few steps into our day out, 'I don't think that the tours musicians make around the world really are like this.'

Hmm, agreed. I can't imagine the E-Street Band going out to look for sheep on one of their stopovers. Little Steven getting all excited because he's seen a badger.

'And secondly, Little Mix are *shit*.'

God, I love this girl. I might be a useless dad, but at least Ella's been brought up listening to The Pixies and Echo and the Bunnymen.

Through the thrum of last night's inebriation, out of the dark the image suddenly comes to me. The soft glow within the zipped-up compartment.

'Who were you texting last night?' I ask.

'What?'

'After you gave your blanket to me, you messaged someone. Was it Mum?'

Scuffling along beside me, Ella's hair is now in its usual place, covering most of her face.

'Ella?' I say, twenty steps later, having still received no response. 'I asked—'

Her head snaps round, mouth snarling, as feral as our surroundings. 'It's none of your business, alright?'

'Hey,' I say, putting my hands up like a bungling bank robber. 'I was only—'

If an expression could attack . . .

In fear for my safety should I continue, I give up my enquiry.

Except when my dad and his boyfriend are pointing out my feminine attributes, people hardly ever recognise any of my features in Ella. The only thing that is indisputable – proving she is definitely mine, and that Kirsty didn't have a secret pool boy or lollipop lady – Ella has the shape of my eyes, the speckles within and the outer shade of my blue irises.

Most people see lots of Kirsty in her, though. Right now, Ella looks like a miniature of her mother in one of her rages, even if part of the fury flashing out of her is through eyes that are so like mine.

Perhaps I'd been out of line. I don't know what is in the rules, and what is not. But what I do know is that it's already thirsty work walking up this hill. I reach into my bag to grab the water, but my hand settles first upon a beer. That'll do.

With Ella carrying the map, we recommence the first hundred yards of our day out in silence. My damp jeans continue rubbing against the insides of my thighs, while the air around Ella prickles, electrifying the hillsides.

twenty-three

Every relationship has its challenges, I get that. I know it very well, in fact. Even when things were relatively good with Kirsty, she could massage my head before going upstairs, and by the time she came back down she would be looking for something to smash over it. I probably deserved it, most of the time. But I simply can't work out how Ella has morphed from offering me such a caring gesture last night and smiles this morning, to giving me the sharp mouth and cold shoulder as soon as we left the campsite.

Behind us, Cannock is out of view, hidden by the depth of the trees and the curve of the hillside. Now that the path has flattened out a bit, the going is easier, the weary body of my hangover mostly walked off.

'Look, there are those sheep again,' I say, the first words spoken between us in the last ten minutes. To be honest, I don't know if they are the exact same sheep.

Ella glances briefly through her hair but pays them little interest. Carrying the map and her silence, she's shown no sign of being even slightly bothered with the glory of the valley that stretches out ahead of us, bathed in the startling light reflecting off the morning dew. Plodding forward, her eyes have been only for the screen of her phone.

I've never liked silence. When I was a kid, I would just run around screaming, or start clanging a broom against a bin lid, or beat one of my toy superhero figures on a plant pot, or bash my hands against my head, whatever was closest at hand. I managed to cave in one side of Spiderman's head, and probably dented a fair bit of mine. I would throw rocks against the fence, use the hose as a whip, swing on the washing line. Even the intrusive industrial chatter of the extractor fan beneath my flat is better than no noise at all.

I grab a stick from the side of the slim, trodden path and brush it along the ground, stomping a beat with my feet. Perhaps inspired by the Welsh countryside, I break into a spontaneous rendition of *Hello Sunshine* by Super Furry Animals.

In anticipation of some kind of response, I keep half an eye on Ella. And I do get a response: she turns up the music that she's listening to. Beneath her hair, I hadn't noticed the earbuds.

Even if I would prefer conversation, the static buzz of her music is at least some kind of accompaniment to the blissful, empty silence. I sing louder, competing with Ella, and together we transform the peaceful countryside into a festival of noise.

The path soon begins to ascend, climbing upward to a break between the hills, rising towards the brightness of the sun. Weird clumps of grassy mounds are dotted about, bounding down the slope that leads into another valley. From this higher vantage point, I can see a hint of glistening water between a dip in the hills, perhaps the reservoir that Nell mentioned yesterday.

We continue further upward, through a broken gate hanging onto a tumbling stone wall. Ahead of us is a convergence of paths, spider legs walking over the hillside. A pair of walkers are halfway up the next hill, but too far away to tell if it's the young couple. Anyone to talk to would be good. While Ella's music continues to deafen her, I throw my stick away and grab another beer. What the hell, there's not much else to do.

Once we have rounded the top of the next hill, I tap her on the shoulder. She watches me open out my arms and range them around at the scope of the view.

In all directions is an uninterrupted panorama of undulating wild land, dots of waters, patterned clumps of trees, shades of every natural colour of the planet. The skies and horizons do not have a defined end, just a blurry infinitude where they meet and merge in a pale mist. It would make a great album cover. The only gloom to be seen is on Ella's face.

Using monkey signs, I indicate for her to remove the earplugs. 'Look at this! Isn't it fantastic?' I say once she does. 'Feel the air on your face. Breathe it in. It makes you believe that God is real, being out here.'

'You don't believe in God,' Ella says, a soft rise of pink upon her pale complexion, given by the wild air. 'You always said that He's an arrogant prick.'

'That does sound the like the sort of thing I'd come out with, I suppose. But I'd be arrogant, too, if I designed this place. *Look* at it.'

With a barely perceptible shrug, Ella does take in some of the view.

'Look at that bird up there,' I say, all keenness this morning. 'Do you think it's an eagle? It must be.'

'It's a buzzard,' Ella mumbles, as we watch it gliding in gentle spirals over the landscape. 'We have buzzards in Tenderbridge.'

'There are two of them!'

It turns out there are, in fact, three, but Ella doesn't correct me. All she does is hand me the map.

'I don't know where we are,' she says.

Upon the floppy tri-fold page are straight lines, curvy lines, coloured lines, and odd place names, not that I can find one that looks anything like Daniwhojamaflip. The hills must be those depicted by the tight patterns of pinkish lines. The deeper patches of green are probably forests. The blue bits must be water. The long, curly grey lines are likely to be roads. It's all kind of obvious. We're just somewhere out in the middle of it.

After being thrown out of gigs, pubs and parties, or after missing last trains and buses, or after finding out that the people who said they would give me a lift have driven off because I've been a dick, I have always managed to find my way. Even on the occasions when I could barely walk. My natural navigational instinct is proven to usually be reliable enough. Standing above the landscape, comparing it to the designs made by some kid with a craft set, it's not like we even need the map.

I notice Ella's eyes flicker a couple of times towards my beer. She has a slightly pouty, Kirsty-like look.

'Do you want a banana?' I ask, remembering that I have some in the bag, wherever they came from.

With a face as miserable as a street urchin, Ella nods.

I search around to see if the pair of walkers are still knocking about, but can't see them anywhere. I fold the map, stuff it into my bag, and point my beer towards a slope that leads down into a woodland. 'I'm pretty certain the waterfalls are in this direction.'

Ella doesn't respond, not a single syllable.

With much shuffling of feet – and Ella slinging away the browned banana, uneaten – we begin our descent towards the broad patch of trees. A bit further down the hillside, I notice a river meandering into the woodland. Again, my logic seems to winning, for there can't be a waterfall without a river. At least I don't think there can.

twenty-four

When I was looking down on the woodland from above, I hadn't considered that it would be quite so thick with trees, more like a forest. The light of day is blocked out by the canopy overhead. Heavy hands of branches reach over us. Twisted trunks wrapped inside chunky vines surround us. Starved of daylight, some of the trees have given up and lay as they fell.

We are standing at yet another junction of paths. As I predicted, trying to work out what's what on the map is of no help at all. Sure, there are clusters of foresty areas on there, but no directions on how to navigate through them. And what's more, I haven't got the slightest clue which of those dark green patches we are in.

I had presumed there would be signposts, like the one outside Tenderbridge Railway Station. *Waterfalls* this way. *Picnic Area* that way. *Exit* over there. Hoping there would be a signpost pointing towards a pub was always going to be wishful thinking. The morning's walk has, at least, dried the dampness of my jeans.

'Which way is it?' Ella says, wearing her yellow coat ever since we entered the confines of the forest.

Patches of light twinkle through gaps left between careless leaves, lacking the energy to dry out the rich, sodden earth. Hidden birds chatter and call above us, all around us. Things rustle unseen through the leafy floor, distracting the attention of my disquiet.

'Dad?'

'Umm, this way,' I say, folding the map and dropping it back into my bag.

It looks nicer this way. More welcoming. Slightly less threatening.

A soft scrunch of leaves answers each of our steps. I breathe in the aroma of compost and fertile growth, the satisfying scent of nature. All my life I've lived in towns, surrounded by fugly civilization. Never have I heard the call of the countryside before – except for the yearning I sometimes get for a cosy country pub when summer turns colder.

'These trees are nice, aren't they?' I say, trying to spark a bit of conversation again.

'What?' Ella replies, just about.

'All these trees. They're nice. They're going on about trees in the news at the moment. I heard some bloke in the pub talking about it.'

Ella stops and gives me the glare. Even in her coat she's no wider than the slimmest of the trunks, but the look I'm receiving is more threatening than the heaviest boughs above our heads.

'Do you care about anything other than yourself?' she says.

'What's that supposed to mean?'

'Every weekend, Josephine's dad volunteers for a charity that helps feed and clothe homeless people, even on Christmas morning. Phoebe's dad is a hockey coach in his spare time. Nicole's mum takes photos that are included in exhibitions, even though she also writes and edits articles for *Harper's Bazaar* five days a week.'

As she lists these achievements, Ella ticks them off on her fingers. Although I'm not sure that they are achievements. Most of the things she said just sound like a waste of time. I don't think I've ever even met anyone who has played hockey.

'I spoke to grandad the other day,' she says. 'He and Julian are volunteering in the tea rooms at Nuffield Place one day a week until the end of the season.'

'Are they?' I chuckle fondly at the thought of my dad and his boyfriend in their pinnies.

Sparing time for a quick glower, Ella continues: 'Bobbi's dad goes for bike rides at the weekends, even when it's raining. In fact, most of my friends' parents do. Other parents go to evening classes or take weekend courses. Like Britney's mum, who publishes poetry on her own website.'

'You have a friend called Britney? Really?'

'You don't *get it*,' Ella says, stamping a foot and slapping her hands against her sides. 'None of them do those things because they *have* to. It's because they have interests, or they like helping people.'

'Don't forget that I've got my music, Els.'

'You do that for yourself!'

'Bobby's dad probably goes on bike rides for himself. Who is Bobby, by the way?'

'A girl at school, not that it's relevant.'

'Bobby's a boy's name, isn't it?'

'Bobbi with an i, you dick.'

'Ella, bloody hell, what's brought this on? You were sunshine and light this morning. Something's been up ever since we left the campsite.'

She turns her back and stares into the endless depth of trees. A bird flutters somewhere above us. Not even that can distract Ella's grumpy glare, so intense that it threatens to set light to the forest.

'I only said that the trees look nice, sweetheart.'

In a blur of hair and yellow, Ella fires back into life.

'No, you didn't. You said *they're going on about trees*. Because *some bloke in the pub* said so. You spent all day yesterday pissed. Then you trashed the tent, fuck knows how, but you did. You just threw your empty cans into the woods—'

Whoops. Busted. At least I don't think Ella saw the one I threw into the undergrowth a short while back.

'—and generally don't give a shit about anything.'

'I give a shit about you.'

Ella's head goes down. Her hand plunges into the mess of her hair. The juddering of her shoulders is the final giveaway.

'Hey. Els . . .'

She must hear me moving towards her, scuffling leaves, but she doesn't shift or snarl. Nor does she shake me off when I wrap my arms around her. All that hair presses into my chest.

'You're embarrassed by me,' I softly say.

'Ashamed,' she sobs. 'Yes.'

My lips press hard against each other. To hear her say that aloud is a knife that grinds against my ribs as it turns around in my chest, not just piercing my heart but shredding it. There is no possible way that I could have known Ella's friends' parents are all out there winning the Nobel Prize for Nobility in their spare time, but how could she not be ashamed? Holding her, I try to think of something that could possibly help to assuage her disappointment.

That I knock on the door of an elderly couple on my delivery route to make jokes about sex toys, because it cheers them up?

That I once pushed a bloke out of harm's way when his mobility scooter broke down in the middle of a pelican crossing, even though I didn't need to cross the road?

That I would do anything for her not to move away. How the very thought of it tears me into so many pieces that my heart physically hurts on each and every one of the ten thousand times a day that I think about it?

'I'm sorry you feel that way, Els. I know I'm useless. I do know. But I've not always been . . . like I seem to be at the moment. The truth is that . . .'

I stop myself from playing The Blame Game. Now is probably not the time. Because of Ella's current indifference towards Kirsty, I am tempted to resurrect The Blame Game at some point before the end of our trip. I don't think that this little bundle of torment could be so upset just because I'm a proven prick. It wasn't only her friend's *dads* who are out there changing the world, one bike ride at a time. Ella might even fancy playing a few hands of The Blame Game herself.

By the feel of her back, she has stopped sobbing, yet still she hasn't separated from me.

'Is this about moving away from your friends?'

'No.' And after a slight hesitation, 'Well, yes. That as well.'

'As well as what, sweetheart?'

'I don't want to talk about it.'

A chorus of voices comes from somewhere up ahead. There must be a fair few of them, judging by the volume. Even though their advance echoes off the heavy sails of the trees, it is impossible to tell where they are.

The long sleeves of Ella's coat disappear into her fringe and she rubs her face. When she brushes her hair back, she looks just about normal, if a bit puffy.

'Has it got something to do with you being on your phone in the night?'

'I *literally* just said that I don't want to talk about it.'

'Okay, okay.'

The first in a line of cyclists swings around the corner. Five others follow, all speeding in our direction.

I ease Ella off the path. We stand to one side, my arm around her shoulders.

'So . . . it's not actually anything that I've done?' I ask the top of her head. 'It's not about the trees?'

Ella half-sobs a snotty laugh. 'No, it's not about the trees. Just shut up, you stupid old knobhead.'

The first cyclist speeds past us, some bloke with a skinny face and skinny legs, wearing tights. His bike hisses over the leaves, mud sprays up his back. With a nod and uncertain frowns, the rest of the cyclists pass by, some of them turning on their saddle to shoot dirty looks over their shoulders.

I have never heard of anything like this before, a father being consistently scorned for associating with his daughter. Still, it's not as if they thought to stop and check that everything is above board. It's reassuring to know that if an actual paedophile was seen in the woods with a young girl in tears, most people would only shake their head and tut.

A thought occurs to me. They might be the owners of the big green military tent, away on their cycling tour. I might go and introduce myself later. When I notice them begining to fidget, only then will I introduce Ella as my daughter.

Another thought: I probably should've stopped them to ask where we are.

'Hey,' I call, semaphoring my arms from the middle of the path. 'Hey!'

The one at the back, just about still in view, glances briefly over their shoulder but keeps on going. I look at Ella, still standing to the side. She looks tinier than ever; a girl who is becoming a woman but is still much closer to a child.

'Are we lost?' she asks, not fooled by my tactical grin.

'Huh? *No.*' I guff at the very suggestion of it. 'Not lost.'

Just not entirely certain where we are.

Alone with my girl and the forest again, I explain to Ella about my internal navigation and how it rarely fails me; that I have this innate ability to know where I am, and a guided centre that directs me where I need to go. I just leave out the bits about the friends deserting me, and the times that I've woken up in fields or in parks or in bus shelters, and all the rest of it.

twenty-five

'You said we weren't lost,' Ella screams from beneath her umbrella. 'You told me you knew where the waterfalls were.'

'The fells,' I call back, momentarily pausing with the log that I am dragging over the soaked ground. It slips beneath my grip, but I manage to keep hold of it. 'That's what they call them out here, the fells.'

'Whatever the stupid bollocks they're called, you lied to me, you absolute useless twat.'

The rain Nell told us would be coming did indeed arrive. It came in fast and it came in heavy, its approach hidden by what turned out to be a very deep and incredibly dark forest. While I attempt to heave the log into the crook of my elbow, it storms around us still.

My feet are slipping, sliding over the sodden earth like a new-born fawn. A final surge and the log smacks into place next to the other branches and boughs I have gathered. Ella's tirade of language continues to batter me with the force of the storm, as if I need reminding that she isn't at all happy. I haven't seen this much life in her since she was a screeching toddler. Not that it helps our healing, I suppose; the bond I'm trying to create before she is forced to leave me forever.

Beneath the shelter of her umbrella, the yellow coat untouched by rain, Ella is pointing the crappy torch in my general direction. I am soaked through to the skin. My leather jacket didn't even hold out the earlier drizzle – or the picking, as Nell had called it – like my pissy jeans, though, it had needed a wash. Through the bleary illumination, I blunder about with another armful of branches.

'What even is that?' Ella screams.

'I told you already, it's a bivouac,' I yell back. 'We used to make them in scouts.'

'I want to get out of here. *Now.*'

'Remember what grandma used to say, Els: I want doesn't get.'

Thick slime of the fallen wood is running down the insides of my sleeves. The daylight must still be there, somewhere above the trees and the storm, yet in here it is all darkness.

I stop once more to look at the huddled yellow figure. The rain funnelling through the canopy bounces off her umbrella like hail from a slate roof. Behind the torch's pathetic glow, I can make out only highlights of her face. It's hard to tell exactly how angry she is.

'How can you *do* this?' she screams. 'How can you get us lost in this absolute shithole?'

Pretty angry, I decide.

'I didn't *mean* to get us lost. It was supposed to be an adventure. It *is* an adventure. What a story we'll have to tell when we get back! You'll see. And stop with all the language now, come on.'

'I can't wait to go to Canada. When I do, I *never* want to see you *ever* again.'

'You don't mean that, Els. You're just being dramatic.'

'I am *not* being dramatic!' she shrieks, stamping her feet. The swinging umbrella knocks a branch. A tumble of rain bounces off the top of the brolly and Ella shudders as if the whole lot had gone down her neck.

Skidding over the sticky mud, the little scene makes me chuckle to myself.

Something thumps against my back and lands in the puddles growing around my feet. I pick up the torch and shine it towards Ella. Her face is now hidden inside the yellow hood, sleeves hugging the brolly. And then I notice that my bag has been kicked out into the rain.

I prop a few more long branches against the sides of the bivouac, slop over to a dead pine, and commence stripping long lengths of bark from the trunk. Some of them I sling inside the structure, and the others I rest against the exterior walls, latticed with spongy rolls of thick moss peeled off nearby boulders. For my final task, I plunge the torch into my mouth and start throwing a thick layer of leaves over the top of it all.

With the torch in hand, I stand back and look at our temporary accommodation. It actually doesn't look that bad. I survey the cushioned interior. Beneath the meagre glow of the torch, it seems as cosy as a home away from home could be. Sure, there might be more woodlice than

I would prefer in an ideal world, but with all that I have learned from life, it is certainly not an ideal world.

The entrance is to one side of a low-slung branch, the supporting beam of our new home. The back wall is the broad base of an elm, its higher-up branches the first line of our defence. Inside, it is surprisingly roomy. In the shallowest part there is even a small area for us to put our bags. But the most remarkable thing is that, except for the odd drip from the wet wood, no rain seems to be coming in. I will certainly be taking a picture of my eighth wonder to show to Brian.

Before I peek under the umbrella, I can already hear Ella's music. It sounds a bit more musical theatre now. Her eyes shirk away from the torchlight.

'Sorry. I've finished the house.'

She removes an earplug. 'Have you found a way to get out of here?'

'No, the house. The . . . thing. I've finished it. It's dry inside, too. *Mmm*ostly.'

As cruel fate should deign, the rain has mostly eased. There is not a bit of me that is dry. At the same time, perhaps thinking the same thing, we both look down at my bag. So I am staying wet tonight, too. At least there's a can of beer left. I think I have one left. I hope I do.

Maybe the argument and aggression has blown out of Ella. Or perhaps she is as tired as her eyes looked when I shone the torch in her face. She quietly approaches the bivvy, half-turns towards me, drops the umbrella, and enters. The rabbit that Kirsty and I bought for one of her birthdays gave me that same sidelong look when we brought it home.

Seriously, you guys, you want me to live in that tiny hutch?

It hadn't survived long. We only have to survive this one night in here.

On her knees, Ella uses the torch on her phone to pay scrutiny to the padded sides. The interior doesn't look quite so good in the brighter torchlight; wet and shaggy, much like me. She lowers herself onto the bark floor, and then quickly lifts her hands. She hadn't seen the wood-louse that was there a moment before, but I had. Even though she is shining the phone vaguely in my direction, through the gloom I can see how grumpy her face is. I don't think I have ever seen a sight as miserable. And I lived with Kirsty for more than a decade.

'Are you going to make your one now?'

'*Ella . . .*' I shake my head, scattering rain. It runs down my neck, though I can barely tell the difference. 'We have to share this. I can't possibly make another one. I'll stay out here while you get comfortable, okay? When I come in, you won't even know I'm there.'

'You can sleep in the doorway,' she says. 'And then tomorrow we're going home.'

'Home?' I say. 'As in, home home?'

'Home as in, back to where I live and don't have to share a twat shack.'

She does make me laugh. Even Ella has her cute little I-shouldn't-find-it-funny-but-can't-help-it smile.

'We'll talk about it in the morning, okay? And I'm sorry about getting us lost. Really, it does help if you try and see it all as an adventure. A pretty unique one, sure, but still an adventure. It could be fun, sleeping in here tonight.'

Ella still doesn't look convinced.

Dry as a bone and wretchedly glum, I leave her alone in the bivvy, before she can start trying to argue with me again or calling me names.

The ground squelches beneath my boots. Pattering rain falling from the trees splats against me. A shiver runs through the entire length of my body. I trip over my bag, pick it up, think for a moment, and then duck back into the bivouac.

I dare to glance at Ella. She is curled up on the bark strips, facing the base of the tree. I rescue a beer from my rucksack – it is indeed my last one, nestled beside my soaked jumper – and then I retreat to the forest.

twenty-six

The rain is still picking, fine drops as mist in the air. The smell of earth is even richer than when we first stepped into the forest. Arcing the torch beam, ensuring there is nothing else to trip over, I see a pair of eyes staring back at me. A large rabbit – much bigger than the one that was murdered by something in our old backyard. Before hopping off, it gives the bivouac a glance. *Good luck, mate*, its expression says. *But I wouldn't.*

I never knew how easy it is to get lost in a forest. Head one way, only to find yourself walking down the same path in the opposite direction twenty minutes later. Try to retrace the route of your footsteps and find that they have disappeared. Say for the fifty-first time that I know exactly where we are, and then the forest twists a new route into the labyrinth. It's like trying to find the way out of a cloud.

Now that my mania has blown away with the storm, I feel flat, completely deflated. No matter how much I enjoyed the adventure of the day, the snips of arguments and the unexpected smiles, this must surely be one of my all-time greatest balls-ups. Maybe one day, when she's in *Dan's* comfortable Canadian mansion, Ella will look back upon this trip with something close to fondness – mostly for having survived. But the reality is that, once again, I have let her down.

Crumpled inside the battered chest of my deepest regrets, I always knew that Ella, my little detached heart, was one day fated to look upon me as other people do. The shame, just like she told me herself. It is not because I don't help fundraise for charities, or have photos in exhibitions, or pour tea for old people; these things must happen to me because I deserve it. I couldn't even not snore to make Ella stay.

Or maybe, just maybe, it is all random fate. Like the fortuity of our very existence, such as being too drunk to use a condom.

I press both hands against my temples and squeeze. The grinding groan of the machine that I can't get out of my head. A perpetual machine. It never stops. All I've ever done is have another drink and blown raspberries at it. The easiest solution. My life in a can.

I crack open the beer. The cold tears of rain have cooled its sides. My first chilled drink of the trip, and it really does taste good. To break the silence, to quiet the noise, there is only one song that comes into my head. Against the log I'm sitting on, I begin to drum Ringo's loose beat. And then I howl the words to the top of the clouds. I hammer on the log. I stamp my feet. I cry to the sky.

I don't know how many times I sing the refrain of

Ticket to Ride. Over and over again, until the forest is finally silent.

My clothes are stuck to me by the heat of my body, a semi-solid suit of sadness. I preferred having just the one smelly damp patch. What a long day. I wish that I had brought more beers with me.

After a quick whizz – I don't really know why I bothered unzipping – I carefully tread my way back to the bivouac, keen to not repeat last night's disaster. It would probably hurt quite a lot more to fall face-first into a pile of wet wood.

To find Ella asleep is of no surprise at all. Hours of tantrums would wear anyone out. She is still curled in the same position as before, snuggled beside the base of the elm. I didn't know that she had brought her comfort blanket with her.

By the weak torchlight, I clamber inside. The spongy bark floor is quite inviting, surprisingly, which helps me to conclude that sleeping in my wet clothes is a better idea than shivering through the night without them.

Beneath the sound of her music, I hear the soft sigh of Ella breathing.

Here we are, once more, the most contented moments of my life, beside my sleeping daughter. I reach out and touch the soft material of her blanket. If only this feeling could stay forever, knowing that she is near me, beside me, the width of a blanket from my touch, I'll store it.

Huddled inside the damp bivouac, a cheerier thought arrives. There's more to come before our trip is at its end. Even if just for now, we are still together. I promise myself that I will not destroy this opportunity. Or I'll try my hardest not to.

I take out my phone to check the time, but the screen doesn't bother coming to life. Whether it's because the battery has run out of juice or is terminal, there's no way to tell. Because this phone was once Ella's, I resist the temptation to throw it out into the night.

The first drops of a new wave of rain begin to land upon our roof. They increase. Until, all of a sudden, it is falling as quickly as Ringo's roll at the beginning of the song. I press my hands against the walls to feel if we are being breached. I smile, satisfied in our cosy, damp nest.

And then, the moment I switch off the torch, from the darkness Ella's phone *pings* with an incoming message, muffled by the earbuds.

It could be nine o'clock in the evening. It could be midnight. Whatever it is, and however busy my mind might usually be, I find myself soon being sucked into a whirlpool of total and absolute exhaustion.

twenty-seven

By the time Ella emerges from the bivouac, wearing her coat and with the comfort blanket wrapped around her shoulders, I am already outside eating crisps.

It isn't sunny this morning, but nor is it raining. I grin as broadly as a cold, tired, damp man can. After rubbing her eyes, Ella gives me a sleepy smile. A shock for this new day.

Daylight finds its way through the leaves and the branches. I glance over to where I was sitting last night, still in shadow. The empty beer can I found there earlier is stored secretly away inside my rucksack.

'Sleep well, Els?'

Yawning, Ella nods. 'Surprisingly, I did. I don't really want to admit it,' she says, looking at the shelter, 'but it was actually quite comfortable. I didn't hear you snoring, either.'

My mouthful of crisps stays un-masticated for several seconds. For the first time in as long as I can remember, I cannot think of a single thing to say. Over the years, my snoring has been loud enough to wake myself up – along with various lovers, colleagues, strangers, neighbours, bandmates, foreigners, roosting pigeons . . .

I decide not to tell Ella about my night. Yet another wave of rain had woken me when it began soaking my backside. And again later, when a puddle chose to creep inside the bivvy. On what must have been the coldest night of my life, I learned that I make quite a handy water break. So maybe I'm not an entirely *absolute useless twat*.

'Do you want something to eat?' I ask, nudging the rucksack with my toe. 'The bananas don't look too good, but anything wrapped in foil seems to be okay.'

Behind two paws and beneath a messy mophead of hair, Ella hides her chin inside the blanket.

'Umm, *Dad* . . .'

Beneath my wet clothes, my blood turns colder than it already was. I can't deal with whatever this shock will be. Not after such a lovely start.

'I need to . . .' Ella twiddles her hips. 'You know.'

'Oh! Erm . . .'

I look around. Surrounding us is only forest. Shall I tell her that I went behind our house? Surely I should send her in the opposite direction.

'We won't be using the bivvy again, Els,' I say. 'Just use that. Giveth back to nature.

'Tell you what,' I say, in response to her repulsion, 'I'll take myself for a walk, give you a bit of space.'

I pour the last few crisps out of the bag, throw the packet on the floor, and head off for a wander around the near vicinity.

When I return ten minutes later, my phone checked and definitely as flat as a puddle, and now boasting an arty mist of condensation behind the screen, Ella is eating an energy bar – another snack I was apparently inspired to buy after drinking by the river.

'Did you remember to text mum?' I ask, plonking myself uneasily down.

Ella looks at me blankly. And then it clicks.

'Oh shit.' From beneath the blanket, she pulls out her phone. She taps it. Frowns. Taps it harder. 'Oh shit!' she repeats. 'I had a text from her, but forgot to reply. Come on, you stupid thing. It was working a minute ago.' She finally stops thumping the screen and looks at me. 'Has your phone got any battery?'

'Afraid not,' I reply. 'It's completely Hovis.'

After explaining what cockney rhyming slang is, and giving a few more examples, I assure Ella that we will find our way back to the campsite this morning, where we can charge our phones, have something proper to eat, and then make our way home. Or at least to civilisation.

If she really does want to leave here, I chance a hand, we could stay in Cardiff for the night. She could even have her own hotel room – an entire ladder of steps up from a bivvy in a storm. I mean, with dad's donation, the trip so far has cost me a minus amount. Rather than trying to imagine some way that I can justify keeping some of dad's cash back for beer money, this entire trip can easily be rescued.

'Sorry about giving you a hard time yesterday,' Ella

says, taking a sip of water. 'It's just, well, it was a disaster. But I have to give you props.'

'Props?' I repeat. 'Is that rhyming slang? I can't work it out.'

'Huh? No, *props*,' she says again. '*Respect*. You built that thing—'

'The bivouac.'

'Yeah, and then you—'

'Darren had a friend in a band called Bivouac.'

'Dad, can you *please* let me tell you what I'm trying to *say*?' Ella sort of yells.

'Sorry.' I put my hands between my thighs, as if that can shut my stupid mouth.

'You built that, the bivouac, in one of the heaviest rainstorms ever. And you didn't stop until it was done so that I had somewhere to sleep. All I did was stand there and give you shit.'

'Lots of shit.'

'No, wait before you say anything.' Ella holds a finger up and, God, she looks exactly like Kirsty – just without all the fake bits, and the expensive adornments. 'You did deserve the shit, and lots of it. But I didn't know that you had it in you to, I don't know . . . do *anything*.'

'Yeah, that's a fair thing to say.' I nod in agreement. 'Props.'

'I've never seen anything like it before, dad. And maybe it did make it seem *a bit* like an adventure.'

How many shocks this day?

'When Dan had the treehouse built, he didn't do a thing except for give them his credit card number. If I'd been stranded out here with him, all he would've done is tell everyone to fuck off and stormed about in the rain.'

'That's terrible, Els.' I puff out my cheeks and shake my head. 'What a knob.'

There's something I want to ask Ella, which I don't have to ask – and I do take a brief moment for consideration – but decide that I have to know.

'Ella . . . do you like Dan?'

'*Like* him?' Ella scratches her eyebrow. 'Not really, no. Dan's totally weird. And he might be even more selfish than you. I mean, you're really selfish, but in a different way. You care, you're just useless.'

'Except for when it comes to building bivouacs.'

'Yes. You did that. But don't forget that you did also get us lost. Dan, he doesn't even care what people think. Like with the taxi driver at the train station. If that was you, it would've made you cry, or have a breakdown, or something.'

I never knew just how well Ella has me sussed. Still, as long as she prefers me to that barrel-chested bell-end, she can think what she likes.

'Your phone went off in the night, by the way.'

'What?'

'You got a message. Was that the one from mum?'

Ella's face clouds over. She pulls the blanket tighter and crosses her legs. Fury rages just beneath the surface of her babyish skin.

Why did I have to mention it? Why couldn't I resist? I spend the next few moments balancing upon a rotting piece of timber, hovering just above a blazing fire . . . But, within a chew of her energy bar, the cloud passes. I am certainly not going to push it this time. Not until I know for sure that we aren't stuck in an actual form-shifting labyrinth.

'I've come up with an idea to get us out of here,' I say. 'When you're ready.'

'I'm ready,' Ella replies, already putting the blanket into her bag, and picking up her umbrella.

The sun disappears again. The sky through the trees is a milky grey.

I pat my soggy thighs, stand up and stretch. The crisp packet crinkles beneath my foot, so I pick it up and stuff it into my rucksack.

'Right,' I say. 'I'm just going to have one last look at the bivvy before we go.'

But before I can take half a step towards it—

'Dad!' Ella cries. She shakes her head. 'No.'

'What? Why not?' And then I chuckle, wagging my finger. 'Ah. Of course.'

With both of our phones killed in action, I'll just have to draw a picture of the bivouac for Brian, rather than take a photo. Perhaps I'll casually leave it on the kitchen island for Dan to see. Maybe I'll pin it to the treehouse.

twenty-eight

With both of us concentrating our hardest – a great deal easier to do without a hangover; and because I haven't got any beers left; and because Ella is in charge – it feels like we are making progress.

Ella agreed with my idea to make a concerted effort to head through the forest in one direction. If the path forces us to diverge, then we will both agree which way we're now facing, and so forth with each new turn we make, using glimpses of the sun as our marker. Working together, me and my girl coupling our eyes and minds, there has been very little small talk between us.

This forest must have an end somewhere. I saw it from on top of the hill.

We have also been checking our phones. Ella's did tease us by almost coming to life, but then fizzled out. I'm not certain it would be much use to us anyway. After yesterday's rain had first started picking, and I finally confessed that, alright, I might not know *exactly* where we are, Ella could find no signal at all. It was around about then that she started screaming at me and calling me names.

After a rehearsal one time, I vaguely remember Brian saying something about three words you can type into your phone when you're lost and it will then send you your precise location, even when you have no signal. But I can't remember what the three words were. All I can remember is that it was three words.

I don't say it aloud, but the longer we are in here, the further we trudge, the more interminable it seems, more hopeless. The green clusters on the map might not look that big, but then neither does the British Isles when compared to the rest of the world. Never have I been as stranded – or stranded quite so far from home.

My thoughts start drifting towards foraging, dowsing, fire building, survival.

Bloody people. When I want to be left alone everyone's there, getting in my way, chatting in my face, being irritating. On this rare occasion that I am desperate to see someone, anyone, they have all disappeared.

I wonder what Nell, Andrew and the other campers made of our absence. Having left the tent in the state it was, I suppose they might think we've just abandoned it. Does that sort of thing happen at rural campsites, or only at festivals full of hippies and teenagers on drugs?

'What was that?' Ella stops in the middle of the path, distracting me from my internal rambling.

'What was what?'

'Shhh.'

'I can't—'

'*Shhhhh.*'

Except for the hiss of leaves moving about above us and the background hum of tinnitus, I hear nothing.

'Els—'

'*There!*' She grabs my arm.

I did hear it. It sounded like: '*Gun*shots.'

'That's what I thought,' Ella says. 'Another one. It is gunshots.'

'I think it came from this direction.'

'*Dad*! What are you *doing*?'

I stop blundering into the forest and look at Ella, still standing where she was, back on the trodden path.

'I was going to find whoever's shooting,' I say with a shrug, as if I've just calculated the answer to the simplest question in the world.

Ella's curled lip suggests that I might, in fact, *be* the simplest person in the world.

'Are you *actually* stupid?' she says.

'Some people think so. That's why I hang out with Darren. To make me look smart. Or, well . . . not as dim.'

Ella's expression of disbelief remains.

'Firstly,' she says, 'if we step off the path, we might never find it again.'

That's a fair point. It's also sort of why we're where we are.

'And secondly, they are firing *guns*.'

'Not everyone who fires guns is trying to kill people, Ella.'

'And not everyone who has a penis is trying to rape someone,' she snaps back, 'but some of them do.'

'Jesus,' I say, heading back to the path. 'Why would you say something like that?'

'Well. It's true, dad. If they have one, they can. I just

198

don't think it's a very good idea to go towards whoever has the gun.'

'Well, now that you've put it like that, neither do I.'

I squint into the depths of the forest, trying to see if anyone, or anything, is lurking there.

Another shot. It unsettles us both.

Had it sounded a bit closer?

'Okay, the person shooting the gun probably is best avoided,' I say, letting go of Ella's sleeve. 'You're right. Let's get the Donald out of here.'

'What does that *even mean*?' she says.

'It's just rhyming slang again, sweetheart. It basically means let's go.'

I peer both ways down the path.

And then check again.

And I check again.

'Erm. Which way was it that we were we walking?'

twenty-nine

I don't know if it is our navigational partnership or blind luck, but the path eventually leads us to a river. Presumably it is the same one I saw from the hillside yesterday; the one that I guessed would lead us to wondrous waterfalls and a straightforward day out.

The trees here are mostly spindly, allowing us our first clear views of the sky. It is dotted with fleecy clouds, just a flock of sheep floating on a flat sea. We watch the pregnant water pouring over the rocks, carrying the rain from last night's storm downstream. I decide it would be a good idea to fill up our water bottle while we're here, which is more than half empty.

'I dare you not to fall in,' Ella says.

Once upon a fairly recent time I would have accepted that as a challenge. Fortunately, with my boots slipping over the sodden slope and with one hand grabbing onto a twiggy tree, I instead accept the dare. Even if it would be the fastest way to travel out of here, I wouldn't fancy my chances against those moody currents if I was a

Channel swimmer, and not an unhealthy middle-aged bloke with a bit of a beer podge.

'It makes sense,' I say, explaining my latest idea to Ella. 'If we travel downstream, eventually we are going to come to some form of civilisation. Surely someone other than us will be out for a walk today. We'll ask the first person we see where on the map we are.'

'Okay,' Ella says. 'Sounds like a plan.'

Well, it's an idea. A plan would have been to study how to read a map before we came out to the middle of nowhere. And at the very least to pack a sleeping bag. The logic seems sound enough, though. Just as it does to follow the river in the opposite direction to whoever was firing the gun.

'How's the band going?' Ella asks.

Small talk is allowed again now that we have a plan, shaped in the form of an idea.

'It's good.' A few paces later, I correct myself. 'Oh, no it's not. We've broken up.'

'What? Why?'

'Because of fish.'

'How can a band break up because of fish?'

'Because Mick loves fish more than actually doing something with his life.'

'You mean that rather than having fun and probably drinking lots of beer, because Mick's focussed on making a living, he's not *actually doing something with his life*?'

'Pretty much,' I reply. 'Yeah.'

Walking side by side, the path is open enough to feel the warmth of the sunlight, whenever we happen upon a patch of it. It's funny that neither of us has complained about tiredness today. We must have walked miles, yet our stride is still in easy step with one another. What's more, I love talking rubbish with my girl.

'Dad, look . . .' Ella indicates a fallen tree just off the pathway.

'Oh yeah, that's a nice one, Els.' I notice that bits are still somehow growing out of the tree, even though it has fallen over. 'Really nice.'

'I didn't stop to show you a tree, dad. Let's sit down for a while. My legs are aching a bit.'

Now that she's mentioned it, my legs are probably aching a bit, too. I think it was the prospect of getting out of the forest that has been keeping our momentum so strong.

The tree is smooth, the bark long-since rotted from the trunk. Sitting next to me, Ella sips from the water bottle. She's giving me an odd look, one of Kirsty's old stares. The one that came right before asking how I spent my day, even though she already knew the answer.

'Mum told me you used to dream of having a house with a battlement on it,' Ella says.

'That's right, yeah.' The thought of my house always cheers me up. 'I still do.'

'But that's *it*, dad. It hasn't happened. You need to move on from the daydreams. '

'That's not to say it can't.'

'True. And it's good to have dreams. But where have your dreams got you so far? Actually, don't say it. I know what you're thinking.'

I don't know what Ella was thinking I was thinking, but I had been thinking that this is the first time I have properly left Tenderbridge in years. Which must mean that, so far, my dreams have got me lost. And the only real reason we're here is because of some wealthy prick taking my daughter away from me.

'I thought it's a cool thing to have a dad in a band.'

'Yeah, it's cool if your dad is Liam Gallagher,' Ella says. 'Sorry to be the one to break it to you, dad, but . . . you're not. And you just told me that you don't even *have* a band anymore.'

'Liam lost his band. Twice! And he's doing alright for himself.'

Ella's expression is now the same one that I get from Brian. The one that demonstrates mature, adult understanding. And also concern. And usually a sprinkling of despair.

'You play cover songs in pubs, dad. That's alright, but it's not much, is it? Can you say that you've ever *really* tried? Or even that you're still trying? You probably think that getting drunk all the time and throwing beer cans into the bushes is living a rock and roll lifestyle. By the look on your face, I think you do.'

Can't lie, I sort of do. She's got me again.

'You're a fantasist,' she continues. 'Maybe, *maybe* you haven't always been, but you are. Being a musician is a cool thing, you're right about that—'

'Thank you.'

'—but it's way cooler to be able to support those who rely on you. Having a proper job. *Being* there for them. Like Mick's doing.'

'Yeah, but Mick does smell really badly of fish a lot of the time.'

Ella stares into the pebbled sky, rubbing her thighs. Again I am left to wonder how this can be the same little person I used to know. I am suddenly overwhelmed by every blink that she takes; each time that her lips move to speak.

'Have you ever thought about getting a proper job?'

'As well as being a musician, I am a postman, don't forget.'

'And have you ever thought about getting a proper job?'

'What's a postman supposed to be, if it's not a proper job?'

Ella swivels to face me, legs crossed on our perch. 'I mean run a business, dad. Or train at something. A job with responsibilities. Aspirations. One that you can't just doss off and get drunk.'

'So . . .' I swivel, too. Ella made it look much easier. 'What would you like me to do? Be a manager like Brian, sitting on my chair all day, losing my hair? What would you think of me then?'

'There's nothing that *I* want you to do. I just want to explain what life is like for normal people. Because you don't seem happy. Ever. All you do is move through the days, snapping away from the real world and living this fantasy of what you're going to be and the things you're going to have.'

I do do that.

Strumming my fingers against my lips, I pick through the pieces of Ella's assessment, searching for things she got wrong about me. I am ambitious. I don't know why everyone always tells me I'm not. That it could apply to a fisherman as much as it could to a rock star is a strange thought, though.

But unhappy?

Am I unhappy?

What *is* happy?

'Dad?'

'Just thinking about what you said,' I reply, gazing at the forest on the other side of the tumultuous water.

'I don't like the thought of moving away, knowing that you're sitting in the pub all day, every day, fantasising while the world passes around you.' Ella's tone of voice has changed for a third time. I have nothing that I can liken it to. She is looking me straight in the eye. Her eyes that are so like mine. 'I don't want that for you.'

'I didn't know that you cared, sweetheart.'

'Of course I care. I've always cared. But no one wants a drunk prick for a dad, that's all.'

Her hair breezes softly away from her face, just a couple of strands lapping at her cheeks. Her expression is shy, almost guilty, as if she said something wrong.

If only she knew.

I put my hands to those cheeks and kiss her forehead. My lips stay a moment against the cool, smooth skin.

'Come on,' I say, getting up. 'Let's go. We don't want to be stuck out here for another night.'

Slipping off the weathered tree, striding towards the river, the truth is that I had felt something begin to burble inside me. The rainfall travelling down the mountainside, pouring into the river, building as it comes, ready to spill over . . .

Not because she called me a drunk prick. She does that all the time.

Before recommencing our journey, I have one last check in my bag for any straggling beers, but find none. My stomach gurgles at me, so I take out one of the now very squishy bananas.

'Can I ask you something, Els?'

She shuffles her feet on the edge of the path, picking at her fingernails. 'What?' she says, a bit grumpily.

'Something I've always been curious about.'

'You can try,' she says, 'but I might not answer. Just so you know.'

'Understood.' I tilt my head downstream. 'But let's keep going.'

After we do, I begin.

'When my dad, you know . . .'

How shall I articulate what I'm trying to say?

'Started having sex with a man,' Ella says, filling in for me.

'Yes. That exactly. I was ten, so a bit older than you were when I, erm . . .'

We share a look and Ella smirks, tempted to do my work for me again, but clearly relishing the thought of hearing me say it out loud. Because we both know it, I bypass the need to say it.

'After dad left, school was hard for me at first. You know, people said things, teased, that sort of stuff. Uncle Paul got it worse than I did. But still, it was tricky for a little while.'

'So you want to know if anyone teased me about you shagging the lollipop lady?' Ella says.

'Not exactly how I was going to put it, but yes.'

'It was the lollipop lady that everyone took it out on,' Ella says. 'Mum's friends were *horrible* to her, not that I really understood why at the time.'

'Yeah, I heard that,' I say, itching the back of my head. 'But you weren't humiliated?'

'Dad, I was only *six years old*. Me and my friends, we

didn't understand what was going on. I just used to tell them you weren't around much because you were a rock star.'

'You told them that?'

'We all used to think that you were a rock star. None of the other dads had long hair and wore leather jackets. It was only when I grew up a bit and you were still wearing the same jacket that I realised you were only pretending.'

Me and my miracle sprat. I make rock star poses and sing some Zeppelin, until Ella tells me to shut up. I was only making a point, showing that what she said hadn't hurt me.

The further downstream we head, the wider the river becomes. Any of the clouds that were littering the sky have blown further off, only visible now on a distant slice of the horizon.

'Can I ask you something else?'

The change billows within Ella's previously bright aura. I knew that I would be taking a chance, especially seeing as we are still kind of lost, but we've already proven what we can achieve when we are walking in silence.

'The text messages,' Ella says.

'Yeah.'

'There's this boy . . .'

Okay . . .

'It's not *like* that,' she says, even though I didn't say anything out loud.

But now I'm thinking, *Not like what, exactly?*

'Josephine kissed him, if you really want to know, even though she knows I like him. And now she keeps texting me *all the time* to tell me about it. Fucking bitch. I hate her. I hope she gets herpes and dies.'

Ella's late-night tales, all spilled in one breath. My grown-up young woman becoming a little girl again.

Herpes, though. That's interesting. Can you die from herpes? I won't rule out wishing that on Dan, then.

'Els—'

'Don't you dare tell me that at my age it doesn't matter, because it fucking does, okay?'

'Okay. Really, I wasn't going to.'

I look at the hair stomping along next to me. 'So . . . this boy. Is this the Bobby that you mentioned?'

'Bobbi's a *girl*, dad. I *told* you that. I'm not saying his name.' Ella tries to spit on the ground, but only succeeds in emitting a spray that lands on my arm and mists across my cheek. Peeking out from her heavy hair, her face is a mess of tears and puffy cheeks and anger and Kirsty's pouting lips.

'Thank you,' I say, wiping my cheek. 'Really. Thank you for being honest with me. But you don't need to kiss anyone at your age, Els. No one wants herpes.'

'Josephine does. Slag.'

Perhaps Josephine does want herpes.

When I was Ella's age, it had certainly mattered to me, the who snogged who and the how far and the rest of it. Ella is right about that, and I would never tell her otherwise. The main difference is that when you're older it affects more than just the central players. At least she isn't stomping quite so heavily now. Heartbreak is so much more energy-sapping than anger.

'Oh, hello.'

'What?' Ella replies, not in her usual grumpy way,

208

but in a curious *You've finally found a way out of here?* kind of voice.

Which I have.

'I spy,' I say, fixing my gaze on it in case it should disappear, 'with my little eye, something beginning with . . . P.'

'Pub,' Ella guesses.

'Well, I was going to say phone box. But since you mention it, the pub probably has a phone, too.'

thirty

Meanwhile, back in Tenderbridge . . .

Kirsty taps the settings button on her phone for the third time in as many minutes. She checks that the Wi-Fi is on, the mobile data, the Bluetooth. They all are. She turns the phone off and on again, the way that Ella had shown her. Her hand trembles as she waits for it to come back to life.

The piece of fruit with the bite taken out of it.

The password: **2006**.

The smiling face on the screen, her bespectacled little wizard, pointing a wand.

And still no message.

Kirsty knows her phone is working alright. Today she has received millions of messages from the girls' WhatsApp groups – Briony trying to organise a night out to go and see *Magic Mike* up the Hippodrome. A picture of Julie's vegetable lasagne, and another of Sharon's curried chickpea soup. Bea endlessly texting about pool boy, the latest one stressing that Barbados, and possibly the entire engagement, is off. Kirsty's had messages from everyone that she doesn't want to hear from.

'What's up, babe?' Dan says, answering Kirsty's third attempt at calling him.

'It's Ella. I still haven't heard from her.'

'What do you want me to do about it? I'm at work, aren't I? — *Alright, Sly. No worries, mate* — Sorry, babe. That was Sly.'

'She still hasn't got her phone on, Dan. Or *he's* done something to it.'

'Babe, he couldn't tell you which end a horse shits from. What's he going to do?'

'Anyone can get rid of a mobile phone. I'm scared.'

'Look, we'll talk about it when I get home — *Yeah, I've got it, Sly, mate . . . Nah, I'll send it to him in a sec . . . I don't fucking know, do I? Ask Maz* — Listen, I've got to go, Kirst. That deal's got to be closed today and no one knows where the IBLs are.'

'But what shall I do about Ella?'

'I told you already, babes! We'll talk about it later. After I get back from the driving range. Kisses.'

The smiling wizard reappears. The time: 14:14.

Inside the empty, echoey kitchen, Kirsty's nails rattle against the Prosecco glass. She drains it. And then heads to the fridge to top it up.

The last message from Ella had come through at two minutes past eight on the first night of her trip. That was nearly two whole days ago, now. And fifty-eight minutes earlier than arranged.

> dad's drunk...had 2 put tent up myself
> ...smh nvm we got here ok...finally :) luv
> u ttyt xxxx

There was no doubt that the message had come from Ella. Just as it was no surprise that Ella said John was drunk. He had been drunk on every trip, night out and journey that Kirsty could remember. He even turned up drunk at the hospital after she had given birth to Ella, serenading everyone in the ward to a rendition of *Rehab*, trying to get them all singing along.

Kirsty opens the thread of messages she exchanged with John before they left for the trip. His messages are always badly written, barely decipherable – if they could be understood at all, and weren't just a jumble of consonants. Especially if he had somehow turned predictive text on – but perhaps he left a hint to suggest that he was up to something.

> stn 815 tomo

That was the last one, sent the night before they left.

Outside the railway station, Kirsty told John how healthy he looked. Also, though, he was happy. John Slade is never bloody happy. Especially in the morning. That *joie de vivre* could have meant all kinds of different things. At the time, Kirsty assumed that John had drunk a beer with his breakfast, or instead of breakfast, or had got laid the night before – as if anyone would have him.

But maybe he had been happy for another reason.

Kirsty scrolls further back.

Fat lot of bloody stupid help that message was.

Although . . .

Actually . . .

When he mentioned the name of the campsite, Kirsty was sure she had written the name on the telephone pad.

Her heels echo through the kitchen, then are muffled by the hallway carpet. She looks from John's text to the name on the pad: Cannock.

all booked campsite called cannock

Stupid bastard.

Kirsty taps the screen and details of the Welsh campsite appear. The website might be shoddy, but there is a telephone number.

'Hello, Cannock,' says a female voice.

'Yes, hello. My name is Kirsty Daniels. My daughter is staying with you, and I am having trouble getting hold of her.'

'What's her name, lovely?'

'Ella. But Ella Slade. Not Daniels.'

'Ella Slade, okay. And is she camping or staying with us here in the cottages.'

'Camping. I didn't know you had cottages. But she's definitely camping.'

'And who is she camping with, pet?'

'Her father, John Slade.'

'Oh, yes. I know who you mean. Just the two of them, isn't it? Did you not fancy a trip up here to join them?'

'It's . . . No. They wanted a trip by themselves. I was just wondering if you've seen them?'

'Well, that's the funny thing. Their tent – big thing, it is – sort of . . . fell to pieces on their first night here.'

'Fell to pieces? What do you mean?'

'Well, one half of the tent looked like an elephant had sat on it.'

'Oh my God.'

'Don't worry, pet. My husband Andrew went up to field and fixed it for them. It does look a bit wonky now. But they haven't returned to the tent at all. Not even in the storm.'

'Storm? What storm?'

'Oh, we had a wild night up here, we did. Rained all night long. Heavy rain, too. We have a group of cyclists staying with us who got back to the campsite just before the storm. When they came in for supper, they told us that they had seen a man with a very young girl out in the forest. We wondered if that might have been them, your missing husband and daughter.'

'He's not my husband. And what do you mean by missing?'

'I don't mean *missing* missing, my love. But, well, out in a storm like that, they must have stayed somewhere for the night, surely. You wouldn't want to be caught.'

'Did they say where they were going? Did they tell you anything? Anything at all?'

'Not really. Just that they were going out to look for the fells – the waterfalls.'

'Really? And there didn't seem to be anything odd about them, other than the fact that they were looking for waterfalls?'

'Well, now you mention it, when they first arrived they did look terribly weary. Your husband, he found it hard to walk properly.'

'He's not my husband. And that wasn't because he was weary. Look, do you know where they are now?'

'I haven't seen them. Let me check with Andrew.'

Kirsty's nail tap-tap-taps on the black glass top of the hallway table.

I'll kill him, she tells her reflection in the gilded mirror. *If anything's happened to my baby, I'll kill him.*

'Hello, love?'

'Yes?'

'Hello. Nell again, here. Andrew says that he hasn't seen them. But it doesn't mean they didn't come back last night, he thinks. Their bags were still there when he fixed up the tent. It's possible they just got up and out early this morning. Because we didn't see them doesn't necessarily mean that they weren't here. Like I say, no one would have wanted to be out in that storm.'

'Do you sell alcohol?' Kirsty asks.

'Yes,' the lady replies. 'Yes, we do.'

'You would have seen them. And there's no way that they would have been up and out early this morning, either of them. Do me a favour, if you do see them, tell them, *tell the girl*, Ella, to call me straight away.'

'Ella. Okay. And you're Kirsty.'

'Yes. I'll leave you my number, just in case .'

'Got it.'

'The *moment* you see them, okay?'

'The moment I see them.'

As soon as Kirsty ends the call, she taps out another number. It is answered instantly.

'Which emergency service do you require?' says the bored voice.

'Police,' Kirsty says.

'Putting you through.'

thirty-one

The river path leads up to a road. Over the road is a grassy triangle, its muddy edges bleeding into a lane. Late summer bulbs are still flowering upon the grassy triangle, wilting heads beside a lichen-splattered bench. Plonked right in the middle of it all is the phone box that I had seen.

A row of cottages, all facing the forest, step away along the pocked road. Among them is a small church. With a cross nailed beneath its eaves, I assume it is a church. If it wasn't for that cross, it could be a scout hut or a village hall. Perhaps it is all three. Past the phone box in the other direction, the road leads into the great expanse of nothing. Even though there is no one around, someone's having a party somewhere.

'Is that noise coming from the pub?' Ella asks.

'That's what I thought. Let's try the phone box first, then we'll go to the pub.'

The grass has clearly not been cut in a while, reaching

up beyond our ankles. I spy a wonky carving etched into the wooden backrest of the bench.

MY CAT HATES JOHNS it says.

AND SO DO I is scratched underneath by an even unsteadier hand.

'Better steer clear of that cat,' I tell Ella, pointing out the random graffiti. 'Probably whoever I is, too, actually.'

'This place is weird,' Ella says. 'I don't like it.'

'It's fine,' I say, even though what she said echoes my thoughts exactly. 'We'll just phone your mum, have a quick drink, then go back to the campsite and get our stuff. We'll be in Cardiff by this evening, I . . .'

Ella looks as grubby, tired and sulky as a girl who has spent the night camping in a bivouac. Even though I washed in a puddle, wiping a bit of the forest off my hands and clothes, she looks pristine compared to me. The difference is that I'm used to it.

'Were you about to say I promise?' she says.

'We'll make it to Cardiff,' I say. And then I pat her on the shoulder, because it seems like the right thing to do.

A cheer goes up from inside the pub. It sounds as though it is hosting a barn dance for bullocks in there.

'What's your mum's number?' I ask, digging in my pocket for coins.

'I don't know.'

'Whose number do you know?'

'No one's,' Ella says. 'No one needs to know numbers anymore.'

Unless you're lost in God knows where.

I rack my brain, as clear as it has been probably since this mouldy bench was first hammered together. Once I get my synapses around it, a phone number does pop into my head; the same one I had when I was a kid.

'I'll phone grandma,' I say.

'*Grandma*? What can she do? I want to get out of here. Now. Phone the police.'

'I can't phone the police, sweetheart. They're not a taxi service,' I say, even though in the past I have considered the police as being a bit like a taxi service. 'Tell you what, I'll see if there's a number for a taxi firm inside the phone box.'

There's not.

Anything that was once flyers or stickers have all been picked at and peeled away. It is clear that the river sometimes pays a visit to the inside of the phone box. The floor is wet. Weeds are growing in the piles of silted mud. I put the first coin into the slot – a twenty pence piece with chewed edges. It travels straight through to the change draw. The next coin isn't even that adventurous and falls directly into the heart of the machine.

I glance at Ella, standing next to the rotting bench, checking her phone again, probably desperate to know what Josephine has been up to, even if it hurts her. She looks towards the latest tumult of noise from the pub. To answer the worried expression she shares with me, I give her a thumbs up. And then I keep feeding the hungry machine until a coin finally grabs.

The line is terrible, but I can hear a faint echo of mum's voice. Just like the hissing and bubbling noises spouting out of the busted receiver, I think she might be giving me an earful.

'Mum? Just listen, alright. *Listen*! Hello? Hello? For fuck's sake, you twat.'

The phone has cut out.

I continue to stuff coins into the machine, but succeed only in getting irritated. Lifting my hand back to smash the receiver against the stupid bloody thing, I notice that Ella is watching, so I calmly hold the phone to my ear. Now there isn't even a faint dial tone. I try the triple nines anyway and am answered by silence. Picturing this stupid, ancient, beautiful phone box floating off downstream, I crack the receiver back onto the hook.

'To the pub, then,' I say, putting my arm around Ella. Not only does she look utterly miserable, I can feel the despondence emanating through her slender shoulders.

The door of the Sir Thomas will barely open for the depth of the crowd packed into the small room. When I finally manage to ease it far enough for us to enter, we are greeted by a swarm of big bastards all wearing red jerseys, watching a sports match on two small, elevated tellies in the corners. Squeezing our way through, no one moves a single one of their bulging muscles. If I were prodding my way in here with a pitchfork, I doubt it would make any kind of an impression on this lot. With an arm wrapped around Ella, we weave our way around the outside of the mob.

A few of the rugby fans turn to glare at us – not that they would be able to see Ella, about five or six heads shorter than most of them, pushed deep into my chest. Something happens on the tellies, so our presence does not distract them for long.

We squash into a space at the end of the bar. The barman's head is covered with tiny prickles of ginger stubble, like a homemade pork scratching. I can't stop looking at his nose, a minuscule button with multiple ridges on it, like the chopped off top of a carrot. A pair of squashed-dumpling ears complete the stew of his face.

'Have you got a phone I can use?' I yell, leaning over Ella.

'Only for incoming calls, mate,' he shouts back.

'What?' I yell. 'Why?'

'Some bugger bunged the slot with bubble gum.'

'Haven't you got another phone?'

'Don't need one, mate.'

'What about for beer deliveries?'

'Fax, mate.'

'Hasn't the fax machine got a telephone?'

'It does, but it can't make calls. The microphone on the handset is bust.'

Curse those bloody tellies. Every few moments, the entire horde bellows at them. Lost somewhere beneath me, I try to manoeuvre Ella into the only vacant two feet of space – a small square in front of the toilets – but she would clearly prefer to stay stuck to me.

'How can I get a cab?' I yell at the barman. 'Can you fax one for me?'

'What?'

'A *cab*. Put bluntly, how the fuck do we get out of here.'

'Won't be no cabs out while the rugger's on, mate,' the barman replies. 'Where to you go?'

'Dannywillywin? Something like that.'

'Danwylliarwean? You're only ten miles away, mate. Be there in about five hours if you set off now. Don't want to be walking that route in the dark, you don't.'

Turning his round shoulders on us, the barman clearly thinks that we've distracted him from the game for long enough. I reach over and prod him in one of his massive muscles.

'Oi. Mate. We need to get out of here.'

'Not my problem, is it?'

I notice that the bloke standing next to us keeps turning around and staring at me. Chubby and not as muscular as most of the others, he doesn't exactly look like he wants to break my face. I can see my reflection in his circular specs, the first time I've seen myself in more than two days. I look like Che Guevara.

'Alright?' I say, a tad more confrontationally than I intended.

His impassive gaze lingers on us just long enough to make me uncomfortable, and then he returns his attention to the telly.

'Oi,' I say, prodding the barman again. 'Give me a pint. Lager. And a gin and tonic for the girl.'

The barman leaves the pint glass collecting beer from the tap, grabs a straight glass, and measures a large shot of gin straight from the bottle. While he tops it up with soda, I continue screaming that I was only joking about the gin.

'And a lemonade,' I tell him, after he plonks the two drinks in front of us.

I down the gin and grab our drinks and we shuffle outside, away from whatever kind of asylum it is that we ventured into. This is my first proper beer in days, yet still we find ourselves as stranded in the arse-end of nowhere as we were before.

thirty-two

The beer has a sharp, rusty taste, as if it was brewed in a barrel of old batteries, not even as refined as a sixty-pence can of unbranded Special Brew from my shit local minimarket. Still, it's a beer. I would have drunk it even if it had been drawn from an animal trough behind the pub. Maybe it has.

'You must be thirsty, Ella. Do you not want your drink?'

Like a girl in a horror movie who has found civilisation after wandering alone for years, from the opposite side of the picnic bench in front of the Sir Thomas, Ella peers at me from beneath the hood of her coat. It's reminiscent of her reaction to gifts I've given her over the years, after unwrapping bits and pieces picked up from some knock-down shop – broken crayons too waxy to draw with, lumpy recycled paper sketch pads, cheap dolls that fall apart when you look at them. One year, when I'd forgotten to get anything for Ella, I wrapped up her favourite plastic plate and some beer mats from the pub. I don't think I've ever seen such a look of disgust, especially from a toddler. This look I am receiving now is possibly even more disconsolate.

'After we've finished these, we'll go door to door if we have to. The number for the campsite is printed on the map, see? I'm sure they'll come and pick us up. We'll be back before you know it.'

Now Ella isn't even bothering to bollock me. Instead, she watches a small family of geese waddling over the bridge, heading out of the sunlight.

'The phone box is out of order,' I call to them.

That wins another glance from Ella, but far from a grin. Even the geese ignore me.

'You're very quiet, Els. Are you okay?'

With one sweeping movement, Ella whisks back the hood, takes a deep breath, and breaks her silence.

'Another promise. There are cess pits less full of shit than you. This isn't just bumbling around town, like you usually do. We're lost. Stuck. Stranded. Can't you get your head around that? You've brought me out to the shittiest place on earth, led me around in the mud and the rain, talking an absolute pile of wank most of the time. You don't care, as long as you get a beer at the end of it all.'

'It's pretty disgusting, actually, the beer.'

The cess pit comment was clever, though. I will definitely have to remember that one.

'Being lost in the middle of nowhere doesn't matter to you. You haven't got anything to return to. No friends, no family. No *life*. I have. And I can't speak to any of them, because they don't even have electricity in this *wonderful* shithole you've brought me to.'

I open my mouth to say . . . *anything* to stop this tirade, fair as it is. But Ella isn't done yet.

'This is the worst trip I've ever been on. I haven't even had a proper meal in a day and a half. I can't wait until I never see you again.'

Not an hour ago we were best pals, chattering along beside the river. But with that, she is finished, retreated beneath her hood.

'I'll see if they sell chips,' I say, trying to build a bivvy to repair the situation. First, though, I down the rest of the horrible pint. Might as well get a top up while I'm in there.

The door of the pub opens, releasing a hubbub of voices. The bloke with the specs, the one who kept on staring at us, steps outside. He gives me a nod. In the speckled light beneath the fast-moving clouds, his rugby jersey is bright blood-red, not quite as worn-in as the varied shades dotted among the clan inside. His tight jeans would be baggy on most people, but on him they just look like spandex stuffed full of dough. With his glasses and his bowl haircut, he reminds me of an inflatable Clark Kent.

'Alright, are ya?' he says in his soft Welsh burr.

'Have you got the time?' I ask him, skilfully skirting around potential chitchat.

'What for?'

'Huh? No, *the time*. The time of day.'

'Oh.' He looks at the Swatch on his pudgy, hairless wrist. 'Ten past three, it is.'

Having studied the timetable throughout the long journey from Tenderbridge, I just about remember seeing that the last departure from the Merthyr Tydfil terminal is at sixish. So I have just under three hours to make things right. A hot meal and a comfortable bed in the city might be enough to prevent the wilting steel of mine and Ella's new bond from crippling completely. I don't think it's a lot to ask for. Not when the alternative is that I truly do lose my daughter forever.

'We really need to use a phone,' I say, sliding out from the bench. 'See that one?' I point at the phone box, just in case this bloke has never noticed the bloody great block of vintage technology plonked on the edge of his village. 'It isn't working.'

'Is it not?' he asks.

'No.'

'Oh.'

'So . . .'

'So.'

Bloody hell. I wonder if this bloke was able to pick his own outfit before coming down to the pub to watch the rugby.

'So . . . have you got one?'

'Not on me, no,' he replies. 'Only the landlines work out here to any real effect. A couple of mobile operators have a fairly clear reception in some places. Like in my house. The reception's alright there, most of the time.' He slithers his hands, knuckle deep, into the pockets of his tight jeans.

'Is there any way, any way at all, that you would be kind enough to let us use your phone? I'll give you 50p,' I say, dipping into my pocket, pulling out a handful of change. 'Tell you what, I'll give you a pound if you let us use your phone.' Plucking one from the small pile, I offer it to him.

'You don't have to do that,' he says, even though I notice a slight twitch in his left pocket, clearly tempted to take my pound. 'You can use my phone for free. I've got an oggie in the fridge you could share, too.'

'Really? I love oggies. Do you fancy sharing an oggie, Ella?'

Ella peeks out from beneath the hood and flickers half an eye towards our new Welsh friend. She doesn't answer my question, but nor does she retreat tortoise-like back into her coat.

'So, you're Ella?' the Welsh fellow says. 'And what's your name?'

Before replying, I consider the graffiti on the bench. 'You don't have a cat, do you?'

'A cat? No. No, I don't.'

'I'm John,' I say, holding out my hand.

'I'm Thomas,' he replies, his hand soft and soggy, wet to the touch.

'Like the pub! It's not named after you, is it? You're not Sir Thomas?'

Thomas lets out a high-pitched squealy sound, which I think is laughter. 'Oh no. That's Sir Thomas Phillips. He was the Mayor of Newport at the time of the Rising. That's him in the photos inside the pub.'

'Oh, *right*,' I reply enthusiastically, even though I didn't spare a glance for a single one of the pictures inside that shithole. 'Some people back home know me as Sir John,' I say, earning a disgusted curl of the lip from Ella.

'*Do* they?' Thomas says, rocking forward on his toes. 'Well, Sir John, my house, it's just along the road here.'

I follow Thomas's gaze along the narrow lane, past

the church and the cottages on one side, and the rural wilds on the other.

'Come on, Els,' I say. 'Time to move again.'

With a huge, puffed sigh, Ella stands and slings her bag over her shoulder. This girl, who needs about eight hours sleep in the day and another ten at night, minimum, looks as exhausted as I feel. I offer to carry her bag, but she silently, balefully declines.

'Umm, Thomas?' I say, waddling along beside us like an overweight wind-up toy. 'I was just wondering, have you got any beers back at your place?'

'Oh yes,' he replies. 'We can have one while we watch the match, if you like?'

'Erm . . . maybe you could watch the match while Ella and I share that oggie you mentioned. I really do love oggies. Especially with a beer.'

I thought that Ella would cheer up a bit now we're on the move again. Instead, there is my little Kirsty, giving me the glare.

Maybe she's forgotten how brilliantly I have stepped up to all of the challenges that have confronted us, so I keep half an eye on her while I am telling Thomas about the bivvy. But she doesn't even look up. Not once.

thirty-three

We are led by Thomas into a curved cul-de-sac, hidden behind the main drag of cottages. It is curtained on all sides by shadowy woodlands, looming dark above the houses. Unlike the cottages – pretty, stone-walled, and suitably rustic – the houses wedged in here, with their cladded walls, misted double-glazing, a horror of flat roofs and frosted glass, could have been lifted directly from one of the south Tenderbridge estates.

'Do you live with your wife?' I ask Thomas, leading us towards a house tucked into the far corner.

'Oh no,' he says over his shoulder. 'I live with my mother. She's down at her caravan in St David's at the moment. The sea air is good for her arthritic joints.'

'Sounds nice,' I say. 'The sea air, I mean. That sounds nice. Not the arthritic joints. Dylan's got arthritis.'

'Oh! My mother used to read *Under Milk Wood* to me when I was a boy. That's why she called me Thomas,' Thomas says, 'after Dylan.'

I was less lost when we were just lost.

We follow Thomas through a once-white front door into an enclosed porch, blotchy with black mould. Before heading in through the actual front door, he asks if we don't mind kicking our shoes off.

Inside the house it is lovely and light, the smell of damp left behind with the smell of our shoes. I look around the hallway at the display of postcards – a mini-tour of Welsh coastal towns, by the looks of them. A few faded watercolours on bobbly, rippling paper are interspersed between them. But hanging upon the walls in greatest abundance are framed photographs, mostly of an elderly woman with a fat kid beside her ballooning ankles.

'This must be you with your grandmother,' I say, pointing at one of them.

'That's me with my mother,' Thomas replies.

'Ah.' I lean in closer to the photographs, searching the resemblance. Perhaps it's the photos that look old, not Thomas's mum. I can't help but notice how they both stand to attention in every picture, completely upright, like cardboard cutouts, and with absolutely no contact between them. 'Yeah, I *see*.'

'If you want to sit down in there, the room at the front,' Thomas calls out, 'I'll get the oven pre-heated for that oggie.'

More photos of Thomas and his old lady are dotted around the sitting room. There are a number of framed crocheted pictures, too: neatly threaded images of fruit, animals, and one that looks like that antiques bloke from the telly. But equally, with the tea cosy hair, it could be a knitted self-portrait of Thomas's mum.

Standing on the mismatched, shiny antique furniture are ornaments and ceramics, all with doilies arranged beneath them. I haven't seen a doily since our childhood holidays to crappy British seaside resorts. Even the net curtains have a pattern similar to the doilies. That bloke from Sound All Round would love it in here.

Walking around the room with my hands behind my back, inspecting the display of ornaments, photographs and pictures, everything I see is old-fashioned, exceptionally clean, and very odd.

'Lovely place,' I call out.

'Oh, thank you,' Thomas says, entering the room. 'We like it. Here's a beer for you, Sir John.'

Thomas hands me a brightly coloured can. A Welsh IPA. I guess that beggars can't be choosers.

'And Ella,' he says, squeezing his hands between his thighs and leaning towards her. 'What would you like for yourself?'

'To get the fuck out of here.'

She has dark rings beneath her eyes and no social graces, my girl. Well, she has been raised by the weird hate triangle that is me, Kirsty and Dan, I suppose.

As soon as we walked into the sitting room, Ella slumped down in the nearest place: a huge, soft armchair facing a wooden cabinet in the corner of the room. Inside the cabinet is an old telly with a bulbous screen, twisty buttons sticking out of a silver panel on the side. On top of the cabinet is a dimpled vase on a doily. I think that the flowers in the vase are plastic.

'And what to drink?' Thomas asks, sliding past the rudery.

'I'm not thirsty,' Ella replies, and then she unzips her

rucksack and proceeds to drink water from the bottle like a baby lamb, while staring at Thomas.

'Just let me know if you do want anything,' Thomas says. 'You can put the telly on, if you like. There might be cartoons. Would you like me to call a cab for you, John?'

Thomas catches me greedily slugging beer. Its taste might be bland, but it is so wet and cold.

'Yes please, Thomas,' I say through a belch – which makes Ella smirk, surprisingly.

'And where to you go?'

I explain where we are staying and then ask Thomas if I can have another beer. Thirty seconds later, I hear him on the phone in the kitchen.

This time when Thomas brings the drink through, he has put it in a beaker, its plasticky taste as strong as the IPA. Less than half an hour ago I was prepared to drink one that might have been watered down by animal piss, so I remain grateful. I'm so grateful that it is pretty much already gone by the time Thomas again disappears.

I slide into an armchair in front of the window. The springs are gone; the seat sucks me in. The relief from finally sitting down somewhere comparatively comfortable drains the life out of me. After having only a few hours of soaking wet kip in the forest last night, I realise just how exhausted I am.

My head lolls towards Thomas when he re-enters the room. He glances down at Ella, curled up on her massive armchair. My head will barely even loll back to centre.

'How are you feeling, John?'

'Sleeep-eee.'

With a smile that broadens, Thomas struggles down

to kneel in front of me. My eyes slowly follow his uneasy descent.

He adjusts his specs. Looks me directly in the eye.

'John,' he says in his lovely, calming voice. 'I've not called you a cab.'

'Whaa yoo meean?' I ask. Or I try to. My tongue feels like a squidgy, marshmallowy flump. My frown won't erase once it has begun on my brow, weighty upon my eyelids. Three beers wouldn't usually make me this tired and slurry.

'Come on, John. You're a man in his fifties, out in the forest with a little girl, *lost*,' Thomas accentuates with four pudgy fingers.

'Onneee . . .' *forty-two*. I know what words I want to speak, but my jaw just won't allow it.

Thomas swivels his bowling ball head. 'There she is,' he says. 'Young Ella.'

My lips part, but only air comes out. My tongue is making clicking noises. My eyes roll down to blearily admire the plastic cup, which I would love to lift and drink the last of the beer from. My hand is still trying its very hardest, bless it.

'Whoopsie.' Thomas takes the cup before I can spill beer over myself. Through my moist, drowsy eyes, his face appears partially pixelated. His porcine smile. 'So. John. Rather than call a cab, I thought you should have yourself a little bit of sleepy-byes. It seems that Ella fell asleep all by herself, though. Doesn't she look cute?'

Again, he half-turns towards my little girl. And then he laughs his awful laugh, as wild as a snared animal.

'Oh, don't worry, John. Don't worry,' Thomas says,

possibly in response to a flicker of emotion upon my slack face. 'Ella is in safe hands with me.'

In my weary state, I can't absorb all of the words Thomas is saying, but enough to follow the general gist. The terror of his intent is trying to take a grip on me, but every sensation has become too dreamy to grab. My eyelashes tickle as they touch against each other. The rapid eye movement as I fight against my eyelids.

'That's it, John,' Thomas says. 'You've nothing more to worry about. Just sleep. Sleep.'

My flickering eyes see a kaleidoscopic red blur turn to face Ella. Now the red blob is rising, standing up, moving towards my little girl. I try to summon strength. Anything to move. Anything to stay awake.

All I can do is dribble.

This is not the first time that I've ended up as a slobbering mess after a few beers, but possibly it is the first time that it has been against my will.

The last moments of my life were supposed to be spent on a revolving bed, two Brazilian sisters giving me the full Entwistle until my heart finally gives out. Not in a broken armchair surrounded by doilies.

thirty-four

The following day . . .

Kirsty runs her fingernails along the thin purple gouge they have carved through the pads of her thumbs. She doesn't feel it. She glances at her phone, on the table in front of her. It remains silent. Since the two police officers arrived at the house, and for many hours before that, all through the night, Kirsty has checked her phone every few moments. Still nothing.

On the opposite side of the table, Officer Nicholls – a thirty-something, blonde-haired policeman with stern, aquiline features – slides the chunky vase along the table. In the centre where it was, it had been a barrier between them and the desperate mother. The vase scratches along the glass, the lilies inside it jangling like Morris dancers.

The young policewoman sitting next to him, Officer Sharpe – dark hair, eyes as big and bright as an anime character – glares at her colleague.

'Lift it, Ollie,' she whispers to him. 'You're scratching the table.'

Kirsty stares absently at the wonky groove leading to the foot of the vase. A few seeds of the lilies have fallen along its line, as if poorly sown. This was Dan's table before she and Ella moved in with him. Perhaps that scratch would finally convince Dan to replace this with the wooden table she wanted. If there was a mark half this size on his car, he would already be on the phone to the dealer.

'Do you mind if we call you Kirsty?' Officer Sharpe asks. 'Or would you prefer Mrs Daniels?'

'What? Call me Kirsty. Call me what you like.'

Kirsty can feel the puffiness in her eyes. Each wrinkle within them, patched up by concealer, digs into the bags of a sleepless night. The familiar salty liquid begins to release from her nasal glands. Kirsty sniffs it down, daps a tissue against her nostrils, and drinks a tiny mouthful of water.

'Kirsty,' Officer Nicholls says. 'We have spoken again with our colleagues at Dyfed-Powys. They've stationed an officer on the ground at the campsite to see if your husband and daughter return.'

'*John* and your daughter,' Officer Sharpe interjects. She gives a slow nod, smoothing a hand over her hair, tied in a tight ponytail.

'We are receiving constant updates from our Welsh colleagues,' Officer Nicholls continues, 'and will keep you informed of any new information we receive.'

Allowing a procedural beat, Officer Sharpe takes over from Officer Nicholls.

'Kirsty, we need to ask you again, I'm afraid. When

you met at the railway station, how did John's behaviour seem to you?'

'He had carrier bags full of beer,' Kirsty replies. 'Not that there's anything unusual about that. John can't walk down the road unless he has a beer with him. But, as I already said, he did seem to be in high spirits. I know he was looking forward to this trip. But John, though, he's unpredictable; capable of anything . . .

'Actually, no.'

Officer Nicholls looks up from his leather-clad pad, where he is making a notation of Kirsty's comments.

'John's not capable of very much at all, really. Not in the real world. But in terms of his mindset, he is often quite desperate. Whether for money or attention.'

'When you told him about the move, Kirsty,' Officer Sharpe says, 'what was John's response?'

'John hates the thought of Ella moving away. And he's not one to hide his feelings. But, even when we were together, John and I, he has always responded to the smallest things in a dramatic and unpredictable way. Rather than just sit down and talk about it like adults, he's always performing some routine.

'To give you an example of what he's like, there was one time we were supposed to be going to visit my parents. John didn't want to go, so he hid in the toilet and broke the lock and said that he wasn't coming out. The only thing was that he hadn't locked the toilet properly before he broke it, so I just pushed the door open and he had to come out. You see, he's childish, John. He has the mindset of a child. A drunk child.'

'I see.'

Officer Sharpe watches Officer Nicholls scribble on

the pad, waiting for him to finish making notes about the lock on the toilet door.

Officer Nicholls places his pen on the table and consults a previous page in his notepad.

'Last year, Kirsty, there were more than one hundred and forty callouts for people who were lost or in trouble in the Brecon Beacons. As it has not yet been two full days since your daughter and John were last seen, because we have had no contact from them – and, as our Welsh colleagues have confirmed, they left most of their belongings at the campsite – for the time being, we will be treating them as missing and in need of rescue. If there has not been any movement by thirteen-hundred hours, they'll send a helicopter up to scan the region. That's in . . .' Officer Nicholls looks at his watch. 'Just over an hour from now. If John has any sense, they'll find their way out into the open and await recovery. That's what we're hoping.'

'That's the problem.' Kirsty drops her hands onto the tabletop, rattling the vase. 'John hasn't got any sense.'

'Let's hope Ella has the sense to search for an open area, then,' Officer Sharpe says, smiling. 'She sounds like a smart girl.'

'She is. She's very smart, not that I know where she gets it from.' Beneath the table, Kirsty presses her finger-nails into her right arm, deep into the skin. 'I'm telling you, they've already been missing for two days. Over two days! He's done something stupid. Or he's hiding her somewhere. I just know he is.'

When Kirsty looks at the garden, dabbing the tissue lightly beneath her eyes, the police officers use the break to exchange glances. Officer Nicholls shrugs, but Officer Sharpe shakes her head. And then she also shrugs.

'Sorry, Kirsty,' Officer Sharpe says. 'In your own time, what can you tell us about the relationship between John and your daughter?'

The anguish seeps from Kirsty's face and resignation arises. 'There's no doubt they would have fallen out by now. That's another thing I'm scared of. They know how to push each other's buttons, those two. And . . . well, Ella has a bit of an attitude problem at the moment.'

'What do you mean?' Officer Nicholls asks.

'Just talking back. Swearing. Nothing we didn't all go through at that age.'

'Hmm,' Officer Sharpe intones, the barest flicker of a frown passing over her forehead.

Finished with his notes, Officer Nicholls places his linked hands onto the table. 'I do have to ask again, Mrs Daniels. Does John have a history of any unreported violent behaviour? Any episodes at all, however insignificant or out of character they might have appeared to be at the time? All the information you can supply us with is helpful for our character profile,' he adds, sensing Officer Sharpe's scour.

'Not towards people,' Kirsty replies. 'I've seen John act violently towards musical instruments, furniture, plants, lamp posts. But never people.'

'His record suggests as much.' Officer Nicholls opens a larger folder and surveys a long form. Drunken misbehaviour and misdemeanours, mostly. A couple of public decency acts, also related to the consumption of alcohol. Nothing of real cause for suspicion.

'Excuse me.' He stands up from the table and leaves the room to answer a telephone call.

'Do you know who John tends to visit or talk to most, Kirsty?' Officer Sharpe asks, an effort to distract Kirsty's half-turned ear harking to Officer Nicholls' low voice in the entrance hall. 'Does he keep in contact with any old university friends or acquaintances? Family? Fans of his band, even?'

'John didn't go to university,' Kirsty says. 'He doesn't really have any friends. And the only one in his family who can tolerate him is his dad, Stanley. As for his band, the only fans they have are in John's head.'

'I see.'

'We have a couple of new leads and updates,' Officer Nicholls says, re-entering the room and standing at the head of the table. 'John attempted to phone his mother yesterday. The call has been located to a phone box in a small village just over ten miles from the Cannock campsite. His mother said that John was quite frantic. She said it sounded as if he had *"got himself into a real tangle"*. And then he swore at her and hung up. We won't be able to confirm what she said until officers visit her at her home. They've been despatched, to the village and the mother.'

'What's the other update?' Kirsty asks, wringing her hands, half-standing. 'Have they found Ella?'

'Not yet,' Officer Nicholls replies. 'But it looks hopeful. Even though the signal is very weak, she has turned her mobile phone back on. Or someone has.'

thirty-five

After going on binges, I have woken up in some weird places. The setting that I have just opened my eyes to discover is as bewildering as any of them. It's as if I have slept my way back through time to find myself in a bed and breakfast from the fifties.

Who the hell uses doilies anymore?

Never have I had a hangover that felt quite like this. I know I need to stand up and unfold my back, which has somehow slipped halfway into this armchair, but my body does not want to respond. My eyes travel left to right over the florally patterned wallpaper, and the glass-topped furniture. The framed photos of some plump kid. In one nearby me, sweating behind his specs; his chubby cheeks swollen by a shy smile.

There's an old-fashioned television set.

There's a yellow coat hanging off the armchair.

'*Ella!*' I croak. My mouth feels as if it has had a sock stuffed in it. I cough and spit out a solid phlegm. It lands on a ceramic frog.

'Ella!' I call out again, a bit clearer.

The ceiling above me creaks.

Putting my hands on the armrest, I slide off the chair, onto the floor.

Someone starts running down the stairs, shaking the house.

On my knees, it hurts my head to clench my fists.

'Hi, dad,' Ella says, bounding into the room. 'Did you sleep well?'

'Sleep well?' I climb uneasily upward. 'Where is he? What did he do? Are you okay?'

'I'm fine, yeah.' Ella brushes her coat to the floor and drops into the deep armchair. 'Oh my God, Thomas is *so* fucking weird,' she says. And then she laughs, an entire body laugh.

'I know he's weird, Ella. But what did he do to you, sweetheart? It's okay, you can tell me.'

'*Do* to me? All he wanted to do was show me his teddies and stuff. He did a performance for me in his puppet theatre. He is *so* weird,' she says again. 'He's hilarious. He's like you, if you were funny.'

'Like *me*? What the hell is going on? I thought . . . I don't know.'

And there she goes again, laughing uncontrollably.

Crouching down uneasily in front of Ella's chair, I am assaulted by the memory of Thomas kneeling in front of me. Swivelling on his knee. The red blur that headed towards my little girl.

Heavy movement blunders about upstairs. I follow it across the ceiling. It stops. Starts again.

I feel my face screwing up. My stomach is sick. The chat about Josephine kissing Bobby, or whatever he was called, was a much more comfortable conversation to confront than this. Ella might not need any consoling about whatever the hell has been going on upstairs, but I bloody do. Something twitches in my guts and I perform a light gag.

Ella pushes back her hair, finally managing to gather herself. Whenever she looks at me, she can barely hold back the brewing laughter.

'Ella, I want you to be honest with me. Just . . . tell me, okay?'

'I *literally* just did.' Ella huffs, again adjusts her hair, and sits back in the chair. 'Basically, Thomas likes to do things that children do. Things like . . .' She takes another moment to compose herself. 'Like . . . playing with dolls, that sort of thing.'

'Playing with *dolls*?'

'Yeah. He loves his dolls.'

'How many grown men do you know who go to the pub when the rugby's on with the intention of picking up children to play with, Ella? Well? Thomas drugged me, okay. *Me*.' I point at the state I'm in for emphasis.

'Dad, what're you talking about? Listen to yourself.'

'No. Where the hell is he?'

In response to the heavy plodding coming down the stairs, the house begins to tremble.

Standing up, I re-clench my fists.

'Hello, Sir John,' Thomas says, filling the doorway.

'Right, you.' I take a feeble step towards Thomas and thump him in the chest.

'Did you just punch me, John?'

'Dad! What are you *doing*?'

'Ella, he *drugged* me.'

243

'Oh yes, I did. I'm sowwy.' Thomas puts a paw to his mouth and shakes his big fat belly.

'Is that a . . . *Winnie the Pooh* onesie you're wearing?'

'It is, yes,' Thomas replies. 'Do you like it, John?'

'Well . . . I don't know,' I say, repulsed, bewildered, but also curiously impressed. 'It does suit you.'

'You should get one, dad.'

'You will not catch me dressing up as any children's characters in the near future, Ella.'

Thomas's flab fills out every inch of his onesie. It ripples beneath the material like hay in a bonfire Guy. He gives me a twirl, bobbing his little black nose about.

Ella is in hysterics. I have never, ever heard her laugh like this, as crazy as a madman building a bivvy on a wild and stormy night.

However disturbing the whole situation should be, I find Thomas hard to stay angry at. Especially dressed the way he is, and how chirpy Ella seems to be today. This morning she hasn't even said that she never wants to speak to me again yet. If we had made it to Cardiff, combined with the inevitable pub crawl, I doubt that she would be all smiles and laughter. Maybe I should even be grateful to Thomas for drugging me. Even though I feel weak through to my nervous system, I haven't slept like that in years, even if I am in need of an osteopath and a nurse. And probably a shrink.

'What exactly was it that you drugged me with, Winnie – *Thomas*?'

'Only a bit of mum's Melatonin,' Thomas replies. 'She gives it to me when I'm feeling sleepy, so I thought that it would help you to drift off. I didn't expect you to fall asleep quite as quickly as you did. You must have been incredibly tired, John.'

'Hey, keep your filthy paws away from me,' I say when Thomas reaches out to touch my shoulder. 'I still don't think it's right to drug someone without asking them first.'

'I know. And I really am sorry, John,' Thomas says, nodding his little black nose with sincerity. 'I just didn't want you to get in the way of our playing.'

'But Ella was asleep, too, Thomas. Haven't you got someone your own size you can play with? This is mad.'

'It's *fucking* mad.'

'Ella, please stop swearing,' I say, rubbing my head.

'Not in front of Winnie,' Thomas adds, patting his paws against his wide sides.

After telling Thomas to book us a taxi right away, I plod upstairs. With an overwhelming urge to check that Ella wasn't also dosed, even with Calpol, I cannot leave this house without a thorough examination.

At the top of the stairs, I walk into a bathroom that wouldn't be out of place in a Mandarin Oriental hotel: all plush, ornate fixtures, fragrances, and a bathtub wide enough to fit . . . well, an adult-sized Winnie the Pooh. In fact, it is so big that there is probably enough room for Winnie to splash around in there with Eeyore.

I take a quick whizz, not caring that quite a lot of it sprinkles over the seat and on the floor, and then throw some water in my face.

Next door to the bathroom I find an old woman's bedroom, which looks ordinary enough. After I also then discover nothing of interest inside an airing cupboard, I move on to the final room.

A huge and bizarre army of Care Bears, My Little Ponies, Barbie dolls, Peter Rabbit and his chums – all the classics – as well as innumerable other assorted soft toys confront me. Alongside various generations of Sylvanian Families, the Animals of Farthing Wood are on a mission along the windowsill. Dangling beneath the lampshade, Teddy Ruxpin waves at me out of his airship.

In a corner is the puppet theatre that Ella mentioned. Considering that he is quite big, I find it hard to imagine Thomas crouching down behind the tiny red-and-white-striped booth. A glamorous princess is on the performing area, leaning up against one of the pillars. Her hair is as white as her sequin dress. There is another doll next to her, lying across the stage, a redhead in a purple cloak. They've got similar faces, those two, close enough to be sisters.

In the corner is a single bed, presumably the one used by Thomas. The headboard is elaborately decorated with finely carved leaves, pink hearts cradled inside detailed heads of flowers. Ornate Pegasus wings spread out from the curved footboard, where more cherubic toys peek out. It is a lovely bed, a soft shade of pink, perfect for a little princess.

In here, it is easy to forget that Thomas is not a little princess. He is a fully-grown man who drugged me so that my teenaged daughter could play with him and his toys.

On the bedsheets, Mickey Mouse's arms are wrapped around Goofy, huge smiles on both of their faces. In the absence of anything that even closely resembles Action

Man, Mickey and Goofy are the most masculine presence in an otherwise very girly room.

However odd it all is, I can see no real cause for alarm. And then I remind myself of the simple fact that this, of course, is the bedroom of a man who appears to be only a little bit younger than me.

What's more, the bastard, I've just remembered that he called me a man in my fifties yesterday.

Yesterday? Who knows?

'Where did you sleep, Ella?' I ask, back downstairs.

'Huh? Oh, in an old woman's bed. Thomas's mum's, I suppose. I assumed that you put me there. I quite liked it. It's soft and smelt of lavender. Look, Thomas charged this for me.'

'I would've charged your phone, too, John,' Thomas says, barrelling into the room in his onesie, 'but I don't have a connector here for something as old as yours. It's rather archaic technology you're using.'

In a remote village where a broken phone box is the most modern thing to be found, and I am still lagging a couple of decades behind.

'I haven't got any signal,' Ella says, lifting her phone above her head. 'Mum will be going apeshit.'

'Probably,' I reply, pretty much dismissing it as standard. 'Say, Thomas, where's that oggie? Did we have the oggie?'

thirty-six

Waiting beside the road for our taxi, Ella's phone still hasn't got any signal. Ella suggested that we could use Thomas's phone, so she can check in with Kirsty, but I don't at all like the idea of going back to his playhouse. He twice offered me a beer before we left, and I'm not sure I could decline for a third time. Anyway, Kirsty's probably too busy spending money online to even notice that Ella's not there.

Thomas wanted to wait with us, but I suggested that wearing his Winnie the Pooh onesie outside, in public view, might not be the best idea. When we were walking away and I looked back to see a Rapunzel doll waving out of the window next to him, I wondered how much Thomas's neighbours might know about the strange man-child in their midst. Or maybe all the burly blokes in the pub are big-little people. If a wanderer turns up on certain days of the week, they might happen upon Baloo, Noddy and a bearded Goldilocks shuffling about in the daytime.

'Still nothing?' I ask.

'No.' Ella reaches her phone up into the blue emptiness. 'How do they do anything out here?'

'Maybe the question we should be asking is *what* do they do out here. Imagine if Thomas is one of the normal ones.'

'I don't want to go to Cardiff,' Ella says. 'I think I'm ready to go straight home.'

'I think I am, too,' I reply, without even needing to think about it. I can't wait to just sit somewhere quiet and wash down the Melatonin pills, which I'd discreetly asked Thomas for, with a cold pint of imported lager. See if lightning can strike twice.

'Look, Els. A helicopter.'

'And our taxi,' she says. 'At last.'

After what happened yesterday, and the beers that he offered today, I had begun to wonder if Thomas would be true to his word.

The cabbie knows exactly where to take us, which I hope is to the campsite and not on some new, alternative adventure – Ella and I have both had quite enough of that. But this certainly turned out to be a trip to remember. I can't help thinking how different it might have been if I had planned it.

A couple of police cars speed past the taxi, lights on, heading towards the village.

'I wonder what that's about?'

Ella is too distracted by her phone to care.

A message finally pings through. It is followed by another. And then a stream of them.

'Is that mum?'

'Hang on.'

Ella taps the screen. Keeps tapping and swiping. With her hair tucked behind her ear, I see her smile. Energy sparkles through her, making her legs bounce and shoulders dance.

'What is it, Els?'

'Norman has dumped Josephine.'

'*Norman*? Seriously? People still call their children *Norman*? Wait. You *fancied* a boy called Norman? Oh, Ella.'

I always thought that Ella would only ever fall for a boy called Zac, or Zeppelin, or Ziggy. Something cool. But Norman? What were his parent's thinking? It's like a joke name for a favourite wooden spoon.

'Mum sounds pissed off,' she says.

'Of course she does. That's her factory setting.'

'Wait. No. She sounds . . .'

'What? What does she sound? Irrational?'

'No. Worried . . . *Really* worried. She's sent seventy-three messages.'

Cruising past the hills and mountains, the stone walls and field gates, Ella reads the messages and listens to the voicemails left by Kirsty. Apparently, Kirsty began by taking out most of her temper on Ella, asking why she hadn't texted as they agreed. And then it softened to:

> Please call me back the minute you get this scrunchie xxxx

> I'm worried about you. It's mum xxxxxxx

But by the end it was:

'See? Told you she'd be being irrational. Don't worry about it, Els.' I smirk at the thought of Kirsty giving me grief via Ella. When she hears how responsible I've been, looking out for *our little girl* ever since we left Tenderbridge, she'll have to take it all back. 'What did you say?' I ask.

'Nothing,' Ella says. 'I've lost reception again.'

Looking out of the window, I snort a laugh.

After uncharacteristically paying the cabbie an extra one pound fifty over the fare, here we are again, standing in the middle of the Cannock driveway. The buildings are ahead of us; the gate that Ella had been clambering on is just over to the side. It feels like we've only been gone for five minutes. I wish that we could do it all again.

Actually, rethinking, bollocks to that.

'Can we just get our things and go?' Ella says.

'Sure we can. We've got plenty of time before the . . . Oh, for—' I turn around and wave like a lunatic at the cabbie before he can disappear down the long driveway, but he must not have been looking back. Idiot.

'Look, there's a police car over there. Maybe they can give us a lift,' Ella says.

'It's worth asking.'

Somewhere, out of sight, I hear the blatting helicopter rotor again. Some poor sods must have got lost out in the wilderness. I know exactly how they must be feeling.

The policeman that the car belongs to is sitting on

the wall of the camping paddock, staring aimlessly at the gate through which Ella and I headed just over two days ago. There's a teacup on the wall next to him. What a job that must be, a copper out here with nothing to do, stopping by local campsites for a friendly brew.

'Alright, mate,' I say as we stroll by.

'Hello there,' he replies dreamily, preoccupied by the view, boredom or some other reverie.

'Look, Els. Someone's mended the tent.'

'Step away from the girl!' the copper screeches from behind us.

Ella and I glance at each other.

'Get away from her this instant.' The copper, now on his feet, holds warning hands out in front of him, telling a pack of wild dogs that, if they attack, they might well find themselves in trouble.

'Sorry, mate? *Me*?' I ask, prodding myself in the chest.

'Move away from her now, sir,' the policeman replies, taking measured paces towards us.

'Look, she's my *daughter*,' I say, staying right where I am, next to Ella. 'I'm *not* a child snatcher. I wish people would stop thinking I am.'

'Seriously,' Ella adds, 'my dad wants nothing to do with children most of the time, believe me.'

Folding his arms over his chest, the policeman seems bemused. 'You're certain?'

'Yes!' I say. 'I'm a musician. In a band.'

'What band are you in, then?' The policeman says, cocking his head to one side.

'Spanky Macaca. You probably haven't heard of us. You might have.'

'You're not in a band,' Ella says, joining the conversation. 'Remember? The band broke up.'

'Oh yeah. I'm not in a band anymore. I've gone solo.'

'*Dad.*' Ella kicks dirt at me. 'Just because the band has broken up doesn't mean you've gone solo, you dick.'

'I have,' I say, turning to face her. 'I totally forgot to tell you. I did a solo show at The Tap just before we left. And then yesterday, or whenever it was, after you said about Liam being cool, I decided that I've definitely gone solo.'

'*Dad.*'

'What are you doing all the way out here with the girl?' the policeman asks, interrupting us. 'I've been told to keep an eye out for you.'

'We're on a trip,' I say. 'A dad and daughter on tour.'

'It's not a fucking tour,' Ella says. 'How many *times* do I have to tell you?'

'Sorry, officer. It's not really a tour, just a trip. And I didn't break a promise by saying it, okay, Ella? I just forgot for a minute. I'm allowed one free slip up. And don't swear,' I add.

'It's been the maddest trip ever,' Ella tells the policeman. 'Mad as frog shit.'

'Your father just told you not to swear, young lady.'

'See?' I say to Ella. 'Go on, officer. Arrest her.'

'I don't think I can arrest her just for being rude,' the policeman says.

'And you can't arrest me for being her father and getting her lost. Even if I did accidentally manage to get her, sort of, kidnapped.'

'The dolls,' Ella says, pinching the bridge of her nose. 'He just wanted someone to play with his dolls.'

It's hard to say exactly who cracks first, but Ella and I both burst out laughing. After all we've shared, what can we really do but laugh?

The copper doesn't know who to prod scorn at next. 'So, who is this kidnapper?'

A pair of police cars tear up to the gates, stark blue and white strobe lights flashing over the woodland trees and the cottages. A smattering of birds flocks out of the trees, startled to the sky. Two police officers – one male and one female – climb out of the first car; another male officer steps out of the second car. With his thick moustache, he looks like a Freddie Mercury impersonator.

From the first car, the female officer removes a handcuffed Thomas, still dressed in his onesie.

'There he is. Hi, Thomas.'

'Hello, Sir John,' Thomas says. 'Ella.'

'Hi, Thomas!'

'This gentleman says that he met you outside the pub yesterday,' the female officer announces. 'Is that correct?'

'Yeah. We were lost and he helped us. I think it was yesterday. Why have you handcuffed him? What has he done wrong?'

'He's a big bugger, isn't he?' the policeman who was waiting for us at the campsite says. 'Apparently, he's a kiddie snatcher.' He nods in my direction. 'That's what this bloke said.'

'He's *not*,' Ella says, stamping her foot. 'We told you already, dickhead. He just wants someone to play with.'

Cheeky little minx. I've never got away with calling a copper a dickhead before.

'He really hasn't done anything wrong,' I say, stepping alongside Ella. For emphasis, I stamp my foot, too.

I see that Nell and Andrew have come out to watch proceedings. They are clearly still a bit unsure about me, and they don't seem entirely surprised by the drama we have brought to their quiet vale. Even so, they respond to the wave I send in their direction. Lovely people.

'You said he kidnapped you,' our copper says.

'*Well* . . . that's not what I meant. We went to his house of our own free will, pretty much. We both fell asleep there, and then this morning he played with Ella. She loved it. Never seen her happier.'

'Thomas put on a puppet show for me,' Ella says. 'He did *Frozen*.'

'Oh, is *that* who those two princess dolls were?' I say, slapping my forehead. 'I thought I recognised them.'

'Well,' Ella says, 'Elsa, the one with the white hair, starts off as a princess. But when her parents drown, she ends up becoming queen. Anna, her younger sister, is still a princess, but she doesn't really care about being a princess – she's kind of awkward, see – and all she wants to do is marry Prince Hans. But Elsa doesn't want them to get married. And *that's* when—'

'Okay, okay, we get the idea,' Freddie Mercury says.

'No, shut up, this is important,' Ella says, shooting authority down for a second time.

I love this girl so much.

'At the end, Hans locks Anna up, even though she used to love him. And then he tries to kill Elsa, but Anna stops him and she nearly dies. Or well, she does die, but . . . Anyway. There's more to it than that, but that's the gist.'

'Doesn't Anna end up with the bloke with the deer?' I ask.

'Yeah,' Ella says, looking me up and down. 'How do you know about what happens in *Frozen*?'

'It's amazing, the things you pick up in the pub.'

'So, did this, err . . . *man* kidnap you or not?' the officer holding Thomas's arm asks, trying to catch up. 'Did he even attempt to kidnap you, or cause you harm in any way?'

'No,' I say. 'Not really.'

'No,' Ella says, another stomp. 'He's kind. Even if he is a bit dodgy.'

'Why did you handcuff him?' I ask again.

'Just because,' the female officer replies with a shrug.

'And well,' says the male one. 'He's a big bloke and he's dressed as Winnie the Pooh. You can never be too careful.'

'He's as harmless as Piglet,' I say.

'Thanks, Sir John.'

'That's alright, Sir Thomas.'

We are finally allowed to stop answering stupid questions and Thomas is taken home. Before that, we found out that he left the house dressed as Winnie, even though I'd advised him not to, just to make sure we got in the taxi alright. Even if that was an insanely idiotic thing to do, it's quite sweet of him, really.

Seeing him standing by the side of the road, the coppers pulled over and asked Thomas if he had seen us, one thing led to another, and he let slip his little secret that he had sort of kidnapped us and drugged me. He might just be a simple bloke, and mostly harmless, but the safest place for Thomas really is to stay hidden away in his mum's house, playing with his dolls.

Once the madness has subsided, I stand alone with

Ella to take one last look at the land of our adventure. I put my arm around her; she leans her head against me. Neither of us says a word. We don't need to.

I don't exactly cry, but I am so content that I could.

Until I start thinking about Canada again. And how close, now, Ella is to leaving.

thirty-seven

Our original policeman, who I found out is called David, agreed to give us a lift to the bus station. Standing by his car, I watch the helicopter fly off over the hills. Apparently, it was called into service to look for us two, when all we actually needed was an active mobile signal or a working phone box. Plonkers.

'David,' I say, just as he is ducking his head into the car. 'This might be lot to ask, but I was wondering if you could take us to the coach terminal in Cardiff instead. It's just, I'm supposed to be back at work tomorrow, and I think we've probably missed the last bus.'

I don't have a clue if we have missed the last bus or not, truth told. I barely even know what day it is.

'Well, it will be a slow day here,' David replies, 'now we've found you two. I don't see that being a problem. Let me check with my sarge.'

'Or maybe you could ask that helicopter to come back and pick us up?'

Whether David ignored me or just didn't hear me, I'm not sure.

Ella is giving me a look that I can't read. She has a twinkle in her eye, accompanied by one of her partially hidden grins.

'What?' I say.

'Nothing,' she replies.

Ella sleeps the whole way to Cardiff. She must have been hungry for it; a bit starved, by her usual standards, of sleep and of food. David gives the impression he's not up for a chat either, so I spend the journey humming to myself and staring out the window, twiddling the Melatonin pills through my fingers.

When she does finally open her eyes, Ella is surprised to find she has woken up at the airport.

Before leaving, I give David twenty quid beer money. He tries to decline, but I insist; so he takes it, of course. A second twinkle and smirk from Ella, but I don't question it this time. If I could win that look even occasionally . . .

Ella phones Kirsty to tell her of our alternative plans: that we have decided to fly home and will be arriving at City Airport just after seven. Not that I'm listening in, exactly, but I overhear her say that it hasn't been a bad trip, even if it was a bit weird, at times.

'No, he's not *drunk*, mum . . .' she adds. 'He might have had one. He always smells like that.'

While Ella was sleeping, David said he didn't mind if I cracked open a couple of my leftover cans. Watching the countryside slipping past the window of his party wagon, I drank them slowly – mostly because they were warm. Tenderbridge could do with a few more top cops like David. He would do well there.

Having teased myself that the journey home would be easy, I assumed that getting a ticket for a plane would be as simple as bunking the fare on a train. Ella is okay and can travel without identification, but as an adult holding a massive bag with a broken tent in it, I need to show ID.

I pull everything out of my wallet. Mangled shreds of paper. Out of date Johnnies. Bundles of leftover cash.

'Ah. Here you go,' I say to Natalie – it's strange to be back in the world of name badges so soon.

'A store card is not a valid form of identification, I'm afraid, sir,' Natalie replies. 'Not just because it doesn't have your photo on it. If you haven't got a passport, we can accept a driving licence or a military personnel card.'

'Hmmm.' With a sideways glance at Ella, I continue picking through the piles of grimy detritus.

When I was banned from driving after joyriding over the bowling lawn, I had accidentally walked away from court, a little bit tipsy, with the driving licence still in my pocket, and subsequently managed to lose it somewhere. The DVLA repeatedly sent letters, ordering that I must surrender my licence to them. They just didn't seem to understand.

"It must have got lost in the post," I kept telling them. "I am a postman, remember. This shit happens."

Still they persisted pestering me. So I was eventually forced to forge a proof of postage, obtained from one of the lads at work. Pulling rank on the gov-dot-co-dot had been a very proud moment indeed.

As with the rest of the junk cluttering my wallet, I had not a clue that my licence was hidden away in there until I was standing at the airport ticket counter, poking through the fluff. A gift of fortuity heading my way, for once.

We arrive safely at London City Airport, a gateway to the world less than an hour away from the town that I hardly ever leave. Kirsty totters towards Ella – who has just woken up, obviously – with hairspray so thick that not a single hair in her bouffant shifts with each of her unstable steps. Her Burberry coat flaps at the sides of her slinky dress.

It's no surprise that Kirsty's dolled herself up to collect Ella from the airport. She used to do the same thing when picking Ella up from school, as if photographers were going to be waiting, all primed to get a shot that they could sell to *Vogue*.

When she's finished pounding Ella with heavy kisses and clawed cuddles, Kirsty reluctantly acknowledges me through her crocodile tears – I mean, even though her daughter was missing, why destroy those delicate layers of expensive makeup?

'Thank you for returning my daughter, even though you did your best to screw it up. Look at you,' she says to Ella. 'Your coat's all grubby.'

'*Mum.*' Ella takes a step away from Kirsty's flailing attempts to pat the dirt from her coat. A step towards me. 'That's not fair. You weren't there.'

'How many fathers would get their daughter lost so far in the middle of nowhere that the police have to get involved? Useless man.'

'And how many stepdads would stay in the car after their stepdaughter has been found?' Ella retorts.

'Well . . .' Kirsty says, her pout protruding to ridiculous proportions, 'we didn't want to pay for parking, if we didn't have to. Come on, darling, we've got to go. Dan's waiting for us in the bus lane.'

'Do you want a lift, dad?' Ella asks. 'We are going to the same place.'

'That's alright, Els,' I reply. 'I need to pick up a couple of things on the way home, anyway.'

In a flash of yellow, Ella crashes into me and reaches around my waist. Gripping onto me, her head rests right against my heart.

'Thanks, dad,' she says; a big smile, huge eyes. 'I'll never have a trip like it again.'

Moments later, I watch her walk away.

Kirsty is owning Ella, smothering the yellow coat within her designer wing. Ella keeps glancing back. I lift my hand, but do not wave. A mime artist trapped inside a glass box.

Using her elbow, Ella manages to shrug off Kirsty's heavily cladded arm, bangles and all. It seems she's now being told off about something. Whether it's the trip, the no contact, the fact that she likes me again, I have no way of knowing. Whatever. It is enough to distract Ella from her backwards glances. Until they are gone.

With Kirsty whisking Ella away like that, it feels like a practice run.

Eventually my fingers curl down towards my palm. I lower my hand. My eyes are fixed on the sliding doors. I bite my bottom lip, as if trying to recall a daydream.

I'll never have a trip like it again . . .

I think that Ella meant it in a positive way. She would have stamped her foot if she hadn't.

I wasn't just declining Ella's offer because I would sooner listen to Take That than have to get a lift back to Tenderbridge with Kirsty and Dan. Nor had I lied. So I pick up my bags and head straight for the nearest place that sells beer.

thirty-eight

Upon waking the next morning, I find myself yearning for a moist, broken tent. Or cold, wet ground cushioned by infested bark. Even Thomas's backbreaking armchair would do. But no, I am in my own disgusting bed.

I'm not familiar with the City Airport area of London. Especially in the tired, smelly and semi-pissed state I was by the time I left the pub. It's not that I got drunk exactly, but drunk enough to make barging the massive tent bag through legions of moody commuters that bit harder.

The odour of damp throughout the flat is even more powerfully pungent than usual, having intensified in my absence. When I finish moping around, I plug my phone in. Waiting for it to suck the pennies from the electric meter, I feel a bit under the weather. It could be because of camping in the rain and walking about in wet clothes, or perhaps my twenty-four hours of abstinence, I don't know.

My phone crackles to life with a steady chorus of

pings. There are a few messages from Darren, but I skip straight to the one from Ella.

> thx again dad :) my bed has nvr felt so
> gd! nite nite luv u xxxx

After reading it for the second time, I can see only a blurry mess of black and white.

Another text pops up.

Wiping my eyes, I hear myself whimper, trying to clear the swelling of my heart, desperate to see what else has arrived on my screen.

> You're late!

Holy shit!

Brian really should've remembered to remind me to set an alarm – not that the message would have got through, I suppose. Thank goodness I was too exhausted to do anything but fall directly into bed when I made it home last night. Too tired to experiment with Thomas's mum's Melatonin, even.

Sitting on the floor, I ponder what excuse to use this time. All kinds of reasons slingshot through my head. I even consider blaming his tent. In fact, I haven't seen the huge red bag this morning, and it would be hard not to notice in this tiny flat. It must have produced a hell of a bomb scare wherever I left it.

Actually, telling Brian that I was caught up in a bomb scare would be a great lie.

> frgt 2 st alrm in sn xxxxxxx

I press send.

Bloody hell, telling the boring truth felt pretty good. The row of kisses was just an accident, though. Perhaps it shows sincerity.

When I head straight through to see him, Brian isn't at all angry with me for being hours late. Having had a few days off, apparently he knew I would be late, so he doesn't even issue me a third third warning. Hearing the cold bug in my voice, and watching me wipe my nose on the sleeve of my uniform, he actually congratulates me for making it to work. It does my head in. If I'd thought about my illness properly when I was texting him, I would have had a valid reason to bunk off.

'Do you think I should go home, then, Bri? I probably should do, really. Rather than spread germs around.'

'I think you should get to work, John,' Brian replies, a glance at the clock. 'You know we're short-handed. And you don't sound that bad.'

'Have you heard anything about Jason's balls?' I ask. 'Are they better yet?'

'Let's talk about Jason's balls another time, yeah.'

He's probably right. Because I have to get to work, I don't mention the tent, either. And Brian doesn't ask.

The messages from Darren were mostly banal, those that even made sense. There was only one that captured my attention. And I need to speak with him about it pretty damn urgently.

'What do you mean my sex tape is trending?' I ask

him in The Humphrey, as soon as I finish work, before I have even sat down.

Darren has a baked bean stuck in his scraggly beard. It looks like a massive, grotesque pimple. I'm not going to tell him. Let him walk around all day with it, for all I care. The baked bean isn't the only difference about him, either. Darren's skin has turned from milky white to the colour of watermelon flesh.

'How was your trip?'

'Darren, I'll tell you about my trip right after you tell me what the hell that means, about the sex tape.'

'Oh, yeah. It's wild, man.'

'I agree. It is wild, Darren. But how is it news again?'

'Apparently, when you were in The Tap you told Kev about it.'

'Did I?' I slap my forehead. 'So *that's* why Kev was acting smug when I was doing my solo show.'

I remember how the atmosphere in The Tap made me feel like there was some big joke, but no one was telling me the punchline; everyone giving me the weird looks. Now it all makes sense.

Oh, *Jesus Christ*.

'It's funny, mate.'

'Funny, Darren?' I'm half-tempted to pluck the baked bean out of his beard and stick it up his nose. 'It might have been funny five years ago.'

Back then, it had taken a while to succeed in erasing all this from my memory. And yet here it is, once again, swooping down, delivered by the stork of idiocy.

This must be Kev's payback for the hanging baskets.

My leg is jittery. It boings against the underside of the

table. My mind races to measure the consequences of the resurrection of my goddamn sex tape.

'How the hell did Kev find it?'

'Don't you remember?' Darren says, sitting there and grinning his stupid baked bean face off. 'You called it *Famous Singer In A Famous Band Shags A Beauty*. Thought it would be good for your industry profile. You know, when everyone was making sex tapes.'

God, I *had*. Putting *Famous* in there twice had been a touch of genius, so I thought at the time. Such would be the intrigue to the browsers of popular porn sites that my sex tape would reach a maximum number of hits. That had been the intention, at least. All that actually happened was it was shared around the pub, and my level of local fame rose from *failed musician* to *failed musician with his own hilariously shit sex tape*. Expounding my delusions, at its peak *Famous Singer In A Famous Band Shags A Beauty* received a consumer rating of twenty-one percent, and had been viewed forty-seven times.

I try to stop my leg dancing. It slows to a bounce, but starts boinging again of its own accord.

'Do you know who's watching it?'

'People in the pub, mostly,' Darren replies. 'But it's easier to share around these days, with Instygram, TitTok and whatnot. People don't really think it's you, though. They think it's Craig David.'

'*Craig David*?' I exclaim loud enough to turn heads.

'That's how bad the video is. I'll show you.'

'Show me? Why on Earth . . .' I stop mid-sentence. If everyone else is talking about it, I probably should watch it. I can hardly remember it. 'Alright. Go on then.'

Darren spins his phone around and there it is, the blurry image of a man, gormless and grotesque, clearly very drunk, and absolutely nothing like Craig David. It's me. On the screen, I can clearly see the image of myself. The only thing that the idiot on the screen has that Craig David has is a goatee – it was a very brief phase, one that's popped its chin up over the years after I've been listening to Nirvana.

Hiding the phone in my hands, I press play.

The screen spins around to show a girl's behind. The curve of her buttocks wink beneath the sparkly, green leather miniskirt. Her long, blondish hair whips against her boob tube and the base of her back. Soundtracked by the heavy breathing of the person holding the phone (a very drunk me), *the girl pushes a toilet cubicle door open. Once inside, the door slams closed behind them and there is a glimpse of her face, this "beauty".*

I remember prettier dinner ladies from my school.

'Who?' I say, narrowing my eyes at the screen.

'Wasn't that Megan?' Darren replies, taking a sip of his beer. 'The girl from The Bell?'

'I have no idea.' But I definitely agree with him about having a sip of beer.

The girl's head dives towards the phone and some very noisy kissing ensues.

"C'mon, darlin'," the voice of the idiot holding the phone says – Rather than sounding like me, or Craig David, the gruff voice is more like a pub darts commentator playing Long John Silver in a small-town pantomime – *"Let's get that up, yeah."*

The cameraman attempts to tug on the girl's skirt and the screen begins to shake. She takes over from his pathetic one-

handed efforts, lifting the skirt herself to show her bare bottom; the big, pink shape of a palm print on one cheek.

I feel myself begin to blush, watching this, the man who thought he had given up on dignity a long time ago.

"C'mon, then," the girl says, a high-pitched cheep. "I ain't got all night."

There is more blurry screen action as he unzips himself . . .

Thankfully, my unsteady camerawork is all over the place here, succeeding in showing nothing more than damp colour and wet tiles. When panting, and all kinds of ridiculous phrases such as *"You bloody love it"*, start blurting out of the speaker, Darren quickly shows me how to turn the sound down. Even when the cameraman finally manages to start having sex with Megan, there is mercifully little on display.

The drunk pest tries his best to slip the camera between Megan's legs, but doesn't seem to understand that the lens is on the back of the phone, so succeeds only in capturing ankles, heels, a jangling belt buckle, the disgusting floor, the filthy language, and the occasional close up of his finger.

"There you go," he says fifty seconds later.

And that is when the cameraman turns the phone around, showing—

my stupid, pitiful face. For a fleeting second, there I am, clear on the screen.

"Spanky Ma-caaa-caaa," he says, eyes rolling around in their sockets.

Following that, there is a bit of rustling, some wobbly visuals, a close up of my tongue poking out as I attempt to work out how to stop recording, and then the video shuts off.

It is not a sex tape. It's a horror.

Before I hand the treacherous phone back to Darren, I notice that the percentage rating has gone down to eighteen percent. And the views have gone up. To over—

'Four-hundred *thousand*?'

'Yeah. That's when it got out that it's Craig David.'

At least it's not as bad as I thought it might be. I just look like a drunk idiot. And also, even though my sex tape is only five years old, I do look quite a bit younger. Anyone watching it would surely need to have known me back then to have any real chance of recognising me. Which is only slightly better than the fact that I was too pissed to reveal anything explicitly X-rated. Watching it back just makes me feel as ridiculous as the prat that I depicted myself to be. And that is before even considering that, at one point in my life, I decided it would be a good idea to advertise myself as a fifty-second stud.

'What's happened to you, then?' I ask Darren, once the waves of embarrassment have begun to ebb.

'What do you mean?'

'You are burnt to crackling, mate.'

'Oh yeah.' Darren carefully touches a fingertip to his forehead. I don't think I've ever seen anyone's skin turn such a devilish colour, except maybe when Bea's really gone for it on a sunbed. It does look very painful. Jesus, even his eyelids are burnt. 'I was collecting money for a charity outside The Forum, wasn't I.'

The best small room in the world.

The Forum is in the posh town just a short stumble down the road. The venue itself is mostly famed as being a converted public toilet. Perhaps it is an irony that we leave our town, which is a toilet, to go and watch bands play in a place that used to be one.

For local musicians, to perform at The Forum is a rite of passage, something to aspire to, treading in the footsteps of bands who were to become legends. Spanky Macaca had our one opportunity, supporting Biffy Clyro when they were just another upcoming Scottish band.

But I screwed it up, of course.

An incident in a multistorey car park that involved whisky, an inflatable unicorn, helium balloons, pre-made gravy, and the police meant that we didn't make it to the show. Those were the days, sliding off the shoulders of giants.

One evening, years later, I was listening to Simon from Biffy chatting to Zane Lowe about their early days. There he was, on national radio, talking about the time their support band nicked most of the rider. It transpires that The Biff never forgave me for thieving their booze. It took quite a long while for the others to forgive me for that one, too.

'Two questions,' I say, warming off Darren's radiance. 'How did you get so badly sunburnt collecting for charity? And *why* were you collecting for charity in the first place?'

'Er, yeah, good questions,' he says. 'I fancy this bird who works at The Forum, so thought volunteering might impress her.'

'Okay, that makes sense. But what about . . .' I spread a hand across the air in front of my face, as if washing it down with an invisible sponge.

'I fell asleep, didn't I. Only laid down for a minute, but dozed off. Next thing I know, I've woken up looking like this and found out that some bastard had nicked my bucket.'

'Did you get a date, with the girl?'

'No, mate. I scared her, walking in all red. Haven't seen her since. Quit the Jungle Gym, too.'

'Have you? I thought you liked working there. All the yummy mummies and the foreign *au pairs*.'

'The incident with the crisp packet hit me hard, man.' Darren holds up his still-bandaged finger and sadness becomes his face. 'I just can't work in such a dangerous environment anymore. Danger everywhere in that place.'

'It surely can't be that dangerous, Darren. Children play there.'

'I can't believe they let them in, to be honest. It's atrocious. What if it was one of them who slipped on the oil I spilt?'

'*So* . . . were you fired?' I ask, reading between the squiggly lines.

'Yeah,' he says. 'I was. Anyway, I asked Brian for my old job back.'

'Oh, yeah? What did he say?'

'Didn't say anything. Just laughed.'

I can't help but laugh at the dopey demon in front of me, too. Sometimes I wonder how Darren has managed to survive into his forties. Sometimes I wonder how he manages to do things like cross roads by himself, and other tricky stuff like that.

'I was thinking,' he continues, tormenting his brain-cell. 'It's weird, isn't it, how we recognise people from their faces?'

'What do you mean, *recognise people from their faces*?' Even if I'd taken a tambourine-full of hallucinogens, I wouldn't have expected him to come out with that. He must have got heroically stoned last night.

'We've not seen each other for, like, nearly a week, yeah?'

'*Right . . .*'

'But you walk in and recognise me straight away, even though I'm all red.'

'Why is that funny? I've known you most of my life, Darren. And you always stick out like a . . . plum.'

'Yeah, but . . . I dunno. I was just thinking about it.'

'You want to watch out, mate, with all that thinking.'

Even so, Darren's eyes are searching around, seeking out his next thought like a butterfly catcher.

'Oh yeah, that's what I wanted to ask you,' he finally says, a bit aggressively. 'What solo show?'

'What solo show what?'

'You said earlier that you played a solo show in The Tap. You know, when your sex tape started trending?'

'Keep your voice down,' I say, glancing at the tables around us. 'Yeah, I did do a solo show. Kev asked me to. It was pretty good, except for everyone giving me the weird looks.'

'But what about the band? Why didn't you ask us to play?'

'Because the band has broken up, Darren. That's the only reason why I agreed to do a solo show. And you've got a broken finger, so you wouldn't have been able to play anyway.'

'Broke up? What, Spanky Macaca broke up? No one told me.'

'You were there when it happened, mate. When Mick said he wanted to focus on his fish.'

'*Oh*, then, yeah. Wack.' Darren scratches his face and the baked bean falls out of his beard, sadly. 'Maybe Mick can give me a job?' he says, picking at the saucy crust left by the bean.

I can't even be bothered to respond to that. In the unlikely event that Mick did agree to let Darren work in his village fishmonger's, there is no way it would last. It wouldn't take long for Darren to slip on a scallop, or accidentally turn the freezers off for the night instead of the lights.

'Hello, boys.'

Toothy Charlie's wondrously bright dentures radiate down upon us.

'Alright, Charlie?' Darren says, giggling. Just looking at Toothy is always enough to set him off.

'Am I alright?' Toothy says. 'Hang on a mo, Dazzler.' Toothy puts two fingers against his wrist, looks up to the ceiling, serious and thoughtful for a moment. I can see right up his hairy nose. 'Yeah, I think I must be alright,' he says. 'I can feel a pulse.'

That sets them both off. I smile, too. That was one of his better ones, which is saying absolutely nothing.

'But listen, right. Listen yeah.' Toothy leans in, as he always does when he's about to tell his next worst joke. 'I was telling the wife the other day she's like a laxative. "Like a laxative?" says she. "Me? Like a laxative? How the hell am I like a laxative?"'

Darren's already giggling. 'Oh, Charlie, man. You are funny.'

'No, Daz,' Charlie says, frowning. 'That isn't the end of the joke.'

'Oh. Sorry, Charlie. How's your wife like a laxlitive?'

Bloody *laxlitive*. Darren doesn't even understand half of Toothy's unfunny tosh.

'Well, Dazzler. Well, I tells her. Like a laxative, she irritates the shit out of me.'

A group at a table over by the pillar further along from us start laughing. Toothy turns around, thinking his joke is the reason for their mirth. Realising that they are laughing at something among themselves wipes half the smile from his moronic face.

I could be sitting at their table. They all have normal haircuts and clothes with buttons. They're drinking wine and enjoying each other's company. While all I have is a friend who marvels at the fact that you can recognise people by their faces.

But this is it. This is the life that I have chosen. Or the life that was chosen for me.

My cold hasn't properly kicked in yet, or it's not a bad one. I just can't stop sniffing. The beer has helped a bit, but this morning's route didn't. Maybe I will take tomorrow off work.

'Is that a cold you've got there, Roger?'

'Not really, Charlie,' I say. 'Just the sniffles.'

'Right, yeah. I see. Yeah. It reminds me of when I was standing there on my wedding day, my wife walking up the aisle. So, when she's walking up the aisle, yeah, I thought I had a cold, too. Turns out that I didn't have a proper cold, just cold feet.'

'I've got to go.'

Leaving the two of them wheezing, I walk past the table with normal people and step out through the doors of The Humphrey.

The grim high street greets me.

I breathe in the fumes.

A little chav is feeding chips to the pigeons. A bald

bloke with long grey hair, wearing a manky dressing gown, is pushing a shopping trolley with a big old box telly and a rusty barbeque inside it along the edge of the curb. In the window of a café opposite, I see an old dear picking her nose while simultaneously eating a toasted sandwich. Outside the betting shop, there is an argument going on between a chubby bird with a pushchair and a skinny, pasty prick wearing a vest, their screams louder than the traffic. A ganja cloud blown out by a stocky, shirtless, tough-looking lad swamps me. The kid he's carrying – shaved head, pierced ears – glares at me over his shoulder. I lift my foot to get the hell out of here, and the sole of my boot peels away from the elastic grab of the chewing gum that it is stuck to.

The trip with Ella might have only been brief, and I have been back here for less than twenty-four hours, but already it feels like I never left this place.

thirty-nine

After work each day, I have been going to the pub by the river, not only to avoid the stares and the smirks. It is quiet here. I watch the flow of water wash by. The people travelling over the bridge, heading into the south side.

I sit here. I sip my beer. And I think.

When we first arrived home from the trip, I wasn't drinking much, by my standards. Yet now, always alone with my thoughts, my consumption is creeping slowly upwards. Watching the world and the days tick by, the fine sand trickles through the hourglass, the grains piling on top of me, rising until the moment that Ella leaves.

We haven't seen each other since we got back from Wales, but Ella and I have been exchanging regular texts. Even so, there have been no more **luv u** at the end of her messages, just the occasional **x**.

These past days, I have barely left the flat without my phone charger, should I miss a message from my girl. I press send and I wait, staring at the river and life passing by. I gaze at the days, drinking while I impatiently study patience, for I've learned that staring at my phone does not make it *ping*.

> wna meet up xxxx

I wrote in the last message, and the one before that.

> hey dad! im sooooo busy catchn up w ppl sayn bye n stuff. deffo c u b4 i leave tho x

And then my heart will leap for a single **x**. Never has one tiny character meant so much to me.

> gotta sort Josephine out 1st

As if I need reminding about the Norman situation.

Watching all the strangers going about their day, I am consumed by nothing but thoughts of Ella. It is now only days until she leaves, and the future keeps coming.

What if she goes without saying goodbye? What if I have already seen her for the last time? Never have I felt so hollow. In an empty cavern it can be heard so much louder, the sound of something breaking.

To fill that empty space, I drink.

And then I drink more.

Being by myself has never much suited me. Even now, sitting by the river, part of me wants to commiserate by getting wasted with a bunch of strangers, and dance on tables, and do other stupid shit. Just like I've always done. But instead, wading through a headful of noise, I drift in the relative silence.

Another daydream about our trip is at its end, so I

finish the last dribbles of my beer, ready to leave here and get a couple of cans from the shop; maybe go and sit on the riverbank. Just as I am pulling the plug out of the socket, a message arrives.

It's from Ella. Asking if I'm free on Friday.

Springier of step, I take a different route home, to bypass the high street. The longer circuit leads me to the Tender Bridge.

Being the fulcrum of the town's divide, most people assume that the Great Bridge, separating the wheat from the chavs, is the centre that the town grew from, leaving this place all-but-forgotten. I used to come here when I wanted to be alone, usually after Kirsty and I had been giving each other earfuls. I don't know why I never come here anymore. The neutrality of its environment, away from the horror show of the town.

I lean on the latticed rail of the little arched bridge, resting my chin on my hands. I watch small birds flitting in and out of the shrubs and trees.

Once upon a long while ago, the last time someone bothered to renovate this place, the bridge was painted a mid-shade of green, partially camouflaging it among the flora, complementing the nature to be found here. A secret delight to discover beneath the huge weeping willow, the tips of its branches dipping into the trickling tributary. The hidden charm of town so lacking.

All alone out here it has been neglected, allowed to become rundown. Even the little plaque on it can't be read anymore, covered in foul graffiti. Beneath my arms, the green paint peels from the splintered wood. I watch a carrier bag fluttering in the stream, its forward course denied by the rusted trolley that it is stuck to. Among the litter on the banks, and also decomposing in the stream, is a confetti of tickets and discarded fines, blown here from the car park on the other side of the pathway. Sorry flowers, spent of life, hang from the shrubs. Why would anyone bother to come out here and deadhead them, when most will visit the castle and the river?

For a while longer I pause here, listening to the birds that share this abandoned view. I stand and I stare. My reflection stares back at me, a hopeless dummy floating in the water.

Walking homeward from the Tender Bridge, I pass the entrance of the arcade, a covered walkway that used to have the coolest shops in town: Our Price, Blockbuster, Barney's Toy Shop. A jeweller's window that sparkled gold and silver. A shop called Pin Ups, with posters of Prince, Debbie Harry, Grace Jones, and Marty McFly in the window. Now there are only abandoned units. Post piling inside doorways. Discoloured frontages covered with graffitied To Let signs. The spiderwebs of cracked windows.

Generally ignoring this slice of the town, in the same way that most people do except for the graffiti artists and the drifts of dead leaves, I'm not sure that I've ever noticed the flower stall in the entrance of the arcade. It is a bright explosion of colour within the drab, monochromatic background.

I find myself wandering towards it.

Upon benches and shelves propped on top of plant pots

and upturned crates is a floral display of every shade that the eye can absorb. Bursting clouds of aroma overpower the stench of fumes travelling through from the high street.

A woman steps out from behind the stand. She sees me and smiles. I double take; my eyes trace their route slowly backwards.

Her hair is tied in a long, thick plait, draped over one shoulder, dark against her tanned skin. Her hand dips into the pocket of a leather utility belt tied at her waist. When she withdraws the hand, now holding a thread of twine, I see no wedding ring.

Rather than browsing the flowers that drew me here, when she looks up again, I am suddenly aware of how odd, possibly even unsettling, I must appear, standing here, watching her.

'Do you need any help there?' she asks, taking a step towards me.

For some reason I take half-a-step back.

'I have a daughter,' I hear coming out of my mouth.

'Are you looking for some flowers for her?'

'Um . . .' I scratch my head.

Am I looking for flowers?

With a hand inside my pocket, I give my balls a quick squeeze to calm me down.

'Sorry . . . Yes,' I say, taking a semi-confident half-step closer. 'I'd like to buy some flowers. For Ella. My daughter. She likes yellow.'

'Okay—'

'I think.'

'Okay. Then I have just the thing,' the woman says, removing a flower from a bucket. 'This is a floribunda rose, a cross between polyantha and hybrid teas. That's what gives it this amazing spray of petals. Even though they're smaller than traditional polyanthus, the bloom has a similar array to a carnation. I think it's a sacrifice worth making for the scent.' Her hazel eyes flicker over the rose, as transfixed as I am on her. 'I just love them.'

'Then I'll take all the ones in that bucket,' I say.

'Sure?' She flashes her smile, luminous and charming. 'You have a very lucky daughter.'

'I do,' I reply. 'Well . . . I . . . Um . . .'

I follow the flower lady to the far end of the stand, where she wraps paper of various colours as a petally arrangement around the flowers. I try to discreetly shake my captivation and look at her in a more usual manner, less of a gawp; in the way that people normally look at other human beings.

'I really like your stand,' I say to fill the silence. 'Tenderbridge needs a bit of colour.'

'Thanks!' she replies, with what what seemed to be genuine appreciation. 'I'd dig up the high street and turn it into a wildflower meadow, if I could.'

That's it. She's adorable.

I have known lust at first sight. After a few beers, I can wander into any pub, or travel agency, or cheap shop in town and easily fall in lust. And I wouldn't even need to bother my balls to stop myself from saying odd or inappropriate things. This feels different.

How can I possibly come across as anything other than an idiot? It would be so much easier if this woman wasn't nice. I wish she was angry, or ugly, or stupid, or something.

'That's going to be eighty-four pounds, please,' she says when she has finished preparing the bouquet.

For a bunch of fucking flowers?

No wonder she said Ella was lucky.

Tugging my wallet from my pocket, still semi-flush with dad's cash, I take out ninety.

'Keep the change,' I say, surprised at how easily I managed to do so after spending nearly a hundred quid on something that will die in days, possibly hours.

'Ah, that's too kind,' she says.

Even if it was too kind, she keeps the change.

I would have done the same thing. If I didn't fancy her, I would have asked for my money back. In fact, I probably would have only bought daffodils.

The flowers don't feel natural in my hand. How am I supposed to hold them? Like a baby? I was never any good at that, either.

I try to think of something else to say; something to keep the conversation going. Anything will do. I look around the arcade, searching for inspiration.

'I really like flowers.'

She smiles, but now it is a pitying smile, accompanied by a slightly confused frown. And that is the exact moment when I realise that I just don't have it anymore. Whatever *it* is. If I ever had *it* at all.

What's Norman got that I haven't got?

She glances at a peeling poster advertising a rave. The sound of a boy racer speeding down the high street echoes through the arcade.

I suppose that I should probably go, but I don't really want to.

'I . . .' we both say at the same time.

'Sorry,' I say. 'After you.'

'I know this is probably going to sound weird . . .' she says, glancing again the poster.

My mouth goes dry. And drier still when she turns to face me.

She lifts the empty bucket Ella's roses were in and holds it to her chest. I hear myself swallow, a gulp that I'm sure travelled around the arcade as loudly as the boy racer's twin exhausts.

'. . . I think that I *know* you,' she says.

'Where do you think you know me from?' I reply. 'I'm certain I'd remember you.'

Charming, John. That's much more charming. Now sniff the flowers.

'Are you a *singer*?' she says, her eyes inquisitively narrowed. 'In a band? I'm sure I saw you playing in The Tap once.'

I dread to ask when that might have been. If she was there on the fateful Christmas with the hanging basket, then I'd really rather not know. Or maybe she's friends with Megan from The Bell, my movie co-star. This could definitely still go one of two ways. If there even is more than one way that it can go.

'That *might* have been me,' I reply. 'I haven't been playing in a band for a while, though. We broke up. I'm working on a new project now.'

'Still in music, I hope,' she says. 'You were great!'

'Well, I was, uh . . .' I begin, before starting again. 'I was, um . . .'

I quickly double-check the wedding finger – because life has taught me some standards, where I have few.

The arcade spins around me. My heart is thrumming like the drone string on a banjo.

Okay. Just say it quickly. Then run away, if you have to.

'I was thinking if you'd like to go for a drink sometime we could talk all about it? If you want. You don't have to.'

When she agrees, it crosses my mind to say that she could get the first round in, seeing as I've already given her the cash towards it. I don't know if I've finally grown up, or what, but it seems like I might have just managed to act like something close to an adult.

What the hell has been happening to me lately? I wonder, heading towards the beer shop with my massive bunch of flowers, and with a scrap of Kraft paper in my pocket, the pretty woman's phone number written on it.

forty

I told Shona, the flower lady, that Friday night is no good for me, but that otherwise I am generally free. When she asked what I was up to, I said that we have band practice. It didn't feel good to tell a lie, the very first time I met her. But it was better than the alternative: that all weekend I am likely to be an absolute mess. I could only hope that, like Darren, she wasn't paying attention to the fact that the band have broken up.

Friday's delivery round seemed endless. When it was finally done, I bought half-a-dozen fruit smoothies and came straight to the park. Sitting on a log, waiting for Ella to arrive, I've drunk three of them and visited the toilet as many times. I am completely buzzing – mostly because I can't wait to see Ella, but also because of how much sugar they shovel into those supposedly healthy, overpriced fruity highs.

My fizzing eyes scan each face that enters the park. I don't recall the last time I was nervous before meeting someone. I'm not even sure it is nerves, exactly. However odd it sounds, I have only ever felt this fluttery sensation in my stomach before a date with someone that I actually like. It is possible, though, that this unsettled, prickling feeling that I have right now is acid reflux after drinking three smoothies so quickly.

It's quite cold today, one of those late summer chills that catches people out. Back in time, I used to bring Ella to this same park nearly every day. Looking around, I can't see any fathers watching over the kids in the playground, there are only mothers. And none of them are drinking booze.

As my mind begins its loud tick towards pessimism, convinced I've been stood up, at last I see her. Nearly twenty minutes late, she is walking along with her hands in the pockets of her yellow coat. I don't think that I have seen Ella wearing a dress since she hit double figures.

My stomach, my heart, everything clutches.

This is a young woman walking towards me. When will I get used to it?

I suppose it's too late to get used to it.

'Hey, dad.'

Springing off the log, I give her a hug.

'Would you like one of these?' I ask, offering Ella a smoothie.

'Maybe in a bit,' she replies, eyeing the bright pink bottle with scepticism.

'So, how's it all been? Caught up on sleep yet?'

'Just about.' She chuckles and messes a hand through her hair.

She's so bloody lovely.

'How about packing? Finished?'

'Just about,' she says again, but without the chuckle.

'I've had to get rid of a lot of the things we can't take with us. Tramp has had his jabs, though, and his passport came through when we were away.'

'Even dogs need passports, huh?' Tramp is one step ahead of me, then. That blows my sneaking suspicion he was named after me right out of the water.

'Mostly I've just been catching up with people. You know, saying goodbye.' Ella's lip twitches. Just a small, involuntary spasm. A bit like Tramp does whenever he sees me standing in Dan's kitchen. 'Mum's absolutely shitting all over the place.'

'That doesn't surprise me,' I say. 'She always did shit a lot, that woman.'

There is a moment of silence, each of us left with our thoughts. I clamber back onto the log. Ella stays standing beside it, hands still in the pockets of her coat, peering around with a wistful half-smile.

'I've got something for you,' I say, reaching behind the log. 'I didn't think it through properly, I guess. Especially after what you said about getting rid of things. But . . . I got you these.'

'Oh. My. God! There are so many of them. They're beautiful.'

Ella is momentarily hidden behind the huge bouquet of roses. Her eyes scan each flower in turn. She runs her fingers over the silky petals.

I consider telling her how much they cost.

'I'm going to take a picture,' she says, searching for somewhere on the long, fat log to place them. She holds them out to me. 'Here. You hold them.'

'Okay,' I say, taking back the roses.

'Nice face, John. Another one, please. But smile this time. And sunglasses off.'

To my surprise, I don't look half bad in the pictures. Maybe there is something I see; a sadness hiding in the eyes. And I am scruffy as ever, of course. I prefer the one with the sunglasses.

Ella climbs onto the log and smooths down her dress. Looking around the park, taking it all in, she snaps a couple more pictures.

'I've got you something else,' I say, again sprawling backwards. 'I thought that it would look good with your coat. They were all the rage when I was a kid. Thought of getting one for myself, too. Probably will.'

'This is totally *sick*. I love it.' Ella slings the retro-style satchel – yellow leather, black trim – over her shoulder. She checks out the match against her coat. 'Is there something inside?'

'Maybe.'

Flipping the satchel onto her lap, she pops the clasp and spreads out the hooded top to read the print on the front.

I 🖤 WALES.

'I bought it when you went to the toilet in Cardiff. Just something silly for you to remember our trip by.'

'Dad, do you really think I could forget that trip?'

'True. I wonder what Thomas is up to. What do you reckon? Dressed as Aladdin, trying to sell trips on his magic carpet to lost travellers?'

Ella laughs, right from her stomach. It makes people turn and look, and she doesn't give a single shit.

I simply smile.

It is only just over a week since I last saw her. How can she have changed so much in such a short time? Whenever I next get to see her, presuming that one day I will, she's going to be an entirely different person. Not a girl anymore, a proper grown up.

A bitter taste begins to creep down the back of my throat, so I crack open a smoothie, even though I already need another whizz.

'I will have one of those, actually,' Ella says.

Together, we sip our sugar juice and shoot the breeze, both of us kicking our heels against the log. I notice that Ella can't stop checking out her new satchel, and that her eyes twinkle whenever she does.

Every day I have sat and stared at the little urn. Last night, I *finally* decided against giving it to Ella. So it will be a Christmas present for mum, after all. Or maybe for Shona, if things go well.

'So, did you manage to *sort Josephine out*?' I ask like an east end gangster.

'It's not like that, dad,' Ella replies. 'Josephine was totally broken by what happened with Norman. She's a complete mess. So I've been helping her to, I don't know, pull herself together, I guess.'

'Wait a second. Josephine went behind your back and you *helped* her afterwards?'

'She's my friend, dad.' Ella is clearly taken aback that I could think any differently.

Not that there's been much involvement on my part in recent years – my replacement being a brash city lout – but how Kirsty and I have somehow managed to raise a child who would do something as virtuous as helping a friend who betrayed her is nothing short of miraculous. In thirteen years, our girl has a better handle of maturity than both of us combined.

'That's amazing, Ella. I'm proud of you.'

'Hang on.' She sits upright. 'I've only just realised. You are drinking a *fruit* smoothie.'

'Yeah. This is my fourth,' I say.

Because one drink is never enough.

'As in, this has no alcoholic content.'

'Yeah. I know.'

'And you haven't put any vodka in it, or anything?'

'No, I bloody haven't, Els. I can be a bit funny with vodka.'

'That's pretty amazing, too.'

Another wordless moment settles upon us, a contradiction of total ease on the surface while a subterranean tide of awkwardness washes away the ground beneath us. The thing that is unsaid, but of which we both know. The thing that will drag this day towards its finality.

'Dad, what's the longest you've ever gone without a beer?' Ella asks, just before I can mention the bivouac.

I twist my lips, trying to work it out, searching backward though the haze.

'Twelve years, probably.'

'Twelve *years*? Why did you take it up again?'

'Oh no, that's when I first had a drink, about the age of twelve. After that, it's hard to say. It was only when I lived with your mother that I began to drink most days.'

'You can't blame her for everything, dad.'

'You're right, I can't. But I can blame her for a lot.'

By the change in Ella's demeanour, I might have said the wrong thing. The gleam disappears from her eyes. It looks as if she is pondering going on the attack. If I had brought the urn with me, I would smash it over it my own stupid head, save her the trouble.

'Have you ever read any Hardy?' she says a moment later.

'Uhh, heard of him. He's a . . . poet?'

'No. Well, yes, he was. But he was better known as a novelist. We've just finished one of his books, *The Mayor of Casterbridge*. There's this scene, right at the beginning, when Michael Henchard, the main character—'

'The mayor?'

'Yes, but not at that point. He's much older when he becomes mayor.'

'How old?'

'I don't *know*, dad. It's not important.' Ella gives the log a heavy kick and I shut up. 'Anyway, right at the beginning, Henchard decides that he has had enough of his wife, Susan. They visit a country fair and Henchard, totally pissed out of his face on rum, decides to auction Susan off to the highest bidder. But that's not all . . .

'Along with Susan, he also sells his baby daughter.'

'How much does he get for them?' I ask after a pause, because I don't really know what else to say.

'Five guineas?'

'And how much is five guineas in today's money?'

'I think that a guinea is basically a pound.'

'He got a fiver? Bargain.'

'*Dad*.'

'Sorry. I know what you're saying, Els.'

Looking across the park, I see children playing, families taking a walk. A couple of drunks that I know are on the swings. Just along from them, a ribby dog is cocking its leg against someone's parked bike.

'Ella . . . I never wanted to give you up, sweetheart. And I never have. I've fallen short in every aspect of my relationship with you, except for one thing.

'Being a father, I'm useless at. Everybody knows that. And what you told me in Wales was right: I've failed at nearly everything in my life. But loving you? I have *never* failed at loving you, Ella, no matter what.'

Ella is staring at the dry ground in front of the log. A stream of ants are carrying tiny lumps of dried bark back and forth. The marbled profile of her eyes follows their progress. They bump into each other. They carry on.

I imagine this is how Ella reacted when Josephine was pouring her heart out. Just sitting there, listening. Not interrupting like I do, Kirsty does, and pretty much every fucking idiot I know. I can only assume she had been listening. It kind of makes it easier to think that she is not.

'Not having you near has always torn a hole inside me, Els. Right through the middle of my heart. You're the only thing that is good in my life, and pure, and bright. If you knew how you are my first thought every morning and my final thought every night . . .'

I leave the words to breeze away down the path.

'Anyway,' I say, taking a glug of smoothie, 'I would have wanted at least ten guineas for you.'

'Dick,' she says, punching me on the arm.

In each other's gaze, I see a reflection of my eyes. Ella is joking around now, mimicking each of my expressions, until it becomes a game. She copies when I twitch my nose like a bunny, and again when I stick out my tongue. It is much more fun than playing the Blame Game.

'Spanky *Ma-caa-caa,*' she suddenly says, crossing her eyes. And then she mimics my open-mouthed shock.

'Oh shit. Have you . . . ? Oh *shit.*'

I didn't think that anything could make me blush, except for Kev's cocktails. I peek through my fingers.

Ella produces another cloud-splitting cackle.

'Why are you laughing? Are you not embarrassed?'

'I *can't* be embarrassed by you anymore, dad. If one of my friends' parents made a sex tape, it might be a shock – the most extreme things that they do is contest proposals at the church AGM – but with you, it's not. I think it's hysterical. You sound like Jack Sparrow.'

'You've actually *seen* it?'

'Well, I didn't want to watch it. But when someone said that it's just you acting like an all-round knob, I had to. All my friends had.'

Again, I hide behind my hands. Possibly even deeper this time.

And then I hear Ella letting go again.

After a moment of watching her, dumb, I can't help but join in.

With both of us clinging onto the log, we raise the sky. The tears that have threatened me all day begin to fall, and never have they felt more wonderful.

Soon afterwards, we leave our log and walk around the park for a while. When the cold begins to get to Ella, she puts on her Wales hoodie. It is not lost on me that we could have been doing this any time I wanted. It hurts my head to think about it.

I don't know when, but at some point – fooled by contentedness; tricked by my happiness – I lost the sense of the day slipping by. Until, finally, Ella tells me that she has to go.

We stand at the entrance of the park, beneath the line of ancient trees. The sun is drawing down behind them. A thin roll of clouds wafts along the broad sunset sky. I don't know what she is feeling, my girl, but she looks timid all of a sudden. A bit awkward, maybe.

'What do you want to do with these?' I ask, holding Ella's roses out to her.

She looks around, as if searching for something. A wicked glint strikes into her eyes.

Ella takes the roses and throws them high up into the tree above us. Eighty-plus quid's worth of flotsam, lying sideways across a branch.

'There,' she says. 'So that no one else can have them.'

She has my spirit, this girl, as well as my eyes.

'Before you go, Els, there's something I wanted to tell you,' I say, performing a soft-shoe shuffle. 'I have, uh . . . I've met someone.'

'You've *what*?'

'Yeah, the woman who sold me the flowers you just threw into the tree.'

'Whoops. Soz. What's she like?'

'Well, I haven't been on a date with her yet. But she's really . . . *nice*. I think you'd get on well with her.'

Ella scrunches up her face and smiles, but sadly. Both of us are thinking the same thing. The subterranean flow that cannot be interrupted.

'Right. Come on,' I say, putting my arm around her. 'I'm walking you home.'

We go slowly. I make sure of that, lifting each foot as ponderously as I can, almost trying to hold us back. Ella doesn't seem to mind. The further we travel, the deeper she rests against me, her satchel hanging by her side.

'We never did get to see a waterfall, did we?'

'Oh no, we didn't,' Ella says. 'And I didn't tell anyone that you wet yourself, either.'

'You knew about that?'

'Dad, you had a big wet patch after getting drunk. It doesn't take a genius to work it out.'

'Why didn't you tell me off?'

'Because I wasn't talking to you at the time. You were being a prick, remember?'

'Stands to reason.'

The north side of the high street is quiet. A few cars pass by. Couples are heading out for the evening. In the background, I hear the faint rasp of moped engines and the call of seagulls strayed far from the coast.

As we round the castle mount, the sun is smothered, taking with it the day.

forty-one

I wish that I had lost the tent, rather than find it propped up next to the bins behind the takeaway. Living in such a cramped flat, a bag of apples takes up four times the space than it does in a normal house.

I messaged Brian with two options of what I could do with the tent. He quickly replied, saying that he and Debs are not going out until this afternoon, so it would be great if I could drop it over. I had hoped that he would agree to the second option.

Shuffling to the taxi rank, I watch the sky and see only one plane up there. It couldn't be the one that Ella is on. Her plane left just after sunrise. Walking home from her yesterday, I didn't blub at all. In fact, I'd felt a strange joy washing through me, picturing her hanging onto the log, rollicking with laughter, clutching her satchel, pure delight in her eyes.

I don't know how long I stared at her final message for.

> thx! take care dad :) luv u 2 xoxo

And then, pinging through right afterwards

> don't get 2 drunk ;p

Cheeky little scamp.

Throughout the start-stop ride along the high street on my way to Brian's, I continue running through the reel of our time together in the park, every moment of each frame.

'Do you know if Tenderbridge has a bookshop?' I ask the cabbie.

The taxi leaves the high street and swings onto a road that leads around the back of the castle. On the tiny one-way lane, he waits for me outside a shop called Mister Books.

No sooner than I step through the door, immediately I feel out of place. I wasn't aware that a bookshop could have so many books to choose from. A youngish guy is sitting cross-legged on a stool behind a low wooden counter, a comic spread out in front of him.

'Are you Mister Books?' I ask.

'I . . . am . . . not?' he replies, half-smiling in a challenging fashion. He glances through the window at the cab waiting in the tight street.

'Sorry,' I say. 'Look—'

'Look?'

'Yeah, I need a book.'

'Right!' He spreads his arms, Jesus after a miracle – even though this guy has short hair, mutton chops and stubble. 'And what *book* might that be?'

'I don't know the title, but it's by Tom Hardy.'

'The actor Tom Hardy?'

'Erm, was he a poet and an author?'

'No? He *is* an actor. I think that you probably mean *Thomas* Hardy.'

'Same thing,' I reply.

'Agreed! The actor and former rapper Tom Hardy is the "*same thing*" as Victorian poet and novelist Thomas Hardy. Because . . . their names? Are the same?'

I wonder how often this guy gets people from the south side coming in and asking for the latest book by *that bloke with a nose*, or *that bird from the telly with the big tits*. He clearly picked me out as being from the wrong side of the bridge before I walked in and proved it.

'There's a book by Hardy that I'm looking for,' I begin again, as carefully as I can. 'At the beginning, the main character, the . . . man, sells his wife and child for a fiver. Five guineas,' I quickly correct.

'Have you Googled it?' he asks, the half-smile again creeping at the edges of his lips. Perhaps satisfied by my dumb response, he says, 'I'm just fucking with you. I've got it right here.'

Simple as that, I walk out of Mister Books with a copy of *The Mayor of Casterbridge*. In the back of the cab, I start flicking through the tiny print, scanning the incident at the country fair. This Henchard bloke sounds like a prize bell-end.

For some reason, I tell both Mister Books and Mister Taxi to keep the change. I'd better not get too used to doing that, just because I have a pile of cash to deplete for the first time in years. It's not like I want to date everyone who sells me something.

The garage doors are open. I see Brian fannying about inside. Tottering over the gravel, I lug the tent through. And then I stop mid-step.

Brian has one hand on his hip. The other is holding a tom-tom mount.

Had he planned for me to witness this, a finality to the end of Spanky Macaca? To see the drumkit coming apart is to see Brutus's knife catching a shimmer of light before the final plunge.

'Have you, what, just given up?'

'Not exactly,' Brian replies, looking at the pieces of his kit. 'I need the space for something I'm working on.'

'Well, here's your tent,' I say, immediately regretting the petulance with which I drop it on the floor. It's all just too much, too soon. At least Brian can't give me any warnings on a day off work. I don't think he can. 'Erm, I've got a confession to make, mate.'

Having thrown the tom-tom mount on the sofa, both hands now on his hips, Brian waits for me to spill.

'It's a bit damaged, the tent. A couple of the poles got slightly, sort of . . . mangled. It does still work. It's just a bit floppy.'

'That's okay, John.' Brian steps around the bass drum and slides the tent under a stack of shelves, back into its designated place. 'I don't think we'll be needing a tent as big as that again. Can't imagine another family camping trip in the near future.'

'Have you given up camping, too, as well as drums?'

'Camping's never really been a hobby,' he says. 'But with the boys grown up now . . .'

Brian gives me an odd look, a bit of the old side-eye.

He knew about the sex tape first time round, didn't he? He must have.

'Do you want a beer?' he asks.

'Uh . . .'

A *beer*? I hadn't been *planning* on having a beer.

'Cup of tea, Bri, if that's not too much to ask?'

Brian has all the facilities out here, of course. Even so, he phones the house to ask Debs to bring a jug of milk out for us. 'And sugar,' he says, calling Debs back after I ask if he has any.

I have always liked Debs – she's kind and non-judgemental, even though I've definitely deserved it at times – so I am perfectly happy when Brian drops a teabag into a third mug. Wearing faded black jeans and a red padded-rib jacket, Debs brings the milk straight over.

Everyone has started putting their jackets on, lately. I'm even wearing my new one. The thought of bumping into Shona while I was wearing my shabby leather jacket was tormenting me. So, when I bought Ella's satchel, I treated myself to a navy parka from the department store next to the car park beside the Tender Bridge. Going to that particular department store also meant I could steal a quick glimpse of the flower stall.

'Did you see Ella off?' Debs asks, sliding onto the sofa next to Brian, squiggling into the cushions.

'I didn't go to the airport,' I reply with a surprising grin. 'But I did spend the afternoon with her yesterday.'

'Debs was a wreck when Jake first went to uni,' Brian says, putting his arm around her. 'Freddie's heading off in a couple of weeks, too, so I'll have to go through it all again.'

He kisses Debs' cheek, them shuffling about on the sofa as if he's trying to cuddle her on a ferry. It's disgusting. I can't watch. Or I shouldn't watch, anyway.

'They'll both be hundreds of miles away,' Debs says, easing Brian off her. 'Jake's in Manchester and Fred's going to Exeter. So, they'll be hundreds of miles from us, and hundreds of miles apart.'

Later today, Ella will be landing an ocean away. But I keep that thought to myself.

'Brian keeps reminding me how important it is for them,' Debs continues. 'You know, they're both growing up now, not babies anymore. They'll make new friends and learn about life. That's what I have to keep trying to reminding myself, too.'

Even the thought of it clearly brings a happy/sad feeling to Debs – a reflection of my own, whenever my thoughts drift to Wales. With Debs already so close to tears, I can hardly look at her. She could fall apart at any moment.

'I've been thinking the exact same thing about Ella, getting my head around the fact that she has a life of her own. I mean, for me she's always had a life of her own. But . . . y'know. Our trip was a blast, though.'

I tell Brian and Debs about the journey, getting lost and camping out in the bivvy I built in the storm. The broken village phone box and being sort-of-kidnapped by a man-child with an impressive collection of dolls. Hitching a lift back to Cardiff with a fuzz and finding my misplaced driving licence.

'So, because we spent one night in the bivvy, and another night under the duress of a lunatic, we only ended up using the tent once. But, erm, thanks anyway,' I say, raising my mug.

'And from such moments, memories are made,' Brian says, being uncharacteristically philosophical, and with all the emotional depth of a slogan for an airline.

'What's the new project you're working on, by the way, Bri?'

'Oh yeah. I'll show you.'

Brian strides over to a cabinet near the beer fridge and pulls out a little contraption. The way he looks at it is how I imagine metal detectorists might examine their discoveries: not quite allowing themselves to comprehend what it is that they have found.

'What is it?' I ask. 'Some kind of pedal?'

'Exactly that,' Brian says. 'One day, the other week, I started playing around, soldering a board just to see if I could, and I got a bit carried away. It's not finished yet – I need to get some plates made, stuff like that – but I'm definitely sticking with the wooden casing.'

'Let me see it.'

'This one is the third prototype,' Brian says, carefully handing me the varnished wooden box. 'It's pretty rudimental, just now.'

'It's very retro.'

I roll the case around in my hands, looking at the fine curved finish on the edges. Glancing inside, I examine the engineering work Brian's put into it, wires leading from some bits and pieces attached to the sides.

'This is awesome, mate.'

'Cheers.' Brian takes back the pedal and again stares at it intensely, before stowing it safely in its place inside the cabinet.

'You were saying you'd like to work on it with some-one,' Debs says. 'You could get John involved, couldn't you?'

'Oh, look.' I put my empty mug down and hold up my hands. 'I don't know the first thing about how pedals are made. I only know how to trash them. Don't put him on the spot like that, Debs. I wouldn't want to mess anything up for Bri.'

'No harm in giving it a go, I suppose,' Brian says, playing with the wiry tuft of hair in his widow's peak. 'You've lived and breathed music your whole life, John. More than anyone I know.'

'But . . . well . . .'

How shall I put it?

'What about all of the other stuff I've done over the years?'

forty-two

Having accepted the offer of working with Brian on his pedals, I declined the offer of a lift. I haven't got much to do today, the sky is clear, and I fancied a bit of time alone with the countryside. It's surprising how easy I find it to breeze past the pubs on the route.

Not only have I chosen to start giving booze a swerve in daylight hours, I have also been avoiding Darren – temptation greets you like a naughty friend, and all that. Strolling happily homeward, my phone rings and it is him, breaking from the tradition of arranging things with sloppy text messages.

With a mood as bright as the day, I decide to answer.

'Where've you been?' he says, straight out.

I consider telling him that lately I have been enjoying the company of people who can boast of more than a single braincell. Instead, I tell him that I've been keeping a low profile, thinking things through. 'You know, with Ella leaving, and that.'

He doesn't respond.

'Hello?' I look at the phone to check we're still in call. 'Darren?'

He sniffs loudly. 'Do you fancy a beer?'

'Uh.' I scratch my eyebrow. 'I don't know, mate. I'm kind of avoiding pubs, because of . . . y'know.'

'What, the sex tape?'

'Yes,' I say. 'That.'

'But I've got something for you.'

'What have you got for me?'

'I'll give it to you in the pub, if you fancy a beer.'

'Can't you just tell me, Darren?'

Darren says that he doesn't want to spoil the surprise, so we agree to meet at The Ivy House, an old-fashioned pub near the posh school. It should be safe enough in there. I haven't played The Ivy in years. I can't be bothered to waste time thinking about what the gift might be. Probably he just wants to give me a beer.

Walking into the pub, it feels strange, as if I am a man returning to a place where he committed a slaughter. Not because anything in particular has ever happened in The Ivy House. I think that I would have had this feeling if I had walked into any pub, possibly in any town.

'Weakest lager, please,' I say to the barman.

I don't recognise him, nor anyone else in here. Best of all is that no one shows any sign of recognition towards me. I wonder if Craig David would've received the same response.

I find Darren at a wobbly table by a window facing on to the road. In a place like this, a flamingo-pink, long-haired moron sticks out like a man-sized Winnie the

307

Pooh standing in the middle of a Welsh hamlet. At least his sunburn doesn't look quite as bad as it did.

'Desert Island Discs,' he says before I have even sat down.

'Do we *have* to do this again, Darren?'

'I already know what songs you'd take. *The One I Love. She Belongs to Me,*' he says, ticking them off on his fingers. '*Angel of Harlem . . .*'

'There is no way I'd take any U2 with me,' I say, irritated he'd even think it. I mean, it has only been, what? forty-odd years that I've known him.

'But what about your luxury item, though?' he says, pointing a finger at me as if he's caught me out. A dim-witted Columbo.

'I don't know, Darren. *Umm* . . . an umbrella. I'll take that.'

'But it's not raining. It's a desert island, remember. That's a new jacket, isn't it?'

'It's going to rain at some point on a desert island, Darren. And yes, it is.'

'Why not take a sheet of tarp, then? Or a tent?'

'Actually, you know what? Forget the umbrella. I'll take a house with me.' I rap my knuckles on the table. 'On my imaginary desert island, I would like to have a house. Thank you. End of.'

Darren's head goes down, defeated, revealing coils of peeling skin in his hairline.

I take my first sip of beer. It is only a sip, too. It turns out that weak lager barely even tastes like beer, more like hoppy water. Since that cup of tea at Brian's, I haven't drunk anything, so it's welcome enough.

'What is it that you wanted to give me?'

'Why wouldn't you take a guitar with you?' Darren replies, evading the question. 'That's what I'd take.'

'Well, I'll invite you over from your island, then.'

'But we couldn't jam, could we, because you haven't got one.'

'I forgot to tell you, I've made a guitar out of a fallen branch and some fishing wire.'

'Have you?' Darren asks, impressed.

'Well, I haven't, no. But the me that's stranded on a desert island has.'

From the cobwebs dangling where the wall meets the ceiling, Darren seeks another stupid question. 'How are you going to call me over to your island if you haven't got a phone?'

'I'll just shout, mate. You're only next door. Or I'll send a message in a coconut. Look,' I say, before he can concoct another scenario from the webs, 'I really don't want to play this game. Not today.'

Seeing him so disappointed makes me feel a tiny bit bad. I can't exactly tell him that I've missed the aimless, drunken ramblings not one single bit, and have, in fact, felt better for their absence. But why should I sacrifice myself? An ache is already forming in my brain.

'What's this thing you've got for me?' I ask again.

'Oh yeah.' Darren takes a flimsy carrier bag off the windowsill. I hadn't noticed it, sitting next to a dusty bowl of potpourri. 'Go on then,' he says. 'Open it.'

'You mean take the carrier bag off?'

After a brief stare-off, I do remove the carrier bag . . .

Finishing a bowl of horrible food in a foreign country, only for the well-meaning host to bring a new platter, that is how I feel, looking at the urn identical to the one I was intending to palm off on my mum.

The ornately decorated sides. The three birds. Oh no, there it is. I had forgotten about the fourth one.

'After we left The Humphrey, on the day you bought yours, I went back and nicked the other one for you.'

'You stole me an urn?'

'You said that you wanted both of them,' Darren says, clearly delighted with himself. 'So, you know. Here it is.'

'Truly, mate, I don't know what to say.'

'You don't need to say anything, my friend, I can see it on your face. Don't well up.'

'I'm not welling up, Darren,' I say, shaking my head, still in a state akin to shock. 'And seriously, I am grateful. Thank you. It's a really thoughtful gesture. But why did you nick it? You make enough cash.'

'It's a charity shop, innit.'

'I don't get it. Why does that make it alright to steal from them?'

'They're all volunteers. Didn't you know? It's not as if you're stealing off someone's plate if you nick something from them.'

'You're not stealing off a volunteer's plate, Darren, I agree. But you are almost literally stealing from the plate of someone that the charity has deemed to be in need.'

'Do you think so? I'm not sure. Gangsters run charity shops.'

'Gangsters? Really? Well, there's another reason not to steal things from them, then. You don't want to be caught stealing from a gangster, do you?'

'Holy shit, mate. That's a good point. I'm glad you've got it now,' Darren says, without a trace of malice, irony, or anything that could even remotely resemble wit. He looks around the pub, checking to see if the charity shop Don's henchmen are searching for us.

'Thank you for nicking the urn, Darren. I do appreciate it. Really. But if in future you're thinking of stealing something for me, please don't.'

'You don't need to tell Emma that.'

'Who?'

'Your *daughter*,' he says. Like I'm the idiot.

'Darren . . . my daughter is called Ella.'

'Oh, right. Yeah. Whatever,' he says, sniffing, picking up his pint. 'Well, you don't need to tell her that I nicked it when you give it to her.'

'I can't give it to her. I can't, Darren.'

I feel a trembling in my bottom lip.

'I can't give *either* of the urns to Ella. Not this one *or* the other one.'

Something clicks inside me. I feel giddy.

'She's gone, mate.'

I grip the underside of the table.

'Ella. She's . . . *gone.*'

I breathe in through my nose. It turns into a massive snort. Another surge rises, from the floor up.

'She's gone so *fucking far away.*'

After shrieking the last bit, I collapse on to the table, knocking my drink over the carrier bag.

The table wobbles.

The glass rolls, drops, and smashes on the floor.

Somebody cheers. '*Weeey . . .*'

'I'll, err . . . I'll get you another beer, Roger,' Darren says. 'Um, John, I mean.'

forty-three

My guitar is on its side with a broken string. My new parka is stuffed under the coffee table. The collection of empty cans dotted around the sitting room floor tell me that I decided to continue drinking when I somehow made it home last night. I got horrendously drunk.

My final memory is of dropping tearfully into the charity shop to make a donation for the stolen urn. As I didn't have any tenners on me, I gave them a twenty – so in the end I did pay full price for the pair, even though I didn't want either of them.

The original urn is in its usual place on the coffee table, but I have not a clue what happened to the other one. Why I have developed a passion for giving people money for nothing, I could not say. I suppose, as a snapshot of my life, because it seemed like a good idea at the time.

The filthy smells from the takeaway, preparing for business, tantalise me. After a bender, I normally can't face food for hours. This hunger pang proves that my hangover is one of those delicious ones, where all I want to do is slump in front of the telly, wrapped up in a duvet, watching shit on the box. In a while, I'll phone downstairs and ask them to drop some of their dirty comfort food up to the flat. Who knows what kind of a healthy tip will await my delivery person?

A knock at the door confuses me, certain that I haven't yet called them.

Wearing my duvet as a cape, mostly hiding my pants, I amble into the hallway. Two figures are silhouetted on the other side of the frosted glass, taped up after I came home steaming one time and slumped too hard against the door while I was looking for my keys. I begin to wonder what happened last night, presuming that this is a pair of coppers.

All kinds of horrifying thoughts suddenly swarm into my mind. Mostly revolving around a certain flight to Canada. If I don't open the door, maybe I'll never have to know. Just spend the rest of my life feeling as sick as I suddenly do.

There is another knock. Both figures shift impatiently.

With a dry mouth, I slowly turn the handle . . .

'Ooo, look at you,' Julian says. 'You look an absolute terror, boy.'

'What the fuck are you doing here?'

Tugging the duvet, I attempt to cover up my pants a bit more effectively.

'We agreed we would come down to take you out to lunch today, Johnny,' dad replies. 'We tried phoning this morning – I thought it would be a good idea to check if you're up – but your phone went straight to voicemail.'

Dad is wearing a pair of red corduroy slacks and a

blue cardigan over a textured white shirt, buttoned-up to the neckerchief. Not just for the lack of colour in his get up, he looks different. Quite stiff. Quite north side.

Julian, however, is wearing a silky purple tracksuit zipped to the top, standing proud, and still not very tall, in a pair of silver glitter boots with two-inch heels. The outfit is completed with a huge gold brooch in the shape a daisy.

Together they look like a weird, aging Europop act.

I tuck the duvet between my legs and lean against the wall. 'When did we agree to lunch?'

'When we spoke a couple of weeks ago,' dad says.

'A couple of *weeks*?'

I can't even remember how I got home last night.

'You'd better come in, then,' I say. 'I just need a quick shower.'

They follow me through to the sitting room.

I stand my guitar against the armchair and kick the empty cans under the sofa. I see my phone, plugged into the charger, dangling against the wall. Whenever I left it there at some point in the middle of the night, I was clearly too wasted to turn on the switch.

'I won't be a minute,' I tell them, switch clicked on with my toe. 'Help yourself to tea, or whatever. I've run out of *Dom Perignon*, I'm afraid. Probably haven't got any milk, either.'

Not that it would be safe to drink if I had.

'Open those curtains, Stanley,' I hear Julian tell dad, while I head to the bathroom. 'And the windows, too.'

I return to the sitting room ten minutes later, hangover mostly washed away beneath the hot water. The not-quite-fresh Sunday morning air carries upon it the scent of exotic, spicy aromas and the echo of church bells. Curiously, the extractor fan doesn't sound as loud with the windows open. Because they are taking me for lunch, as we apparently agreed, I'm glad that I didn't waste any money on a crappy takeaway.

Julian has the urn in his hands. He is turning it over, stroking one of the birds.

'You can have that, if you want.' I down the last of my cold, black tea and sit in the armchair opposite them. 'Hang on, when did you get rid of the moustache, dad? I knew that there was something different about you. *Huh.* I always thought it suited you. Like Clark Gable, but not as smug.'

'John.' Julian peers at me over the invisible frame of his bifocals, cradling the urn as one would a bird with a broken wing. 'Where did you get this?'

'From the charity shop.'

'In *Tenderbridge*?'

'Yeah, yeah, I know. I sometimes go there on a whim. That's where I bought that canvas, too.' I nod towards Warhol's Marilyn Monroe, with the big dent that accentuates her beauty spot.

Julian pays Marilyn not even a split-second glance, just enough time to sneer at the bad imitation.

'If I'm right, John, this is an original Meissen *Schnee-ballen*. And, in fact, I am right. You can tell by these blue crossed swords.' Turning the urn, Julian lightly wipes the pad of his thumb over the maker's mark on the base. 'Oh, it's sticky.'

Beer spillages often make anything that stands on my coffee table for more than a few seconds a bit sticky. In fact, any surface in the entire flat, except for the bottom of the shower. That's just mouldy.

'It's a who and a what?'

'A mid-nineteenth century Meissen *Schneeballen*.'

'It is pretty,' Dad says.

'It is,' Julian agrees. 'Very. And not only is it pretty, this is a quite collectable piece that you have here, John.'

For the next few minutes, Julian tells me about the time when he "*helped out*" at Christie's auction house in King Street. While he was working there, he developed a special interest in collectable porcelain items. Part of his job was to help clean and restore a number of these easily identifiable Meissen creations.

'See, Meissen were the first manufacturer in Europe to develop this brand of hard-paste porcelain, back in the eighteenth century. And this,' Julian says, again showing the crossed swords on the base, carefully cupping the lid, 'is their signature logo. Even though it would not be one of the very earliest examples, of course—'

'Of course.'

'—they still remain quite collectable. Quite collectable indeed. You're very lucky, John.'

'What does that mean, collectable? Like . . . valuable?'

'Yes,' Julian nods, his cheeks giving a wobble.

Stroking his phantom moustache, Dad's nodding too.

'I'm not certain of the exact market price, but of late the auction value of Meissen has continued to rise. And, of course, this being an individual piece and not part of a pair. That affects the value, too.'

I sit up from my slouched position. 'A pair?'

'Like many antique porcelains, Meissen sell for much higher prices as a pair. By itself, this might fetch up to a few thousand on the open market. But if there were two of them, and I can only guess here, I would approximate that you could be looking at over ten thousand.'

'Ten thousand . . . *pounds*?'

'Well, yes,' Julian replies with a frown.

My guitar clangs to the floor. I skittle over the carpet to my phone. In the interminable wait for it to spring into action, I do a quick spin around the flat. In my stomach, though, I know that I no longer have the other urn.

While I was in the middle of my breakdown in The Ivy House, I spent a while desperately cuddling the urn in the beer-sodden carrier bag. Knowing how quickly my moods can change after a few drinks – and certainly did last night, I recall now, when at some point I was surfing on the counter in a kebab shop – there is every chance that I attempted to deposit the urn in the night safe at the bank, or, more likely, launched it into the river. The night safe would've been an accidentally wise move. But if the urn ended up in the river . . .

'Bollocks!'

'Are you alright, Johnny?' dad calls.

I trip back into the sitting room and skid over to my dangling mobile.

Darren doesn't pick up. It goes to voicemail.

'Call me back, Darren,' I blurt into the piece of junk. 'As soon as you get this.'

I hang up and punch myself in the face.

'What on *earth* is the matter with you, boy?' dad says.

'I had it. I did have two urns. I had a pair.'

'Well, where is the other one now?'

'That's the problem. I *don't know* where the other one is.' I clutch fistfuls of my hair. My body is tingling with urgency. And self-hatred. 'I was in the pub last night. Not with this one, with the other one.'

'What were you *thinking* of, John? Taking a valuable urn to the pub.'

'I didn't *know* that it was valuable, dad.'

'Well, it still doesn't make sense,' dad says, 'carrying an urn about as if you're showing off a new puppy. Even if it's not valuable.'

'It's not like that. Please, can you just . . . *shut up*.'

I squeeze my eyes closed and press both of my hands against my head, but I don't think I'm strong enough to crush my own skull, no matter how hard I try.

Think, you stupid shitbag.

My eyes pop open. I stab the air, which makes dad and Julian flinch.

'I'll call them. I'll call the pub. The pubs. The ones I went to. And the kebab shop. One of you, give me your phone.'

'Why don't we just go down and ask them?' Julian says. 'It might still only be the morning, but they're probably open. It is Tenderbridge, after all.'

'Yes, Julian!' I punch a fist into my palm like a frustrated superhero. 'If I call them, there's no way they'd actually bother checking to see if it's there, anyway. Brilliant idea. Are you ready? Go and start the Rolls. I'll get my coat.'

'It's quite warm out today, John,' dad says. 'Are you sure that you need a coat?'

I can't be bothered to reply. Snatching my new parka out from beneath the coffee table, I whip it on and something heavy swings round and hits me in the nuts. I smile carefully, unable to celebrate until I know that the second urn didn't smash against anything more substantial than my redundant genitals when I was staggering home last night.

Easing the pocket open, I find the urn safely cushioned beside a leftover kebab, no worse for wear than when Darren originally nicked it. Discovering that I also have my Hardy in the other pocket, I decide that this day could not possibly get any better.

With dad and Julian cradling my valuable twins, and while I am snacking on cold lamb and soggy tomato, my phone *pings* from the other side of the room. Now that I have my urns together, safe and well, assuming that the text is from Darren I almost don't bother looking.

But I do look.

Throughout my adult life, I have proved many times that I simply should not be allowed access to a mobile phone after a few beers – never more than with the Craig David sex tape. So to discover that at some point late last night I sent Shona a message, my stomach plummets three storeys into the ground.

Tentatively scrolling upward, all I can surmise is that Darren must have helped me craft the message.

> hey shonA! if your free do you fancy
> cofee tomorrow X

Two spelling mistakes, and probably missed pieces of punctuation, but otherwise it is much better than any message I would usually bother crafting. I wonder how long Darren and I debated whether it is too cheeky to put a kiss on the end, or too understated not to put a row of them, to show how keen I am. Goodness knows how we managed to put an exclamation mark and a capital **X**. Perhaps more surprising is that we asked if she would like to go for a coffee, and not straight to the pub.

Either way, it seems to have worked.

Sounds good x

Still marvelling at what I see, the phone begins to ring. It's only Darren returning my call, so I hang up.

forty-four

Rather than celebrate Julian's revelation in my usual fashion, I went alcohol-free on my lunch date with him and dad, only joining in with a few spritzers and an Irish coffee with dessert. Content with the knowledge of my investment in the urns, it meant that I could go on to meet Shona later without first needing to perform the manic laughter routine, and with only the most minor of bowel movements. By the time I returned from the toilet, she was at the table.

Unlike the first time we met, I immediately felt easy and relaxed. Our conversation led forth without pretence or awkwardness and no need at all for me to punch myself in the bollocks. It must have gone alright, because she agreed to a second date.

The only moment of slight discomfort was on our third date, when Shona suggested that we could go to The Ivy House for a drink – now another establishment on my list for temporary avoidance. Instead, I took her to the pub by the river.

The taste I've found for white wine could become a concern, I suppose – too much white wine has led me on rampages in the past – but now I am drinking to enjoy it, and the company I share. Jazz plays in most of the places we've been, and I've not even asked them to turn it off, or tried to rip the speakers from the wall.

Approaching the end of our latest date, hand in hand through misty rain, we head beneath the damp street-lights back to my place for the first time.

I settle the wine glasses onto the coffee table and sit next to Shona, grateful that it is now acceptable to not be able to take my eyes off her. We're still only at second base – although what could be classed as second base has changed quite a lot over the years. With no easy explanation that comes to mind, I just don't seem to be in a hurry with her.

Lounging against the plump cushions – bought with the latest of dad's loans, secured against the urns, which are now under his and Julian's care – I gaze at the new curtains, and the plants bringing life to the corners of the room. My guitar, dusted down, polished and restrung, is on its new stand. I can smell the air fresheners doing their job, too. Yet, despite feeling insanely happy, anxiety is breeching. And it has nothing to do with this beautiful woman and her hand rubbing over the lower parts of my belly.

As well as buying a few other bits and pieces for the flat – including a spare set of bedsheets – I also invested in a new mobile phone. Brian chose one for me and then showed me how to use it. Somehow, tech genius that he is, he even transferred the pictures of Ella and her mates from the old phone, assuaging a slight panic within me. But nothing can calm the unease that still bubbles my blood.

For each of the first twenty-three days after she left, Ella and I either messaged or spoke to one another. She even sent photos – we joked that Canada looks sort of like a sunnier version of Wales – and she seemed happy enough. But something has changed. And I have no way of knowing what.

For nearly three days, she has not responded to my messages. I can see that she hasn't even looked at them. On my most recent attempt to call her, before meeting Shona this evening, Ella's phone didn't even ring.

I became certain that something serious is wrong when I couldn't get through to Kirsty, either. Now I know exactly how she must have felt when I managed to get Ella lost in the Welsh hills.

Earlier today, I considered contacting the Canadian police, just as Kirsty did with the local rozzers when Ella and I were accidentally kidnapped by Thomas. If there is still no word tomorrow, I have already decided that I will call them. And then I'll ask Brian what else I should do. Right now, my mind is as unsettled as it has ever been. A subterranean tidal wave that is distracting me from this incredible woman.

'It's *really* weird,' Shona is saying, sitting sideways on the sofa with her knees up. 'I mean, I admire anyone who tries to think innovatively – and I *love* cake – but the main focus of a record shop should always be on the music. Maybe I'll ask them if I can put a flower stand in the corner.'

I love the sound of her laughter. We might have only met weeks ago, but I adore everything about her. Even so, I don't join in. Running a finger over my lips, I look at the partially concealed mouldy patch on the ceiling, still visible through my bad job of painting over it.

'John, are you okay?'

'Sorry.' My trance breaks and I land back on the sofa.

'I asked what you think of Coldplay.'

'Erm. They're okay. Their music is just a bit too vegan for me.'

She laughs again – even though it wasn't intended as a joke – but quickly her laughter becomes a smile. Even that doesn't stay for long.

'What's up?' she says, massaging my belly. 'Have you still not heard anything?'

'No,' I say, glancing again at my phone. 'It's not just that, though. There's something else.'

I place my wine glass on the coffee table, twist round, pick up her hand, and place mine over hers on her knee.

'Look . . . Shona, I really like you.'

She hesitates before swallowing her wine. I hear the gulp as it slides down.

'I thought you seemed a bit distant tonight. It's okay,' she says, sliding her hand out from beneath mine. 'I understand.'

She swings her feet from the sofa and places her glass next to mine. Then she moves to stand up.

'I should go.'

'*No*.' I reach for her hand. 'It's nothing like that. The problem is that I *really* like you. A lot. And truthfully, I'm not too familiar with that feeling.'

Is it too early to tell her that I'm in love with her? In

the past I've told strangers standing at the bar next to me that I love them. And they've not always been girls.

'Because I . . . *like* you so much, there are a few things you should know before we, um . . . take things further, that's all. And because I want to be the one that you hear it from.'

Yeah, I'm thinking about Bea.

I pick up my wine glass and down it in one.

I'm all in, now.

Jesus, even my internal chatter has started to sound like a Craig David song.

'Okay.' I muffle a burp, resettle myself, release a puff of air, and begin. 'There was this lollipop lady—'

A knock at the door interrupts me before I can properly start reeling out the scroll of my confessions.

'*Maybe if we're quiet . . .*' I whisper.

And then another knock. A few of them.

The lamplight and candlelight will be shining clearly through the window. Even though the curtains are new, they're cheap.

'You should see who it is,' Shona says. 'It might be important.'

Sighing like a disgruntled horse, trilling my lips on a breath, I reluctantly get up. 'Don't go anywhere. Okay?'

'Ah, you got me,' Shona replies. 'I was thinking of sneaking out the window as soon as you turn your back.'

The moment I switch the hallway light on, my smile becomes dry. There is a silhouette behind the patched-up glass. A shadow cast by the orange streetlight.

I am crippled by the same convulsion as when dad and Julian arrived that Sunday morning.

No response to my messages.

Missed calls.

It might be important . . .

The knocking starts again; a dull splodge that beats against the door.

I can't not answer. I know that I must.

It takes all of my courage to creep closer. Weak knees. Trembling heart. Anxiety. Paranoia. My unsettled mind. Too much Melatonin. Whatever it is, to be answered.

My hand reaches for the lock. I can't seem to stop it. I'm too terrified to consider anything but the rapidity of my heartbeat.

I ease the door open, so slowly . . .

'Hey, dad.'

Peering from beneath the hood of her yellow coat. *Ella.* It is her.

But it can't be her.

'Hell*ooo*? Earth to John. Why are you looking at me so weirdly? Are you pissed?'

I drag Ella in from the rain and spin her around, knocking her boots against the freshly painted hallway wall. The wetness upon her coat soaks into my shirt.

'Stop smothering me, dad. I can barely breathe.'

'Sorry, sorry, I'm sorry.' I step back and stare at her. 'It's really you.'

'Yes, it's me. *Dur.* Sorry I didn't call. Can I take this off? It's soaked.'

While I hang up her coat, Ella stamps the rain from her boots and brushes herself down. Adrenaline is still struggling against my nerves and punch-drunk confusion. Why does she seem smaller?

'Oh . . .' Ella says, ceasing her stomp. 'Hi.'

'Hiya.' Leaning on the jamb, Shona is peering around the doorframe.

Ella gives me a cheeky grin.

'Ella . . . this is Shona. The lady I told you about.'

'I heard that . . .' Shona glances at me, uncertain how to say it.

'Yeah. What are you doing here, Els? You're supposed to be in Canada, aren't you?'

'Ooo, I hope I'm not interrupting anything.'

Both Shona and I chuckle, indicating that Ella probably is standing between bases of some kind.

Is that what she meant? Is it okay that Ella might've thought she could be interrupting the same thing that Shona and I are thinking she was?

'Your dad was about to tell me a story,' Shona says. 'Something to do with a lollipop lady.'

Ella's eyes, huge and wide, turn with comic stiffness from one of us to the other. 'O-*kay*?'

'Now that Ella is here, it can wait for another time,' I say, packing away my confessions scroll. 'Come through, Els. Tell us why you're not in Canada.'

'It was the weirdest thing ever,' Ella says, following Shona through to the sitting room.

We leave the rain to drip down the hallway walls.

The first thing Ella tells us, sliding into the armchair next to my guitar stand, is the reason why she couldn't call before heading over. Apparently, when he found out that they were returning to the UK, Dan took Kirsty and Ella's phones away. In fact, he had *demanded* them back.

'But why have you returned? I mean, it's amazing to see you, but . . . what are you doing here?'

'Um, you might want me to tell you in private?' Ella says.

'I can go, if you want,' Shona says for the second time tonight, from her place on the sofa next to me.

'No!' Ella replies, just before I can.

We agree to head through to the kitchen for a quiet chat, leaving Shona with Chet Baker and his parping trumpet.

Ella leans her back against one of the now non-sticky countertops. Her gaze cannot settle upon a single thing for more than a second, and she can make only fleeting eye contact with me.

Maybe she does look a tiny bit more grown up.

'So?' I say, leaning on the cabinet opposite her.

'Dan didn't choose to move to Canada,' Ella begins quietly, even though the sound of the music stops her voice from travelling beyond the doorway. 'He didn't have a choice. Or well, the choice was to either accept the role over there or be fired.'

'What do you mean?'

'He was sent there, dad.'

With Chet tootling in the other room, Ella proceeds to tell me that Dan was busted after he installed hidden cameras inside the women's toilets of the London office. Apparently, he installed cameras in the men's toilets, too. He claimed it was to wind up his mates, but his bosses weren't having it.

Dan was already not very well liked. There were new complaints about his behaviour on an almost daily basis. So when still images of him making fascist gestures at a football match began circulating online, his bosses finally reached their ceiling. If he didn't make so much money for the company, Dan would have been fired.

It was Canada or nothing.

'He tried to deny that it was him,' Ella says. 'But the pictures were taken from television vision footage. Then he tried to argue that he was just waving at the camera. But . . . well.'

'Did mum know all this before you left?'

'Mum knew, yeah. She didn't like it, but she knew.'

Ella looks at the clock above the doorway, which now tells the right time. Confused as I am, I wait until she decides she wants to continue.

'Mum irritates Dan quite a lot, dad.'

'Sure,' I say. 'I understand.'

'No.' Ella gives me quite a stern look. 'I don't think you do. Haven't you noticed that her make-up has got thicker over the years?'

'Of course I've noticed.'

It would have been hard not to notice. The make-up got thicker. The lips became plumper. The lines on her face became fewer . . .

If she couldn't look at me before, now Ella is staring straight at me.

'Dan hits her, dad.'

'He *hits* her?' I straighten up. My fingernails dig into the chipboard of the cupboard I'm leaning on. 'He actually . . . *hits* her?'

'He always has,' Ella says. 'I've never seen him do it, and mum is always making up excuses, telling me that she's walked into something, or been bitten by an insect, or had a reaction to some new brand she's using. But . . . yeah.'

'Hmm.' It's all I can say. Kirsty might have a gob that is bigger than most UK estuaries, but she actually allows that flash prick to beat her about? No amount of wealth is worth that.

Well, I wouldn't know. But it can't be.

I ponder upon what other allowances wealth permits as concessions; whether an indiscretion with a lollipop lady would have been forgiven if I had been putting jewellery in the household kitty. Of course, all I ever did was take from the kitty and replace it with empty beer cans. But still . . .

Poor Kirsty.

'Is she okay?' I ask. 'She's back here with you?'

'Take a few deep breaths,' Ella tells me.

'Why?'

'*Dad* . . . just do it.'

I picture Kirsty when she was younger, how she was fun-loving good company, but the image of Dan clobbering her keeps filling up my vision. I try to shake it off, but I can't. Angry? Sickened? Terrified? It is hard to say exactly what this feeling is.

When Ella looks at me, I remember I am supposed to be taking deep breaths.

'The other day, Mum was at the nail bar, or something, and I was home alone. Or that's what I thought, at least. I was standing in the kitchen, making something to eat—'

'Dan hit *you*?' I interrupt, letting go of the counter, seeing where this is heading.

'He tried to,' Ella says. 'But I stabbed him before he could.'

'You *what*?'

Ella nods. 'I already had the knife in my hand – I was cutting up a melon. Then Dan started having a go at me, something to do with not washing Tramp after we came back from a walk, and he raised his fists—'

'So you *stabbed* him? Jesus, Ella.' I run a hand through my hair. 'Well done. Where did you, um . . . you know?'

'In the arm. The same one that he'd hit mum with.'

At first, I think Ella is crying into her fist: her shoulders are heaving and tears are running down her cheeks. But then I notice she can't help giggling at the thought of stabbing her stepfather.

Wrapping her inside in a hug, Chet parping on, I find myself chuckling, too. I don't really know why.

Oh no, she is crying, actually.

With all that I've learned about Dan, Welsh Thomas and a kid called Norman, knowing that my diminutive daughter can stand up to them is amazingly reassuring. That there seem to be plenty of them living among us, however – the bloke at the checkout next to you, the one sitting on a bench in their M&S suit, daily travelling companions, colleagues, counsellors, bosses, *stepfathers* – is not.

It isn't the way that I would have chosen to have Ella back. Even the thought of her knowing of someone who went through what she and Kirsty did is repulsive enough. And I would very much rather that my teenage daughter hadn't had to stab anyone. Even if it was Dan.

Holding my girl, I try to work out if I am in any way

331

responsible, but I decide that I can't be. It wasn't me who chose to marry him.

Oh no. Wait a second.

Did Kirsty only put up with Dan's fists so that . . .

I don't want to think about it, right now.

Ella is here.

Kirsty is safe.

Dan's fucked up badly.

That's all that matters.

forty-five

Life is very different for me now. I have mostly forgiven myself for the poor judgements I made in my past, the numerous ways in which I have failed, and the many times that I have let people down. Like the bloke said at the meeting I went to: *We can only take what we learn from our mistakes and use them to move forward. The past might be set, but our future can still be changed.*

I never went back, though. It wasn't really my crowd.

As the sale hadn't yet completed, Dan gave Kirsty the big house in north Tenderbridge, just like dad did with our family home after he left mum. Perhaps that is a way of rewarding someone after you've committed wrongs, as if everything left behind can simply be swept away with the family broom.

The house was immediately put back on the market for an obscene amount of money. I guess Kirsty deserves it as compensation for her terrible taste in men. We still speak regularly, her and I, and on a level that is friendly enough. But we do still make time for a good, healthy argument. In that way, I will always be there for her.

The Canadians couldn't tolerate Dan in the same way they did in the London office. Not long after Ella and Kirsty returned home, he was finally fired. The last thing I heard is that he's moved back in with his parents in Colchester, while looking for a new job and somewhere to live, which must be trickier now he has a hate crime on his CV.

Apparently, the injuries that Dan sustained when Ella stabbed him were only surface level – it turned out that he wasn't so much as pricked by the knife, which seems about right – so it hasn't affected his golf swing.

Fighting against the odds, the other day Kirsty told me that Bea is indeed going to be marrying pool boy. Good luck to you, mate. With all I have learned, the only advice I would give pool boy is to make sure that they don't enter the property market together.

Having had a haircut and bought a trimmer, Darren now sports a neat beard and a fancy quiff. After he got a job teaching at Goldsmiths University, working in the Department of Music, he surmised that a change of style would make people take him more seriously, bless him. He only took the job because the uni said that he could continue his session work, and soon he's heading off on tour with either Sheryl Crow or Cheryl Cole, I'm not sure which. I got the impression that Darren's not entirely certain, either.

Even with all the other stuff he's got going on, Darren still finds the time to resume epic games of Warhammer with Mick, who I haven't seen for a while. Although I do need to buy some fish soon for the six-month anniversary dinner I've been planning for Shona.

Why celebrate six months? I celebrate every day.

Julian was right when he approximated that the pair of urns could fetch over ten thousand pounds. In fact, he would have been right if he'd said double that. Even after the fees and VAT were deducted, my two lovely urns earned me just over twenty-four thousand pounds.

I offered some of the cash to Darren as a thank you for stealing one of them for me. I also attempted to pay dad back a few of the loans from over the years. Neither of them accepted – dad having his wealthy boyfriend, and Darren with more jobs than the combined population of an entire street in south Tenderbridge.

Some of the cash I have invested in mine and Brian's business, *Spanky Twang*. The name was just a joke at first, but seems to have stuck. We like it, and business is good. The other day, Brian showed me our company registration on the government website: *Spanky Twang*, up there for all to see, and with my name listed beneath his as a director. We haven't told our colleagues at Royal Mail yet, as it is still early days, but soon we should be able to go full time on it.

The pedals and delivering people's post are not the only things I'm working on with Brian. One day when I was round there, we took the sheets and boxes off the mixing board and started playing around. At first it was just to test out our pedals.

'I've written a new song,' I said to Brian, 'if you want to hear it?'

'Sure, yeah. Are you not going to use a Spanky?'

'It's acoustic,' I said, picking up my battered guitar.

The song started off as one of my singing shopping lists, originally sounding like a parody of the *Only Fools and Horses* theme tune – *I need a new toothbrush, an avocado from the corner store . . . chicken, prophylactics, melatonin, Parma ham.* Walking around town, singing away, the melody began to alter. By the time I was back home it had become a song called *Pick Me Up.*

'Seriously, you wrote that?' Brian asked.

'Yeah, I did. Do you like it?'

Not only did Brian say that he did indeed like it, we have now run nearly all of my new tunes through the desk – as well as some of the other ones that the band could never be bothered to play. Sitting down with a cup of tea, listening back to them, we decided that we are going to make a solo album. Or rather, I'm making a solo album and Brian is going to produce it in his garage. Ella has already demanded that I have to use her picture of me sitting on the log in the park, holding the massive bunch of roses, as the album cover – not the sad-eyed picture; the one with the sunglasses. Obviously.

The only thing that brings me close to tears now is seeing Ella and Shona getting on so well. In fact, so much that Ella has started helping at the flower stall, which frees up time for me to struggle through more of the books that she says I should read.

Hearing the door go, I fold my copy of *Little Women* closed. I'm loving the weekly arrival of freshly cut flowers. Shona's vases were bought from the same charity shop as my urns, apparently. Without knowing what I was looking for, I inspected them for brand indicators. And I found them, too: those of a well-known high street retailer.

My girls spill into the room, laughing at something, as usual.

'How did it go today?'

'A boy asked Ella out on a date!'

'Did he?' I smile easily, content with the knowledge that Ella will commit ABH upon anyone who attempts to do anything she doesn't agree with.

Shona said I can't really get Ella a Swiss Army knife for her next birthday, but I'm still tempted to.

Ella drops her yellow satchel against the soft leather sofa. The new plait she wears, tied back from the bangs of her fringe, flips over her shoulder.

I do like being able to see her face.

'He goes to the posh school,' Shona says. 'And he was very polite.'

'He was alright,' Ella says with a dismissive shrug. 'He's got good hair.'

'Never underestimate a man with good hair, Els,' I say. 'Michael Stipe used to have a huge curly mop.'

'No one *cares*, dad.'

'You're probably right. Are you staying tonight?'

'I'm going to mum's in a bit. I don't like the thought of her alone in that house, especially now everything is boxed up again. But it's Bea's hen party tonight, so I'll be back later, if that's okay?'

'You've got your own room here, Els,' I say, 'free for you to use whenever you want, you know that. Before you go, though, let's sit outside for a minute before the sun goes down. I've made lemonade.'

Ella's phone *pings* and she disappears into her room, saying she'll be back in a minute.

I slide off the sofa and head to the big American-style fridge-freezer.

Ice plops out of the dispenser and splashes into the jug. If I had wanted ice a number of months ago, I would have had to chip it off the inside of the fridge in my old flat, the freezer frozen shut for as long as I can remember. The only buzzing fan in our new place comes from the back of this monster, a soothing whirr that kicks in from time to time.

Walking past, I spare a glance for Marilyn. She might have a dented face, but I wasn't prepared to let her go, even if pretty much everything else had. Leaving the jug with Shona out on the balcony, I dip back inside and head over to the record player. Shona's copy of *Automatic for the People* is on the deck. That'll do. I still get an odd temptation to sign the sleeve for her each time I see it.

Ella must have slipped outside behind my back. She's sitting with Shona on one of the rattan sofas, the sun in their faces. Before joining them, I look down at the river – Toothy Charlie's there, telling a terrible joke about his imaginary wife to an unfortunate passer-by – and then over the rooftops towards the south side.

Once upon a time, I would have done terrible things from this balcony. We've not lived here long and already I'll sometimes take a secret whizz over the edge, rather than go to the toilet. I can't promise I will never misbehave again, and I have warned Shona of as much. But I have, at least, let my pet rabid dog off its lead to go and pester someone else.

After all, I live on the north side now.

Leaning on the railings, my girls chuckling at something behind me, I peer out, taking it all in. Visible over the buildings is the top of the willow that guards the Tender Bridge. Further towards the backdrop of the horizon, beyond the town borders, are the ancient forests that I never even knew existed.

I can't see the battlements on top of the castle from here. They are hidden just around the corner. I don't need to see them to know that they are there.

Thank you!

ü

Milton Keynes UK
Ingram Content Group UK Ltd.
UKHW030631270924
1879UKWH00015B/51